DESIGN FLAWS

DESIGN FLAWS

A GRAYSON DYLE MYSTERY

JOE GOLEMO

LEVEL
BEST BOOKS

To Melissa, thank you for your encouragement and support. Love you Always and Forever!

Praise for Design Flaws

"I love how tightly wound this mystery is as two brothers keep circling around a knotted past. A great read with new author Golemo totally nailing the ending."—Mary Logue, author of *The Big Sugar*

"This was great fun to read. Breezy and smart and funny and compelling. You've given us a likable hero, two brothers, a dead mother with a secret, and the promise of more mystery to come. Very entertaining and engaging, and we want to keep on reading. Which is the whole point, to keep the reader reading. Well done!" —Paula Munier, *USA Today* bestselling author of the Mercy Carr Mysteries

Chapter One

Thursday, March 9

I was spying on my mother as she leaned over the casket, her white hair, dark-blue dress, and small frame lost among the floral sprays and bouquets. Technically, it was more of a welfare check than actual surveillance, as the grief at losing her constant companion of over fifty years threatened to consume her.

Mom leaned in, and tears fell as she brushed her hand against Dad's cheek. At first, I thought she was praying. Then I noticed a small beige envelope clutched in her other hand.

"We never could agree on giving this to the boys." Her voice was so soft I had to open the visitation room door a few inches more to hear her.

"So, I'm going to honor your wishes…and your memory…and leave it with you." With that, she tucked the envelope in next to Dad, then smoothed out the fabric of his suit, her hand lingering, not wanting to let go.

"Is everything all right, Grayson?" A voice boomed from behind.

"Jesus Christ." I banged my head on the doorjamb and then turned.

Jamie Cross glared at me over her readers with her arms folded across her chest.

"I think you'll find it's more comfortable to pray in the visitation room." Great—a Funeral Director with attitude.

"Hi, Jamie. I didn't hear you come up." My face suddenly felt hot, so I held the visitation room door open for her, hoping she wouldn't notice me

1

blushing.

Mom was struggling to accept Dad's death, and she didn't seem to notice us come in as she stood near the casket, undoubtedly wondering if she would ever feel cheerful again. Dean and I suggested she move to the Twin Cities to be closer to us, but she would never leave Rochester, Minnesota, not while she still had a strong circle of friends here and the memories of the life she and Dad had cherished for so many years.

I put my arm around Mom's shoulders, which felt delicate and frail. "Are you okay?"

She leaned her head on my shoulder. "I'm fine." Typical Mom, not wanting to burden someone else with her woes.

I looked at my dad for what would likely be the last time. Ben Dyle had been diagnosed with Type 1 diabetes while in his teens and had learned to manage his condition so well that few people realized he had it. But the disease extracted a heavy toll over the years, and heart disease took him in the end. Watching the slow decline of the man that taught my brother, Dean, and me to ride a bike, play baseball, and drive a car had been agonizing. Realizing we would never share a glass of wine over a nice dinner again was devastating.

"Come on, Mom, let's get you home."

She looked around the room. "Let me get my things."

Jamie closed the casket lid and locked it with a small tool, which was much like a hex key. I helped Mom collect her purse and sweater and held out an arm. She latched on for support.

"Thanks, Jamie," I said over my shoulder.

"You're welcome. Good night, Mrs. Dyle. Night, Grayson."

We stopped at the coat room to bundle up when my cell phone buzzed. Dean's text said he was waiting for us at the main entrance. As a home automation consultant, my brother was on-call 24/7 and insisted on driving separately in case he needed to make a speedy exit. Imagine the inconvenience if one of his clients had to get off the couch to turn on the lights manually instead of barking a command at a Google Assistant.

The beige envelope kept nagging at me as we strolled to his car. I was shocked to hear my parents couldn't decide what to do with it. They rarely disagreed about anything important. What was in that damn thing, and why did my mother want to bury it forever?

Maybe it contained a fortune in stock certificates that Dad didn't want to pass along to his sons, so we would have no choice but to be self-reliant. I could see him thinking that way. But if it was something valuable, why wouldn't Mom just keep it? She could sell them off, and we would be none the wiser. No, I figured the envelope held some documents related to our family, which opened up unlimited possibilities.

I suddenly realized I had to have it. I promised myself I would only examine the contents long enough to figure out if it involved Dean or me. If it didn't, I'd bury it next to my dad's grave in the middle of a moonless night without another thought. But, if it did concern us, I had to know what secrets it contained. After all, if Mom and Dad couldn't agree, and she was respecting his wishes by leaving the envelope with him, she must have wanted to give it to us. That was good enough for me.

Having served as an altar boy at more Catholic funerals than I cared to remember, I knew there was no way to retrieve the envelope tomorrow without having Dean create a diversion during our father's funeral. That didn't seem appropriate, so I would have to make the recovery tonight.

I helped Mom into the car and leaned in. "See you at the house in a few minutes. I need to stop for gas." Dean gave me a curious look but didn't say anything in front of Mom. After he drove off, I walked to my car, threw in my gloves, then went back to the funeral home to look for them, switching my phone to vibrate to be safe.

The foyer and main hallway were empty, but the lights were still on, so I walked to the visitation room and peeked in to find the coffin was gone. The funeral home staff must have moved it to a cooler for overnight storage. I crept past the other visitation rooms and a small chapel, which were all dark inside. The hallway was wide enough to accommodate a coffin with pallbearers on both sides, but there were no plant stands or side tables to block their progress or for me to hide behind. My natural penchant for following the rules was working against me, and the possibility of being caught in a place I shouldn't be was causing my heart to thump so loudly it seemed like someone had set off an alarm.

A visitor's lounge sat at the end of the main hallway, and side hallways led to the left and right. I inched around the corner to the right and saw light from an open office door. Jamie Cross must be in there, plotting the next funeral to direct. Down the hall to the left was a closed door marked "Office Personnel Only." The frame had a seal to prevent air from leaking out, so I figured it must house the prep rooms and cooler. I knocked but got no response, then opened the door a crack to peek inside and was hit with the foul smell of formaldehyde. Thankfully, no alarm went off. I bolted in, closed the door, and turned on the fluorescent lights.

To the left were oversized garage doors in front of two stalls, one of which contained a hearse with the funeral home's logo on its passenger door. The other stall was empty but spacious enough to hold an ambulance or emergency vehicle. There were a few smaller rooms on the right and storage racks at the far end. I found the cooler, which contained three caskets lined up side-by-side. I tried the lid on my Dad's casket, but it was still locked. I was desperate for a hex key and searched the shelving units to find one. They held a bewildering array of curved saws, scalpels, wire threads, hooks, pumps, and plugs. For a second, I wondered how well-designed they were but quickly decided I'd be better off not knowing. I spotted a spare key, grabbed it, dashed back to the cooler, and unlocked the casket lid.

"Sorry to have to do this, Dad." I held my breath while searching between his arm and the lining with no luck. Maybe she put it between his arm and torso? I gritted my teeth, trying not to think about how creepy this was, and reached past his arm. Something was wrong. The arm was too skinny, and his suit was thin and silky, almost like a dress. I peeked in to find a withered, gray-haired lady inside and snatched my arm back in shock, dropping the lid with a resounding bang. Oh, that wasn't good. I consoled myself by thinking the cooler room's insulation also made it soundproof.

Not wanting to leave this person disturbed in any way, I reopened the lid to smooth out her dress. A moment later, someone yanked open the cooler door. Jamie stood at the entrance pointing a fire extinguisher at me. I froze.

It took a moment for the scene to register, then she shrieked, "Grayson Dyle, you scared the daylights out of me. What the bloody hell are you doing to Mrs. Farnsworthy?"

"Mrs. Farnsworthy?" I yanked my hand out of the casket, and the lid banged shut again, sounding like the gavel of the judge who would soon be sentencing me for grave robbing.

"What are you doing in here?" She pointed the fire extinguisher toward the floor.

"I thought this was my dad's casket," I said as if that would explain everything.

"Leave now, or I'll call the police."

"Let me explain—"

"NOW!" She pointed the fire extinguisher right between my eyes. Honestly, with all the money Dean and I spent on the funeral, you'd think she would be treating me better.

At five-foot-three, wearing her work uniform of a black skirt and jacket over an off-white blouse with minimal jewelry, light makeup, and sensible shoes, Jamie wasn't much of a threat, but it seemed better to negotiate than fight.

"Wait a minute. This is important to me. I put something in my Dad's casket right before you locked it up, and I realize now that was a mistake. I'd like to get it back before we bury him."

Her face screwed up. "You changed your mind in the last half hour."

"I acted on an impulse, and now I regret it. I didn't think I'd be able to get it back tomorrow, so I had to get it tonight."

"How do I know you're not trying to steal his gold watch or wedding ring without your mother finding out?"

"I'm not that kind of person."

"We get all kinds in here, Grayson." The extinguisher was getting lower and lower as she calmed down.

"Then why don't you retrieve it for me? It was a small beige envelope, and it's by his right arm."

She pointed the extinguisher at the opposite side of the cooler. "Stand over there. If there is an envelope, I'll get it back for you. Toss me the casket key."

I tossed it to her, then slunk to the designated corner for a timeout. I considered facing the wall but didn't want to provoke her any further.

Jamie locked Mrs. Farnsworthy's casket and then opened my dad's. She reached in, snatched the envelope, handed it to me without glancing at it, then relocked the lid. "You know, you could have just asked."

"I figured you'd say no because of some obscure regulation about not disturbing the dead or because you'd think I was weird."

"I do think this is weird, but we get oddball requests all the time. A few months ago, someone wanted me to cover an entire casket with duct tape to be absolutely certain the deceased could never escape. You should check out some funeral industry blogs. They're far worse than this."

"Maybe I'm not so bad after all." I could tell she wanted to make a snarky comment but was maintaining a professional demeanor, and it was killing her. Good thing we were in a mortuary.

I considered ripping open the envelope as soon as I got to my car but figured it was something Dean and I should do together. I took out my phone to see a text from Dean saying Mom had turned in for the night, and he was already at the hotel. I drove over, and he let me in as soon as I knocked. My brother hated wearing a suit as much as I did, so it was no surprise to find he'd already changed into a workout T-shirt and shorts. It had been over five years since he slimmed down, and it was good to see he was diligent about staying that way.

Dean's room had a king-sized bed that a maid had already turned down, an oversized leather couch, and a worktable where he'd set out a bottle of water for each of us. I pushed the phone and hotel directory to one side of the table as I sat, then slapped down the envelope for effect.

"What's that?"

"That is an envelope Mom slipped into Dad's casket right before we left the funeral home."

"What?!"

"Just before we left the funeral home, I observed Mom putting this into

6

Dad's casket. I overheard her telling Dad she thought they should have given it to us, but because he didn't want to, she was going to leave it with him."

"You 'observed' her?"

"I was worried she wasn't coping with Dad's death very well, so I was keeping an eye on her to be sure she was okay."

"You surveilled our mother while she was saying goodbye to Dad." It seemed so untoward when he put it that way.

"It was a simple welfare check. Nothing to get excited about."

Dean frowned. "How did you get it back?"

"Jamie retrieved it for me." If I had admitted to being busted by a funeral director wielding a fire extinguisher while breaking into a casket, I would have never heard the end of it.

"Didn't she think that was weird?"

"Maybe, but nowhere near as bad as the stuff other people have requested. You should check the funeral blogs sometimes." I held the envelope up. "Anyway, don't you want to know what's inside?" In my excitement, I hadn't noticed the writing on the front. I put it face up on the table so we could both read it.

Printed in large, meticulous script were the words "To be delivered to my son, Kieran, on his 21st Birthday." Who the hell was Kieran, and why did Mom have a letter addressed to him?

"Holy crap, I'll bet Mom had a child with someone else before she married Dad." It was the only explanation I could think of.

Dean shot me a menacing look. "That doesn't make sense. She could have given this to him without consulting Dad first."

While that was a good point, I was having second thoughts and was about to suggest we check with Mom first when Dean slit open the envelope with his pocketknife. He took out two pages of matching beige paper. He handed them to me. "Here, you retrieved it. You do the honors."

I gingerly unfolded the pages. The message had been handwritten in the same careful script as the envelope, and I began reading aloud:

"'To my darling son, Kieran,

"'I love you so much. I've decided to name you Kieran. I know that's silly because I'll only be with you for one more day, but you'll always be Kieran to me. I love watching you sleep. Your steady breathing, your perfect little fingers and toes. You remind me so much of your father.

"'I love him, too, your father. He's such a wonderful man. He's already committed, so we can never be married. But we still love each other deeply. We always will. I know you'll grow up to be just like him.

"'I'm not worried about you, Kieran. We've found a wonderful home for you, and I know you'll be happy. It's a good Catholic family that will raise you right. Please don't be mad at us when you find out. It was the only choice we had.

"'I'm miserable here. The nurses are so mean. I couldn't bear it without Sister Anna visiting. Sister snuck in a pen and paper when no one was watching. She's going to give this letter to your new family when they meet you.

"'By the time you're reading this, I know you will have turned into a fine young man, and we will be so proud of you. I told your father it's a miracle you were born on the same day Pope John Paul was selected, but he thinks that's silly. Wouldn't it be wonderful if we met one day? But I doubt that will ever happen. They made me sign something saying I'm not supposed to go looking for you.

"'Am I doing the right thing? I must be because your father says so. You must promise not to look for him. I can't say any more. You must trust me on this.

"'I will close now. All my love, always and forever,

"'Maggie.'"

I put the letter down and closed my eyes to think. There was something familiar about Pope John Paul, but what was it? I opened my eyes to Google it, then noticed Dean staring at his phone, turning as white as the pope's robes. Then it hit me. Dean was born on the day Pope John Paul was elected. This letter was for him.

Chapter Two

Friday, March 10

As the initial shock of Dean's new status was setting in, the first thing we wanted to do was drive to Mom's house, wake her up, and demand some answers. But that would have been cruel. Instead, we wasted a few hours arguing over the why and wherefores of Dean's being adopted. In the end, even though we couldn't be sure about anything, there were two things we agreed on. First, if Dean was adopted, it made sense I was too. Second, we probably had the same birth parents.

When we were kids, strangers at the grocery store would stop Mom and ask if she was exhausted from raising identical twins. Dean's growth spurt at ten stopped that, but we still looked like brothers. We both had green eyes, chestnut blond hair, and the same prominent jawline. How could we not have the same biological parents?

We soon got tired of inventing new conspiracy theories and called it a night.

The funeral service the next day was a torrent of emotions. I vacillated between happy memories of the vacations the four of us took to various theme parks throughout the country and grief over the simple things I'd never do with my dad again, such as golfing or playing chess. I made it worse by beating myself up every ten minutes for retrieving that letter. I should have left it alone.

After the graveside service, Mom, Dean, and I hosted a luncheon. To me, the usual social pleasantries one shared with family and friends had taken on a toxic undercurrent as if each table was speculating among themselves whether losing an adopted father was somehow easier than losing a birth father.

What had seemed like a normal upbringing only yesterday morning was now tarnished, as if some unknown force had loosened life's anchor bolts, and I was floating around in a smoky haze of uncertainty. Childhood scenes kept popping into my head, which now took on more nuanced meanings, none of which were good. Like the countless times my parents took Dean and me to family parties, and our cousins refused to play with us. Or the nasty comments that Aunt Phyllis, Mom's sister, always made just loud enough to be overheard. "Those boys were just born bad," she would say to one of the other grownups while looking straight at me.

I hated those parties. One Easter Sunday, when Dean was eight, and I was six, we were all in the backyard looking for eggs. Stuart, Aunt Phyllis's oldest son, who was two years older than Dean, was lurking in the background, as usual, waiting for an opportunity to mess with us. Stu called me behind the garage, saying he had a present for me. He pointed to an elaborately decorated egg on top of the garage bin and said it was mine if I could reach it. I put down my basket, jumped up a few times, and finally grabbed it. I turned around triumphantly to put it in my basket when I found all of the other eggs had been crushed. It was bad enough that Stu stood there innocently pretending he had no idea what had happened, but then he started yelling that I was hiding behind the garage, smashing my eggs. Mom came running, of course, and bawled me out for ruining them. Stu stood behind her, smirking, and I wanted to punch his face in. Aunt Phyllis chose that moment to appear, saw what had happened, and gave Mom a haughty look. 'What's wrong with your kid?' it said. I wanted to punch her in the face too. Did they treat me that way because I'd been adopted and wasn't a real family member? Or were they just bullies who would have treated me that way no matter what? There was no way to tell.

As I begged the rock-hard hotel mattress for mercy that night, the questions wouldn't stop coming. Were Mom and Dad unable to have kids of their own, or did they adopt us to give some poor unfortunate kids a loving home? Why didn't they bother telling us? Who was Maggie, and where was she now? How did they connect with her? Why did she give us up for adoption? Who was the birth father, and where was he? Despite the seemingly endless list, one question stood out. Why wasn't there a letter in that casket intended for me?

I desperately wanted to know about the past, but that meant confronting Mom, which would be a lengthy process. We'd have to give her a respectable amount of time to grieve first, but we could waste years trying to milk her for tiny scraps of information, and she'd probably refuse to talk out of respect for Dad. It seemed so futile.

Just past two A.M., I resolved to submit a DNA sample to one of those ancestry websites. I would share this decision with my brother, who wouldn't be happy, but I couldn't wait any longer.

The next morning, I met Dean at the hotel's complimentary breakfast bar, his haggard look suggesting he'd also had a sleepless night.

Dean sat across from me with a coffee, a bagel, and cream cheese. "Adopted. How freaking weird is that? I keep wondering why they never told us."

"It sounds like Mom wanted to, but Dad didn't, so they kept kicking the can down the road until they figured it wouldn't matter anymore."

"You have to wonder where that letter has been all these years." Dean stopped talking and became blank and unfocused, with the same thousand-yard stare exhibited by combatants or trauma victims who have become emotionally detached from the horrors around them.

I jarred him back to reality. "I'm going to take a DNA test to see what I can find out."

Dean folded his arms across his chest and gritted his teeth. "If you don't knock it off, I'm going to pound you."

The sudden flashback to our frequent childhood fights didn't deter me. "Dad is dead. Mom may or may not know anything and may not tell us even if she does. I need to know, Dean. I don't know how to explain it. I don't want to go behind your back, so I'm letting you know now."

Dean was shaking his head in frustration. "Maggie specifically said not to look for our father. How can we ignore that?"

"That's the whole point. She asked you to promise not to look for your father. And she said she's not supposed to look for you. But she never said anything about you looking for her. I think she purposely left that out, hoping you'd realize it and then do exactly that."

"That's insane! First, you're reading way too much into this. Second, what if the DNA results end up outing her or the father? What if they went their separate ways after having us? They could both be out there, married to other people, maybe with their own kids. Do you really want to disrupt their lives?"

The other coffee shop patrons started noticing our dispute, so I leaned in and lowered my voice. "Why not? I could let it go if it only happened once. But to have a second child, out of wedlock, in the seventies is about as irresponsible as you can get. If we do end up outing them, they will just be getting what they deserve."

"So, you want to hurt them? Is that what this is all about?"

"No! You're twisting my words...." I took a deep breath, lowered my voice again, and started over. "Okay, let's think. What are the odds that one or both of our birth parents took an online DNA test and are just waiting for us to reach out and find them."

"Hard to say. It depends a lot on their circumstances. If they still want to keep us buried in their past, which seems likely, there's no way they would take a chance. So, you'll only find them if they want to be found."

"Agreed."

"So the deck is stacked against you."

"Maybe, but I don't have to find them—not directly, anyway. Remember how the California Police tracked down that serial rapist, the Golden State Killer, through a partial match with a relative's DNA. I should be able to find a cousin or uncle and explore the family tree from there. It shouldn't be a problem." At least, that's what I was convincing myself would happen.

"No good will come of this, Gray... I can't talk about this anymore."

It was scary how much he sounded like Dad just then.

"I can't explain it anymore either. I just need to do this."

After we got back to the Twin Cities, I bought a DNA test kit and mailed in a spit sample, despite Dean's objections. I set up an account with the username "DesignGuy" and paid extra to rush the results. While I scanned their privacy policy to make sure I could delete my profile, I came across an interesting disclaimer: "Your DNA test results may provide unanticipated evidence about your family or yourself, such as discovering unknown genetic family members, surprising facts about your ethnicity, or unexpected information in the public records. You can delete this information from our website at any time, but you may not be able to prevent its dissemination once it is available online." Perfect. Just what I was hoping for.

Almost three weeks later, Dean and I were in a short line at a restaurant called The Concord, waiting to have dinner with a relative I'd connected with through the ancestry website test results. I bought Dean's letter along just in case, and as I checked for the third time to make sure it was still in the breast pocket of my suit, I couldn't help wondering if this meeting was a mistake. Maybe I should have listened to Dean and left the past alone. On the other hand, what was the worst that could happen? Besides, I couldn't help myself—I had to know.

"Right this way," said the maître d' when I told him we were part of the Brennen party.

The Concord opened in 1935 and had been an icon of the St. Paul crowd for many years. It reopened a few months ago after a much-needed facelift. We walked past large stained-glass windows that faced Grand Avenue to the Chef's Dining Room, which was gray with large mirrors on one side and had windows looking into the kitchen on the other. He indicated a table for four with one of the place settings removed. "Mr. Brennen, the rest of your party has arrived."

"James Brennen, at your service." As he rose to shake hands, James closed an expensive-looking leather portfolio and put it on the table. He was about six feet with gray eyes, conservative glasses, and dark hair graying at the temples. In his dark suit, old-school blue tie, and white shirt, Central Casting could have sent him to play an attorney in the latest courtroom drama.

"Hello, James. I'm Grayson, and this is my brother, Dean."

The family resemblance was remarkable, especially with Dean, and it was all I could do to stop staring at our new family member.

"Is this your first time to The Concord?"

I looked around to take in the atmosphere. "The first time since they reopened. It looks great."

James's face had a broad smile. "Yes. I'm a regular. It's still a good place to celebrate winning a case."

"Grayson and I looked you up. It looks like you have a family law practice near here," Dean said.

"I'm one of the Senior Partners at Murphy, Brennen, & Murphy. I've been practicing since 1977, and one of these days, I will get it right."

Attorney humor. We chuckled to avoid an awkward silence.

"I believe you're the owner of a product design firm, and Dean is a home automation guru," James said.

He'd done his homework, too.

"Isn't the Internet a wonderful thing?"

James's smile faded as he turned serious. "Your email said you'd found a letter from your birth mother, and then you connected with DeeDee Miller. How did that come about?"

Despite his reluctance to confront the past, Dean was willing to strategize about our approach. We had agreed to assume we both had the same birth parents and divulge as little else as possible until he had gained our trust.

I took the lead. "Our adoptive father passed away a few weeks ago, and I thought maybe I should look into our birth family before...."

I hesitated, not wanting to sound boorish, and James must have realized where I was going. "Before any more of your biological relatives passed, and it would be too late."

"Exactly. I submitted a DNA sample to an ancestry website, and DeeDee's name came up as a close family match. I think she's a cousin, but it's hard to say for sure. She must spend a lot of time on that website as she sent me a message almost immediately."

That seemed to pique James's interest. "She must have mentioned my name?"

"I haven't spoken with her yet. We've just been emailing. She shared a few of the surnames in her family tree to see if I knew any of them, one of which was Brennen. Dean did some web searches and found your website, so I emailed you, and here we are. Thanks again for agreeing to meet."

Dean chimed in. "As soon as I saw your picture, I figured we must be related. As you mentioned, I'm a bit of an IT nerd, so I used a facial recognition app to compare our pictures. There was a seventy-eight percent match, which implies we're close relatives. How did you meet her, by the way?"

"I met DeeDee a few years ago at my grandmother's fiftieth wedding anniversary. Once she found out I was an attorney, she latched on to me. She was semi-retired and spent most of her free time building her family tree at that ancestry site. Some potential relatives, who turned out not to be related, thought she was a little too persistent and threatened to take legal action. She asked for my help, and I had one of my partners intervene. I suggested she find another hobby, but she persisted. Did she share her family tree with you yet?"

"Not yet," I said. "She said she likes to meet people in person first. Why do you ask?"

"Let's just say it's amazing how many famous people she seems to be related to. She can be a bit of an acquired taste."

"Sounds like there's a lot more to this story." It was an invitation to keep talking.

"Quite a bit, I'm afraid. You must visit her home in Anoka. It's quite the experience."

I was about to ask what that meant when the server stopped by to drop off a tray of bread wrapped in white linen and take our drink orders. James moved his leather portfolio to the seat of the empty chair to make room. He said he had to get back to the office afterward to prep for a court hearing in the morning, so we placed our dinner order at the same time.

Dean helped himself to bread and passed the tray. "How do you fit into all of this?"

James seemed pensive. "Do you mind if I ask you why you're asking?"

"It's hard to explain…" After pausing to think, I decided James seemed trustworthy enough. "We didn't know we'd been adopted until we found the letter."

"That must have been quite a shock."

"It was. Until a couple of weeks ago, Dean and I thought we knew what we were about and life was good. I want to feel that way again, and I don't know how to get there without discovering who my birth parents are and how I ended up here."

James sat back and looked at us for a moment. "Grayson…Dean…I can tell you about your birth family, but it must stay between the three of us. It's a bit complicated, but this information, this truth, if it got out, would cause tremendous heartache for people I care about. I…."

Just then, the server stopped by with our drinks. His timing was lousy, but James didn't seem deterred.

As the server left, he looked back and forth between us, his face softened, and his eyes twinkled with pride. "Boys, I am your biological father." He seemed to relish the idea of having two sons.

After hearing the horror stories about biological parents or their offspring rejecting each other, I was somewhat relieved to have a biological father with whom a normal adult relationship seemed like a real possibility.

Dean smiled before I could get a word in. "I knew it. I knew a seventy-eight percent match wouldn't lie." Leave it to my brother to make this a technology issue.

"You do mean both of us, right?" I asked.

"Yes. Both of you." James's smile faded a bit, and a hint of shame emerged. The implications of having not one but two children out of wedlock must have hit home.

We all stared at each other, not knowing what to do or say. Should we get up and hug? Fist-bump? High-five? No one seemed to know the proper social protocol when meeting your birth father for the first time.

I was getting a queasy feeling but didn't know why. "So, what happened?"

James looked down, squirmed a bit, then fidgeted with the flatware so they were parallel with the table side and even across the bottom. "It's complicated. I've thought about reaching out many times over the years, but I didn't want to create any issues for you two and your adoptive parents."

"You mean our real parents, right?" Dean was no longer smiling now that his technology triumph was over.

"Yes, yes, of course, your real parents—the only parents you've ever known." James squirmed some more. "You can see why I was concerned about reaching out. There's no easy way of handling something like this."

The server stopped by with another server, who carried plates. "Here we are, sir. I believe you ordered the Steak Diane. Here is the Salmon Oscar and the Beef Pot Au Pho for you. Is there anything else I can get you? No? Great—I will check back with you in a bit. Enjoy!"

The break in our conversation gave me a moment to think, and the realization that he deliberately chose not to reach out to Dean or me merely for his convenience was jarring. I needed to try a different approach before anger shut down all rational thought. "We're not trying to place blame. We're just looking to understand how things ended up the way they did. What can you tell us about Maggie, for example?"

A smile broke across James's face. "She was wonderful. Such a free spirit. She made fast friends with everyone she met. Something in her easygoing nature made you feel good about yourself just being in her presence." Maybe he really did love her.

"She sounded like a very caring person in the letter," I said between bites.

"Did she mention any names?" That struck me as odd. Why was James concerned about Maggie naming names?

"The only name I recall was a Sister Anna," said Dean.

James seemed relieved. "I'm not surprised. Sister Anna took Maggie under her wing, even though she was only a few years older. Anyone else?"

"We don't want to discuss that right now." I jumped in before Dean could answer, and now he and James were both looking at me funny.

"Okay, I understand. Will you let me read the letter at some point?"

"Maybe the next time we get together." I was developing severe trust issues with our newfound father. "What was her last name?"

James squinted as he shifted his gaze between Dean and me. He seemed to be mentally calculating the odds of making a deal—we show him the letter, and he tells us her last name. But then he relented. "Fitzgerald. Her name was Margaret Fitzgerald. Everyone called her Maggie."

"Thanks," I said. "What did you mean when you said the truth would cause tremendous heartache for people you care about?"

James pushed his dinner plate away and leaned forward on his elbows. "This is embarrassing, but my wife, Cathy, doesn't know I have children from a previous relationship. I planned on telling her right after we were married, but the timing never seemed right. It's been over thirty-eight years now. You can imagine how much of a shock this will be. To make matters worse, she's our office manager, so she has full access to my work schedule and emails. I told her we were meeting to discuss a lawsuit. If you speak with her, please stick with the story, at least until I figure out how to tell her the truth. If she finds out on her own, it could ruin our marriage. Let's get back together in a few weeks after we've all had a chance to think about things. Maybe you can bring the letter with you."

Dean was consoling, which wasn't like him. "That's fine, James. We're not going anywhere."

Something was seriously wrong here. Why was this guy so obsessed with reading the letter? I started thinking this was his sole purpose in agreeing to meet with us. I could feel my face turning red and shot my brother a dirty look. "No, it's not fine, Dean."

Then I turned to face James head-on. "How can you sit there and lie like that? Maggie said she couldn't marry Dean's father because he was already in a committed relationship. You were already seeing Cathy and having a fling with Maggie on the side when she got pregnant, weren't you? You have no intention of telling Cathy anything. You're just trying to pacify us until you can see the letter, make sure there's nothing incriminating in it, and then make this whole thing go away—make us go away so you can go back to leading your perfect little life. What is wrong with you?"

I must have been getting louder as the people at nearby tables were glancing our way. I didn't care.

"Hang on, Grayson, that's not fair..."

"No, you hang on, *Dad*. Do you really think you can tell us what to do here? You cheated on your girlfriend, knocked up some poor girl, twice, and probably forced her to have her babies in secret and then give them up for adoption, all so you wouldn't have to deal with them. Then you abandoned her, right? Did you ever talk to her again, our mother? A girl who was so madly in love that she slept with you again after you knocked her up the first time. Do you know where she is now? Maybe send her a Mother's Day card or two, you heartless bastard."

Dean was clenching his teeth so hard it looked like they might crack. "*Grayson!* Will you knock it off?"

"Wait, just a minute...I can explain everything. Grayson. Let me explain...." James's Irish face was ruddy with anger and fear.

The restaurant was getting eerily quiet, and some of the patrons were staring while whispering conspiratorially. I had no idea where this rage was coming from, and it wasn't stopping now. "Well, where is she, James? You have no idea, do you, Jimmy? You had your fun, she had your children, and you got rid of them—got rid of us—so you could go on living your carefree life, right, Jimbo? Did you ever even think about her anymore? Wonder how she feels walking through the park watching other mothers playing with their children or if she grieves on our birthdays?"

James erupted. "She's dead, Grayson... Your mother is dead." He seemed shocked at his brazenness, but he kept going anyway. He looked me straight in the eyes. "She died, giving you life."

It was as much an accusation as it was an admission—as if I were somehow responsible for causing her death.

"I want to see that letter. I will contact you in the morning and will arrange to have it delivered to my office. Don't make me take legal action to get it."

Who the bloody hell did this guy think he was, demanding the letter and threatening us with legal action? Father or not, rage turned to fury.

Despite the rubbernecking by most of the other diners, I jumped out of my seat and lunged across the table at him. "You cold-blooded son-of-a-bitch. I ought to kill you right now."

Dean had quick reflexes, and he caught me by the shoulder before I reached James. He pushed me back into my seat, and the three of us sat there, stunned and breathing hard.

The maître d' wisely choose this moment to intervene. "It's unfortunate that you don't have time for dessert, Mr. Brennen. We can settle your bill the next time you dine with us. Thank you all so much for choosing The Concord. I hope you have a pleasant evening."

I'd never been kicked out of a restaurant with so much aplomb. Actually, I'd never been kicked out of a restaurant at all—another item to cross off the bucket list.

James must have decided to try saving face while making a speedy escape. He stood, thanked the maître d', mumbled a quick goodbye to us, then hurdled toward the exit with his head down and his suit collar up.

As we stood to leave, the dining room seemed to return to normal, if normal meant people were gawking at us and whispering. Dean needed to use the restroom, and I told him I'd wait for him out front. I'd never lost control like that before and was still wondering how it happened.

As I waited in the lobby, our server tapped me on the shoulder. "I found this on a chair at your table." He handed me James's leather portfolio and retreated into the safety of the restaurant. I walked outside to see if I could catch James, but he must have already driven off.

The steady flow of traffic on Grand Avenue was having a calming effect on this city boy, and my heart rate was returning to normal as I waited for Dean on the sidewalk. I held up the portfolio when he appeared.

"Bummer. I guess you'll have to take it to him."

"Me? I just threatened to kill the guy—Why don't you take it?" I tried to hand the portfolio to him, but he crossed his arms behind his back. Why did I always have to do the dirty work?

"Fine." I figured I should apologize anyway, now that I could see what a jerk I'd been. As Dean took off, I opened the portfolio and scanned the documents, finding James's handwritten notes on a few legal briefs. Since they didn't pertain to the adoption, I closed it and tucked it under my arm.

I found James's cell number at the bottom of an email message and texted him about the portfolio, also expressing my regret for overreacting. He texted back, advising me not to worry about dinner as he hoped there would be many more. He also said his office was nearby and asked if it would be possible for me to drop it off on my way home.

Sure, I replied.

I planned to apologize in person for threatening to kill him and hoped this act of contrition would make me feel better. He texted the address and his thanks. Then my phone buzzed again.

Can you bring the letter with you?

I lied in response. **Not possible. Dean has it. He already left**. What the bloody hell did he think was in that thing?

Chapter Three

Wednesday, March 29

James's office was less than a mile away, near the intersection of Selby Avenue and Dale Street in St. Paul, which had some of the city's worst crime and poverty in the late 1960s. Today, gentrification created bursts of upscale development, with cafes, delis, gastropubs, and boutiques popping up next to empty lots and rundown housing.

I decided to walk to clear my head and think about what I was going to say. On the one hand, my concerns were well justified—it did seem as if James wanted to contain any threat Dean and I made to his perfect little world. On the other hand, I shouldn't have blown up at him and resolved to express my concerns with more restraint going forward.

Ten minutes later, I entered James's building and checked the directory to see his office was on the third floor. I used the elevator next to the stairs but soon regretted that decision as it was slower than rush hour traffic.

On the third floor, a gilded sign was set into one of two highly polished, solid-wood double doors indicating the Murphy, Brennen, & Murphy law offices were lurking behind. Did you knock on a door like this or open it and walk right in? I decided to be polite and tap to see what would happen. As I did, the door opened an inch. James must have left it unlocked for me, so I walked in. The reception area was appointed with classic wood paneling and heavy, Queen Ann-style, high-backed chairs arranged behind a small coffee table that was littered with *Time* magazines.

"James?"

Nothing. A hallway led past the built-in reception desk, so I inched along in that direction.

"James? Are you there?" I called out again. No answer. Maybe he was in the restroom.

The offices along the hallway were all closed except for the last one on the left. Thinking he probably hadn't heard me, I walked down, confirmed James's name was on the door and looked in.

"Hello?" I could barely make out someone's head over the top of an oversized leather office chair, which was facing away from me. It was a few feet off to the side from a large, heavy mahogany desk near the back wall of the room. Still no response. Was he ignoring me as punishment for my outbursts at the restaurant? Maybe he didn't want to make amends, and I should just drop off the portfolio and walk out of this guy's life for a while.

"Yo, is that you?" Never one to leave well enough alone, I walked over to face him.

James was slumped down—his unblinking eyes staring at the ceiling. The two bullet holes in his chest had oozed enough blood to cover most of his shirt. I stared in disbelief, hoping he was still breathing. I held two fingers to his neck, but there was no pulse. James was dead.

"Dammit!" I slammed the leather portfolio on the floor in frustration. The office seemed eerily quiet after that.

How could I have lost two fathers in just a few weeks? Why was God doing this to me?

Just then, the muffled sound of a door closing came from down the hall, which could have been the killer making their escape. Of course, he could also have seen me entering James's office and was coming back to clean up a loose end. Then again, maybe it was a random office worker who would later testify in court that they witnessed me entering the law office holding a large binder, which must have concealed the murder weapon.

I listened for a minute but didn't hear anything else. Then, all those years of watching *CSI* kicked in, and I realized I had two choices—call the police and wait for them to arrive or bale out without leaving any evidence. I was horrified James was dead, but staying here seemed like a no-win situation. Considering I'd just had dinner with the victim, where he admitted he was my biological father, after which I threatened to kill him in front of a restaurant full of witnesses, and I was now standing over his body, the cops would award me first place on their list of suspects. Hell, I'd put myself at the top of the list if I didn't know I was innocent. Sure, I would test negative for gunshot residue, but the results would take hours or even days to process. I couldn't do anything more for James, so I decided to bale and report the murder anonymously from another location in case no one else had.

I noticed a slight coppery smell, looked down to find the sole of my right dress shoe sitting in a pool of blood on the carpet, and instinctively took a few steps back, leaving bloody prints as I went. Fabulous—my first time witnessing a real crime scene, and I just stepped in it. I made a mental list of all the things I might have touched since arriving and made a note not to leave prints on anything else.

There was a box of tissues on a nearby credenza, so I hobbled over with the tip of my right shoe in the air and took off my shoe, noting with some relief that only the front two inches of the flat sole were bloody. The heel, which had a distinctive pattern, was clear. I used a few tissues to wipe as much blood from the sole as possible, wrapped a few more clean tissues around the bloody ones, and stuffed them all in my pocket.

I didn't have much time. If the person I'd overheard earlier wasn't the killer, they would have heard the gunshots and would have called 911 by now.

From this angle, I noticed the wall behind the desk contained two bullet holes spaced a few inches apart and about three feet off the ground. James must have been sitting, and the shooter must have been standing across the desk when they pulled the trigger. This implied James was comfortable having the person in his office and ruled out an attack by a random stranger. Since his chair had been pushed away from his desk and the bullet holes and was facing away from the desk when I arrived, the killer must have moved it so they could rifle through the file drawers. I also noticed a display, mouse, and mouse pad on the desktop and a keyboard on an under-desktop tray, but no laptop. He might put it away during client meetings, but I had a hunch the killer took it with them. It turned out that crime scenes were fascinating and gut-wrenching all at the same time. Who knew?

I fought the urge to continue investigating as it was way past time to leave. I put my hand on James's shoulder and lightly closed his eyes as a way of saying goodbye. Picking up the leather portfolio, I decided to take it with me so forensics couldn't get my fingerprints off the leather. I grabbed a few extra tissues, went back to the office door, and turned to recheck the room. Everything looked clear except for those damn bloody shoe prints, but I couldn't do anything about them now. I double-checked my shoe—it seemed like the blood had sunk into the sole and wouldn't leave a trail in the hallway.

James's office door was open when I arrived, so no prints there. I strode back to the reception area and scanned the ceiling for security cameras, but none were in sight. I wiped down the front door and took the stairs to the lobby, Googling "payphones in St. Paul, MN" along the way. I found no security cameras here either.

The nearest phone was at a grocery store on Selby, just a couple of blocks away, and I walked over to prevent any cameras from recording my license plate. The phone was at the store entrance, and I kept my head down while dialing 911 to avoid being seen.

Almost immediately, an operator answered. "Nine-one-one, what's your emergency?"

"There has been a shooting at the office of Murphy, Brennen, and Murphy on Selby." I used a croaky voice, then hung up and left the store. I headed back to my car, feeling distraught but also like I'd dodged a bullet, then stopped dead in my tracks. There was a trail of texts on James's cell phone that led to me. I would have to go back and erase them or risk spending the night and perhaps many more nights behind bars while my very expensive legal eagle tried to justify my release on bail.

I dashed back to James's office building. No squad cars yet, but the sirens meant they were closing in. Then again, in this neighborhood, sirens were still routine. I ran up the stairs to the law office, pushed the door open with my elbow, and peeked in. The reception room was still empty, so I walked in and closed the door partway with my other elbow.

James's office was just as I had left it. His suit coat was hanging on the back of the door. I searched through the pockets. No phone. The sirens were getting louder. I was getting nowhere. Panicking seemed like a good plan. I scanned the room in desperation. The phone was charging on a small side table across the room.

I raced over and realized I would need his password to get in. I toyed with the idea of just taking the phone and running, but that would force the police to pull his text messages from the cell carrier, and I didn't want that. I had no choice but to delete the recent messages here and now, but how? I heard tires squealing, and the sirens suddenly stopped howling. The police must be in the parking lot.

I looked over at James and figured out how to get into the phone. I put his index finger up to the Home button, which I'd read somewhere would work within a few hours of death. Except, it wasn't working for me. I tried it again, but still nothing. I tried the thumb next, and it worked on the first try. I guess some people really did use their thumbs to access their phones.

I brought up the text messages and deleted the ones James had sent me. I considered deleting the emails but thought it would be better for the cops to find them and feel like they'd accomplished something. I wiped the phone down, put it back on the charger, and raced to the front door of the office. Using a tissue to open the door, I ran through, leaving it open to draw the cop's attention.

I heard footsteps on the stairs. I used the tissue to push the elevator button, got into the car, and let the doors close, hoping they wouldn't hear it. I counted to sixty to give them time to enter the law office, then pushed the button for the first floor with my knuckle. If one of the cops had stayed in their squad car for any reason, I was toast. As I rode the slow boat to One, I realized that in my haste to leave the first time, I'd forgotten to wipe down the button in the elevator and the call button on the first floor. When I got to the first floor, all was clear, so I wiped both buttons with the tissue and walked out unnoticed.

When I got back to my condo, I called Dean to tell him James was dead. I didn't want him to see it on the news, and I couldn't text him without creating another evidence trail. As he got over his initial astonishment, I walked him through the steps I'd taken to get rid of the evidence. I told him I'd tossed the shoes and tissues into a random dumpster but kept the portfolio—if I were ever questioned, I could always tell the cops I hadn't had a chance to return it yet, and I might be able to use it to weasel my way back into the law offices.

I also told him I'd deleted the texts on both phones and concluded James's laptop had been stolen. He agreed I'd done everything I could to avoid detection, which was high praise coming from him. It made us both realize the murder could still have been a drug-related theft gone wrong.

After we ended the call, I poured myself a small whiskey and sat on the couch, staring at the partially unobstructed lake and thinking about my birth father. I realized, ever since submitting the DNA test, I'd been wondering what he would be like. Was he rich and famous? A hardworking tradesman? Or maybe a homeless person who was down on their luck? It occurred to me that in each of these imaginary lives, I had given him the benefit of the doubt. I had assumed that, deep down, he had good intentions but found himself in circumstances beyond his control. I never once thought he would have hidden our existence from his world and be terrified of his current family finding out about his previous family. They said you should never meet your heroes—now I knew why.

Chapter Four

Friday, March 31

Two days later, I took the elevator from my condo to Design By Dyle, a small product design and engineering firm my business partner, Paul Cameron, and I started in 2010.

At first, it was just the two of us working out of the first floor of my duplex on Fremont Ave. in Uptown to save money. We were bidding on product design work and losing far more deals than we won. We learned a lot from the school of hard knocks and then hit a bit of luck. A former college roommate, who was CEO of a local medical device start-up, called with a thorny design problem. Paul and I devised an innovative solution that catapulted their product to success. Word of mouth spread, and work soon became steadier. In a few years, we were able to hire more designers, and we moved into an actual office on Lake Street just off Lake Calhoun, which let us show off our design sense and made us feel like a real company.

Since I lived and worked in the same building, I was usually the first to arrive, which meant I had to make the coffee. The shock of finding James dead hadn't worn off yet, and, over the past two days, I'd jumped every time my cell rang, or someone knocked on the office door. As I waited for the brewing to finish, the events of that night and the potential consequences swam through my head...again.

Considering my outburst at the restaurant, the cops would get around to questioning Dean and me. Not to mention we were probably the last ones to have seen James alive, except for the killer, of course. My ruminating was interrupted by a sharp rapping at the front door. *Please let it be Paul saying he forgot his keys.* Instead, a serious-looking man was standing there, and my gut clenched. I opened the door a few inches. "Can I help you? We don't open until eight."

"Detective Aaron Copeland." He flashed his badge. "Are you Grayson Dyle?"

"I am." I croaked out the words like I'd been smoking two packs a day for years.

"Mr. Dyle, I have a few questions for you. Do you mind if I come in?"

"Not at all." The detective was a six-one black man in his mid-thirties in a navy-blue suit, white shirt, and light-yellow tie. He must be hitting the gym as he appeared to be in great shape. "Can I offer you some coffee? I was just pouring myself a cup."

"Sure. I'm sorry to call on you so early, but it's rather important." He followed me to the break room.

I poured him a cup and motioned toward the cream and sugar, but he passed. I led him to my office, which provided the best home-field advantage, just in case I needed it. I wanted the police to solve the case quickly, but that didn't mean I wanted them breathing down my neck to do it. I frosted the glass as we entered and sat down.

The individual offices and conference rooms had floor-to-ceiling, electro-transparent windows, which meant the glass could be switched from clear to frosted using an iPhone or Amazon Alexa. There was a motion sensor with a timer that would switch the windows to clear after 15 minutes if no movement was detected in the room. It was an unwritten but well-established rule that we respected the privacy of anyone in a conference room with the glass frosted. Unless someone else needed that room for a business meeting, in which case the single person could be kicked out on their butt. Hey, we're trying to run a business here.

"You have a nice office—near the lake, too. I'll bet the view from the upper floors is spectacular." The detective briefly looked around. "The frosted glass is a nice touch."

"Thanks—we were lucky. This space hit the market just as we started looking, and we snatched it up. Did you say your name is Aaron Copeland?"

"Yes, sir, Detective Aaron Copeland—no relation to the composer."

"You must get that a lot."

"Not after they meet me. Besides, I spell my name with an 'e' in the middle. That usually clears things up." His brief smile telegraphed a clear message. He'd been through the routine many times and wanted to get down to business. "I assume you know why I'm here."

"Yes. I noticed the story about James Brennen's death on the news. Since my brother and I had dinner with him on Wednesday night, I figured I would be hearing from someone soon."

"We will be talking to everyone he recently met with, and you are two of the last people to see him alive."

"If this were *CSI: St. Paul*, we'd be at the top of your list of suspects for that reason alone, right?"

He ignored my weak attempt at being glib. "According to his schedule, he met the two of you for dinner at The Concord. Is that right?

"Yes, that's right."

"What was the meeting about?"

"We were meeting to discuss a lawsuit Dean and I were considering."

"What was the lawsuit about?"

"That's a private family matter, and I'd rather not discuss it. Doesn't attorney-client privilege cover this?"

"No. Attorney-client privilege prevents the attorney from disclosing the client's confidential information, which is no longer an issue in this case. The client is free to discuss the case with whomever he likes."

Beads of sweat broke out on my forehead. I considered lowering the thermostat a few degrees but decided against it as it would appear to be a sign of weakness.

"That's good to know, but I'd still rather not discuss it. Where is all of this going?"

Copeland ignored the question. "How did you come to meet with him?"

"I found him using a Google search. He seemed like a well-qualified attorney. Also, he worked in St. Paul, which meant I probably wouldn't run into him over lunch, which could be awkward."

"Okay. Did it seem as if Mr. Brennen was nervous or acting strangely?"

"It's difficult to say since that was the first time we met, but I didn't notice anything unusual."

He was silent for a few moments. "Mr. Dyle, did he say anything about someone threatening him or that he was concerned for his safety?"

I had been thinking about our dinner ever since I discovered the body. As far as I knew, the only person that might have had a reason to kill James would have been his wife, and that was only if she'd found out about Dean and me. I realized the detective was watching me intently and figured I'd better answer his question quickly to avoid suspicion.

"No. There was nothing like that. We discussed the lawsuit, and that was it. Did you speak with his wife, Cathy? She's their office manager, you know."

"Yes. I am aware of that."

"Of course."

"Did you disagree or argue about anything?"

I figured this line of questioning would come up and had my story ready. "Not really," I answered as naturally as possible.

"Not really. Is that a yes or a no?"

"It wasn't really an argument. I got a little cranky about some of the things James was implying about my family."

"What was he implying?"

"I can't tell you that without disclosing the nature of the lawsuit Dean and I were considering, which I'd rather not do."

"Did you threaten to kill him?"

"I got angry, something I rarely do, and might have said a few things in the heat of the moment… I don't remember what exactly."

The detective checked his notes. "Let me see if I can help you with that. 'I ought to kill you right now' seems to be the consensus from the other diners." He looked up and stared.

I reached for the coffee cup and realized my hands were shaking. I had to get my act together fast, or I'd look even more suspicious. "As I already stated, I was upset. I don't remember what I said exactly—It may have been something like that. But that doesn't mean I killed him."

"What happened after that."

"There wasn't anything left to discuss, so it was time to go. James left first, then Dean and I left together."

"And?"

"That's it. There's nothing else I can tell you."

"Tell me about the portfolio." Holy crap—of course, the server would have told Copeland he gave it to me. Good thing I hadn't chucked it after all.

"Oh, that's right. James had forgotten it, and a server handed it to me as we were leaving."

"What did you do with it?"

"I didn't know what to do with it, so I brought it home and figured I'd follow up with James the next day, but we never connected. I think it's sitting on my kitchen counter at home." Good ad-lib—points scored for the home team.

He stared at me for one long minute and must have decided to let this ride for now. "Will your brother have the same story?"

"I'm sure he will. I set up the dinner with James. Dean just came along for the ride." These intense stares from Copeland were bugging me.

"Interesting. Did you set it up over the phone or through email?"

I thought about the email messages and texts again and hoped I'd made the right decision about leaving the original set of emails intact. Wait a minute. I didn't kill him. Why was I acting this way?

"I found his email through his law firm's website."

"Okay. Mrs. Brennen is setting us up with access to her late husband's emails and texts, so I'm sure we'll see your messages."

"Whatever helps with your investigation."

"It would help if you would give me Dean's contact information. He's done a pretty good job of keeping a low profile."

"Of course."

Then he hit me with his ace in the hole question. "If we were to go to your home right now, would we find a shoe with a bloody sole?"

32

I almost lost it over that one. "I walk around the lakes all the time. There's no telling what's on the soles of my shoes. Why do you ask?"

"Do you often walk around the lake in dress shoes?"

"Sometimes, if it's been a stressful day, I can't wait to get out here."

"Right." The detective reached into his coat and pulled out his business card. "If you think of anything else."

The meeting must be over. "Thanks. Let me get you Dean's contact info." I took out my cell phone and gave him the details.

As we stood to go, he looked at his coffee cup.

"Just leave it. I'll get it later." I unfrosted the glass and walked him to the door.

Looking across the cubicles, I could see Paul was the only other person in the office. He must have arrived while I was receiving the third degree. He walked over and gave me a bemused look. "Who was that? Is there something you're not telling me about your affinity for strong black men? Don't worry. I'm not offended. A lot of my friends struggled with coming out at first."

Paul was tall and thin, wearing a dull orange sleeveless jacket over a light blue work shirt, light blue jeans, and cowboy boots to round out the look. Add in dark hair and the requisite three-day stubble, and he looked like he could have been on the cover of *Designers Quarterly* if there were such a thing. I've heard that his life partner, Richard, privately called me Paul's "work wife." I wasn't sure if I should be flattered or insulted. They amused themselves by setting me up with single ladies. It was sort of a "Queer Eye for the Minneapolis Guy."

"You know I'm still straight, right? Not that there's anything wrong with it. That was Detective Copeland from the St. Paul Police." We walked back to my office, and I explained what I could about the meeting with James and that he was now deceased. I neglected to mention I was the one who discovered the body. The fewer people that knew, the better. I couldn't believe he thought I might be gay, especially after all the crazy dates he'd set up for me. Okay, not all of the ladies were crazy. Some of them were nice, but they never worked out. No wonder he wondered. Still, he must not know me very well.

Paul looked concerned. "Are you okay? You seem shaken up." Okay, maybe he knew me a little too well.

"I'm fine. It's weird to think someone you just met and had dinner with is now dead." Especially when that someone was your father. "I just need time to process this."

"No problem. Just don't forget we need to talk about acquiring some new clients soon."

What a worrywart. After Paul left my office, I did a Google search for James Brennen. The *Star Tribune* reported he was killed in his office between eight and ten P.M. on Wednesday. The police thought it was an attempted theft, probably drug-related, as he'd been shot with a small-caliber gun at close range. Guilt came flooding in—could I have caused his death somehow? Maybe he finally fessed up to his wife, and she killed him in a jealous rage? No, that was crazy. It probably had nothing to do with Dean or me.

I tried to put the whole thing out of my mind by getting caught up on work emails. After handling a few, I noticed a new email from DeeDee Miller through the ancestry website.

"DesignGuy: Since you live in the Twin Cities, let's get together tomorrow at my home in Anoka. I'll tell you all about our family. It's fascinating! I can't wait to meet you in person, DeeDee."

Considering James's comments about people threatening to sue her, going to her home seemed unnecessarily risky. She had already inadvertently led Dean and me to our father, so she couldn't be trusted with personal information. Since our biological parents were dead, who else really mattered at this point? But there was no one else on the website that I was closely related to, and her promise to tell all about our family hooked me.

I realized that one of the pitfalls of family-origin websites was they were sterile. They could tell where your ancestors lived and whose DNA matched yours, but they couldn't deliver personal connections. Sure, you could email someone and share information or anecdotes, but it wasn't even close to bonding with a newfound relative over dinner or drinks and telling family stories. Assuming you could handle that kind of thing, of course. Right then, I decided to meet her in person, even if it was a bit risky or a waste of time.

But that didn't mean I was crazy enough to go alone. I forwarded the email to Dean using the subject line "Sibling Unmasked by DNA Results Kills Newly Discovered Brother." That should get his attention.

Sure enough, two minutes later, he texted me. **Meeting new relatives. Is that still on your bucket list?** It was a good thing he added a smiley face emoji, or I would have thought he was being sarcastic.

I figured I'd never text him into going, so I rang his cell. "I may need some backup. Those little old ladies can be unpredictable. We should go together."

"No way, Gray. I was against this from the beginning, as you may recall. Now that James is gone, why bother? What else can she possibly tell you?"

"But that's the whole point—to see what else she can possibly tell us. Besides, there doesn't seem to be much of a downside—we can always bale if it gets weird."

"You should go then. I can't. I'm on a tight deadline for Mr. X."

I knew I'd regret it but asked anyway. "Okay, who is Mr. X, and what is this crucial new project?"

"X is a working-class guy who got very wealthy doing high-tech start-ups. He just bought a fourteen thousand square foot mansion on Lake Minnetonka. You've got to see this spread to believe it—five acres, three outbuildings, two pools, and over four hundred feet of shoreline. He wanted to retrofit the place with a bunch of high-end electronics but didn't want to bring in a team to do the install because it doesn't square with his image, so I'm out there in stealth mode. I told our team to call him Mr. X so no one accidentally says his name when we're in public." Dean scoffed. "The crazy part is he liked it and insists we all call him that. It's a bit pretentious, but anytime he gets the slightest whim, we're the only company he calls, so we don't complain."

"O-kay. So, what's the project?"

"X was on a business trip to Dubai recently and saw a fantastic aerial show put on by a company called Skymagic. They simultaneously fly a fleet of over five hundred drones in various formations, including 3D animations.

It truly is remarkable. There are videos of it online if you're interested. Anyway, X wants to be the first one on Lake Minnetonka to have a personal drone squadron, and he wants our team to set it up for him."

"Is it legal to fly drones over a lake like that?" I wondered.

"It is as long as the operator has a Remote Pilot Certificate. I'm in the process of getting certified now."

Of course, you are, I rolled my eyes. Good thing he couldn't see me over the phone.

"Plus, it's a greener alternative to fireworks, and they don't scare family pets or disrupt people with PTSD." Dean must have sensed my skepticism. "Hey, it's a living. Anyway, X plans to hold his first show in a few weeks, and he wants to start testing flight patterns on Monday. Apparently, he wants to be able to spell out words on the first production run, so my weekend is shot."

He didn't seem too upset about it. A mental image hit me of Mr. X's poolside, bikini-clad, undoubtedly buxom girlfriend chatting up Dean about how brilliant he was for making all those silly drones draw pictures in the sky. I quickly shook that off and gave it one last, desperate attempt. "Don't you want to find out how DeeDee is related to us?"

"Not really. Speaking of which, why didn't we ask James while we were at dinner?"

"No idea." Apparently, I was going to have to be crazy enough to go alone after all. Time to move on to other topics. "By the way, I just had a lovely meeting with a very nice Police Detective named Aaron Copeland."

"I thought he was a composer?"

"No, he spells Copeland with an 'e.' Anyway, we should get our story straight because he will probably call you next. Are you free for lunch?"

"Afraid not. Dinner?"

I offered to bring dinner. We agreed to meet at his place in Eagan at six, and I ended the call.

Turning back to the email, I set up the meeting with DeeDee for one o'clock on Saturday. If I could figure out which of the people in her family tree were actual relatives, it should be easy to find them on social media and decide who to approach from there. I suspected younger single people would be good initial targets as they probably shared information online all the time, and they would be nieces or nephews, not sisters or brothers.

Of course, nothing was ever that simple, and I was nervous about the possibilities. What if DeeDee was a hoarder, and we'd be scrambling over a layer of junk so high our heads scraped the ceiling? I decided to stop thinking about it and clicked the down arrow to open the next email.

"Let James's death be a warning. Burn that letter before anyone else sees it. Don't make me come after you."

What the bloody hell? I recoiled from the screen in horror, then figured I must have been mistaken and leaned in to reread the email. It still said the same thing.

My hands shook as I took the letter out of the top drawer and searched it for clues for about the tenth time. I found nothing but the ramblings of a confused young girl who just wanted to do the right thing. Even though I couldn't see it, something on this page was a reason to kill, and connecting with James must have pulled the trigger on his life.

I turned to stare at the traffic on Lake Street in shock and disbelief. Some wacko was hell-bent on destroying Dean's letter. Even though our biological mother and father were both dead, someone still wanted to keep our existence a secret. But why?

A sudden surge of affection for my brother raced through me, which was quickly followed by rage at the nameless monster who was threatening us. I wanted to punch a hole in the window so I could scream through it. I realized that if Dean had been brutally slain, I would never stop searching for his killer until I'd either brought them to justice or killed them myself. I resolved that James's killer would be found, no matter what it took. If the police couldn't do it, I would.

A few deep breaths helped restore a small amount of calmness so I could think this through. The killer must have been in the office right after James returned from our meeting. The only controversial thing James did at dinner was confess to being our biological father. He must have admitted this to the killer and was then shot for it. The email was from James's personal email account, so the killer must have hacked into the stolen laptop—so much for the drug-related theft gone wrong theory.

It seemed likely that digging into the past would uncover some twisted events that led to adoptions and skeletons in the family closet. While I was grateful to have met my biological father, even if just for one night, learning more about the rest of the family in the very near future was critical to keeping Dean and me alive.

Chapter Five

Friday Night, March 31

"What do we do now?" Dean's face turned white after I told him about Copeland's visit, which was amazing to watch, considering he spent way too much time hunched over a laptop and rarely got out in the sun.

I had driven to Dean's home in Eagan after stopping at a sub shop to pick up dinner. Dean had given me a copy of his house key for emergencies, and I'd let myself in. The divorce was hard on my brother, and after considerable thought about his priorities, he decided a modest lifestyle suited him better. He let his ex keep their upscale home in the swanky Twin Cities suburb of Edina and moved into a relatively pedestrian split-level ranch house. I figured I'd find him typing away at the souped-up desktop computer in his home office, which was the most expensive thing he owned after the house. I also knew what was coming next.

"You know I can't be involved in anything untoward."

"I know. You've told me that a hundred times."

"If you hadn't started this whole DNA search thing, none of this would have happened. This is all your fault," he growled. "Our fault..." He sank further into his office chair with the sudden realization that we were in this together. "I told you this whole DNA thing was a bad idea."

So much for him being on board after we found James. If everything were peachy, he would be claiming it was his idea in the first place. I opened the threatening email on my phone and held it up for him to see. I might as well give him all the unwelcome news at once.

Dean leaned forward to read the email, then crashed back into his chair and smacked his forehead hard with the heel of his palm. That had to hurt. "Oh my gosh. It really is our fault! Cathy must have sent that. James probably confessed about us. She must have flipped out and killed him on the spot. None of this would have happened if you didn't start with all the DNA testing stuff."

I sat in his leather guest chair. "Wait a minute. We can't just assume it was Cathy. Any of his relatives could have killed him, and we have no idea how big his extended family is—there could be dozens of possibilities. This whole thing may have nothing to do with us."

"Why would the killer send you a threatening message if it has nothing to do with us, and why are they so desperate to destroy the letter?"

"I don't know, but there's only one way to find out." I held up the bag of subs and started toward the kitchen. "Copeland doesn't know about the family connection, so he doesn't know where to look. He's either going to think it's one of James's clients or some drug-related robbery, so he's not going to find the killer. If we don't tell him the whole story, someone will get away with murder."

Dean followed me and got drinks for us from the fridge while I set out the subs on the island, then sat at a barstool to eat.

"Are you nuts? We can't say anything. I'll bet you're already their top suspect because of your little outburst. Telling him now will make you look even guiltier." Dean unwrapped his sub and took a bite.

"Fine. But if Copeland is looking at the wrong people, he'll never figure it out. We're the only ones who know where to look, so we'll have to investigate the family angle ourselves."

"Yo, Columbo, James was shot, as in, with a gun, twice. You have Dad's old Ruger in that box in your closet, right? Are you going to run out and get a concealed carry permit? Even if you did, your gun is a revolver, so you have to load each round separately. I can see you in a firefight with some bad guy and then calling for a timeout so you can reload. Sheesh."

"Said the IT nerd who's paid to be suspicious. Besides, I've been thinking about getting a carry permit for years, and this is a good reason to do it. Look, if we don't consider the family, no one will. If we find something suspicious, we can let Copeland know, which will make us look less suspicious. Or we can tip him off anonymously—you would know how to do it without getting any blowback. If we really are to blame, we owe it to James to figure this out."

Dean was still skeptical. I sensed this because I'm his biological brother. I'd been reading about adoptees and was saddened to learn some of them never develop the ability to feel their siblings' emotions if they don't have the same biological parents. Of course, it could also be the way he folded his arms across his chest and was staring at me over his glasses. I decided to appeal to his sense of moral decency...and paranoia.

"If someone killed James to keep that letter hidden, some relative we haven't even met yet could be next. Worse yet, it could be me or maybe even you."

That got his attention. "What do you have in mind?"

"Let's see if we can figure out who sent that email."

"Fine. We're fairly sure James's laptop was stolen, presumably by the killer, to see if James sent us any family history info. Since the killer emailed their threat from James's laptop, they'll have to monitor it to see if you reply, which gives me an idea. I should be able to create a backdoor on the laptop using a phishing email."

"What's that now?"

Dean became exasperated. "You're kidding, right?" He could probably tell by my sheepish look that I wasn't. "Okay, pay attention. I'll use your laptop to reply to the threatening email and will add some of my homegrown malware code. When they open the email, it will load the code from my server without them knowing it. This code will create a backdoor to the laptop I can use to search through the files for anything related to the murder."

"Really? That's awesome."

"One thing is bugging me, though. How did the killer know we contacted James in the first place?"

I hadn't considered that. "I suppose you have a theory."

"Yep. You can take your DNA results down anytime you want, right?"

"You can either make them private, so only people you approve can see them, or you can delete them altogether. Why"

"Can you set up an alert where the website will send you an email when they post new DNA test results that match your results?"

"Yeah, so?"

"Did you set up an alert?"

I was suddenly feeling defensive. "I never got around to it."

"What if someone else had their DNA tested on the same site and had set up an email alert, which was triggered when your DNA results were posted, indicating some family relationship with them? They saw your results, realized it would cause trouble, and immediately made their results private. You would have never known they were on the site."

"That seems like a stretch." I finished my sub, crumbled up both wrappers, and took them to the garbage. "It was only about thirty seconds from the time I got the email saying the DNA results were available to the time I checked the website for matches, hardly enough time for that to happen."

Dean didn't seem ready to abandon this theory, and the odds were good that he had already set up an app monitoring his Gmail account that would send him a text message if he ever received an alert email of any kind. He didn't seem to realize the average person didn't know they could do that or have the inclination to figure it out if they did. I jumped in before he could argue.

"Speaking of the ancestry website, how hard would it be to hack in and see who else DeeDee has claimed for her family tree?"

Dean shook his head. "I'll take a look, but countries like Russia and North Korea target ancestry sites to uncover private family relationship data for leverage over U.S. politicians, so they have to be hack-proof. It will be a lot easier to cozy up and get her to add you to her tree."

"Didn't James say she'd been harassing a lot of people on the lineage site? She probably has a lot of false connections."

"I'm betting she just pretends to be a bit slow so no one questions her motives. Doesn't it seem odd how quickly she contacted you after the site posted your DNA results? Then she dropped those bread crumbs in her supposedly innocent messages to make sure you'd find James. Doesn't that seem suspicious?"

"No. It seems like she's somewhat dotty. Plus, why would she want us to find James? She couldn't have been planning for us to kill him."

"I don't know. That's what you need to find out when you visit her. By the way, I think I may have a Kevlar vest you can borrow."

I knew he was just messing with me about the vest, but he seemed serious about the rest of it. I couldn't see DeeDee being the killer, but she still could have been involved somehow. I had to admit it did seem odd she contacted me and led us to James so quickly.

"I'll be sure to ask why she wanted James dead before I leave. I think I'll also reach out to Cathy to see what she has to say. It probably wouldn't hurt to call his partners at the law firm either, just as a precaution."

Dean frowned. "Wait a minute. What are you going to say when they ask why you're calling about James? You can't tell them he was our biological father."

"Good point. I could pretend I didn't know he was dead and say I'm contacting James about a case."

"That won't work. It might get you in the door, but they'll just try to steer you to a different attorney, so you won't go to another law firm. The focus will be off of James and on your case in the first two minutes."

"I'll say I recently found out he was a relative and then ask about going to the funeral. Maybe we can find out more about the family at the same time."

Dean was still frowning. "That still sounds lame. Stopping by his office to ask about the funeral? Why wouldn't you just call them or look up the funeral information online?"

Inspiration struck. "How about this? I'll bring the portfolio along and tell them I'm returning it."

"I don't know. I wouldn't do it, but you should go for it."

"Why don't you research James's past just to see what's out there."

"Okay. Speaking of the funeral, I'd like to go, too."

"I'll let you know when they schedule it."

Dean had a sad, faraway look in his eyes. "Who knew being adopted could be so complicated."

Chapter Six

Saturday Afternoon, April 1

I arrived at DeeDee's home on McKinley Street early, which gave me time to drive around the block a few times on a reconnaissance mission. She lived in a small gray bungalow with a small deck on the front on which a couple of lawn chairs sat facing the street. It has a detached one-car garage, and the antenna mounted on the roof made me wonder if she had high-speed internet. I chuckled, thinking she was using the time between webpage loads to convince herself she was related to some random person or to plot the murder of more family members. Everything seemed routine, so I pulled onto her gravel driveway next to the house.

"Grayson!" exclaimed DeeDee, who must have been waiting near the door for me because it opened immediately after I rang the bell. She looked exactly as I expected—about five-foot-two, with short curly white hair and hazel eyes, wearing a light blue dress with a pattern of small red flowers. She stood on her toes for an awkward hug. "Come on in—we're all waiting for you."

"Thanks for seeing me, DeeDee." She had a mischievous smile, and I liked her almost immediately despite my previous apprehensions about her involvement in a murder.

As we walked through the living room toward the dining room table, I wondered who else was waiting for me. There didn't seem to be anyone else here. Perhaps various pets were lying in wait? She could have been a cat person, but my dander allergies weren't kicking in, so I figured we were clear.

I couldn't help but notice the decor could have used a bit of updating. Perhaps a subscription to HGTV would give her a hobby other than scouring the internet for people she wished were her kinfolk. There were quite a few fancy vases, though. There had to be at least ten in the living room alone, each on an individual doily, with fake plastic flowers and various religious items affixed. Most had plastic rosaries draped over them, and some had holy cards leaning against them. Others were adorned with various plastic icons, including Praying Hands, Virgin Marys, and my personal favorite, Touchdown Jesus, a figure raising his arms straight up like a referee when a football team scored.

"Sit right here at the table, dear."

"Thanks, DeeDee."

Heavy drapes stopped every last ray of sunshine from entering the dimly lit dining room. The curio cabinets that lined the dining room contained more decorated vases and left little room to maneuver. I had to squat and scoot across the chair to sit at the dining room table while I tried not to disturb the copious newspaper clippings, pictures, and scraps of paper with notes scribbled on them. I wasn't claustrophobic, but it suddenly seemed difficult to breathe. I cursed Dean for not being here, and I somehow knew we hadn't gotten to the weird part yet.

"Would you like some coffee or tea?"

"No thanks. I had some in the car on the way over. What a lovely home you have."

"Thanks, Grayson. You seem like a nice person. I think we're going to like you."

I couldn't tell if there were other people in the house or if she was using the royal we. Then she hit me with a verbal barrage about how excited she was to meet me, how she recently became semi-retired and now spent many hours building her family tree, and how much I resembled other relatives. I tried to interrupt to ask who I looked like, but she didn't seem to have heard the question.

DeeDee started talking to the vase in the middle of the table, which had no flowers in it but seemed to be in a place of honor, saying how wonderful it was that I fell right into her lap and then nodding as if it had agreed with her. I stared at the vase, wondering why there were no flowers in it, plastic or otherwise.

Then DeeDee asked, "Where are my manners? Harry, meet Grayson. Grayson, this is Harry."

My autonomic nerves kicked in, and I raised my hand to shake. Then I realized the top was sealed, so it couldn't be a vase. Holy crap, it was a cremation urn. Some dead person's ashes, no, Harry's ashes, were sitting on her dining room table, and she was conversing with them. By now, my hand was out, and I wondered about the proper etiquette for greeting an urn.

I ended up mumbling "Hi" while softly patting the top.

DeeDee seemed oblivious to my dilemma. "Harry is my late husband." She leaned in to whisper in private as if he could no longer hear. "He died eight years ago. These are his ashes. We still talk, though. It's been a great comfort knowing he's still around, watching over me."

She smiled as she leaned back and stared at the urn. I wouldn't have been surprised if it had answered me back just then.

I glanced at the vases in the cabinets and confirmed their plastic flowers were glued to their lids, too. We were completely surrounded by cremation urns. Did DeeDee fill these up herself? Maybe she had a heavy-duty oven installed in the basement and had set aside a special family urn for me. I wondered if she'd let me select the shelf where my ashes would reside. She suddenly seemed like a cross between the nice old ladies in *Arsenic and Old Lace*, who killed their lodgers and buried them in the cellar, and H.H. Holmes, the serial killer from *The Devil in the White City*, who incinerated tenants in his basement furnace.

I fought the impulse to bale out because I hadn't asked her why she killed James yet. *Calm down. Just breathe—you can do this.* I hoped DeeDee and I were far enough apart on the genetic scale so I had avoided contamination by the crazy genes.

DeeDee started picking up seemingly random pieces of paper from the table and telling me about the people listed on them and how they related to the family tree. I tried to ask a few questions, but she didn't seem to notice. I resigned myself to sitting in silence for half an hour, plotting my escape. Did I know Madam Curie and the pop singer Madonna were related to each other? Nope. She assured me they were, and they were related to us, too. I realized that, if anything, James had downplayed her family tree-building obsession.

My curiosity kicked in, and I finally got her attention long enough to ask, "Is it okay to have so many cremation urns? I thought they had to be sealed in a mausoleum or something."

DeeDee looked at me with pity and gave me her mischievous smile. "Mausoleums are for caskets, silly. Urns are stored in a columbarium, which has much smaller niches. Most people don't realize the ashes don't need to be interred. Loved ones can do whatever they want with them. Secretly spreading them near the deceased's favorite ride at Disneyland is always popular, but don't let the park workers catch you doing that. They'll kick you out of the park for the day, ticket or no ticket."

"You certainly know your urns and your urn-related terminology."

"I used to work for a crematorium, dear, but I'm semi-retired now. I guess I just got used to having ashes around. You'd be surprised at how many people abandon their loved one's ashes because they think it's creepy to have them in the house. Can you imagine?"

"Crazy." Kind of like this whole ordeal.

As DeeDee was educating me on the funeral customs of North America, she was moving the papers around on the table and inadvertently uncovered a picture of James. I wondered if she'd heard he was deceased. I thought about telling her but didn't want to cause her any distress—who knows what that might trigger. Of course, if she was involved in the murder, she already knew.

"This is James Brennen, right?"

DeeDee squinted at the picture for a moment, then exclaimed, "Yes, that's him. He's an attorney and a marvelous man. One of his partners has been helping me deal with the crackpots. He's been a godsend. James has a brother named Thomas, you know. Thomas is a bishop. He's a very wonderful man. I see him at the church from time to time on Bingo Night."

She seemed very proud to have a very important person in her family tree, but how did I know she wasn't just making this up? "Wow, that's great. How are you related to them?"

"I think they're second cousins. Would you like me to ask my father? He's over there on the mantle."

Oh boy. "No thanks. It's not that important."

We talked for what seemed like another hour. Well, DeeDee told stories, and I listened. I didn't mind—it was fascinating. But she kept the house quite warm, and soon I was getting drowsy. Falling asleep seemed like a terrible idea since there was no telling what state I would wake up in, if I woke up at all. It was definitely time to go.

"Would you mind if I took a picture of us for my home album?" I interrupted.

"Of course not, dear. You can take pictures if you want. Do you mind if Harry joins us? He doesn't like to be left out." She slid the urn over.

As she moved Harry over, a smaller urn came into view. I couldn't help myself. "Who might that be?"

"That's my ex-husband, George." DeeDee banged the table loudly with her fist. I was so startled I nearly knocked Harry over. "To tell the truth, that's only half of him. His second wife has the rest." She leaned toward me again and whispered with a conspiratorial grin. "But I got the better half."

I had no desire to find out what that meant. I just needed to leave. I took a quick picture of DeeDee and Harry and got up to go. "This has been fascinating. Thank you so much for inviting me into your home and sharing all this with me!"

"Do you have to go?" DeeDee pouted. "We were just getting to the good stuff, and I thought we could have dinner together." She motioned toward the kitchen. "I made a lovely meatloaf, and I can pop it into the oven anytime we get hungry."

I carefully sidestepped the people in the living room as I inched toward the door. "That sounds delicious, but I really have to be going."

The urns now seemed like unconcealed landmines, and an image of me accidentally spilling her former dog, Skippy, flashed through my head.

"Wait, wait, I put together a care package for you." As she headed for one of the back bedrooms, I seriously thought about running for it.

"Oh, you didn't have to do that. I hope you didn't go through any trouble." I was hoping she wasn't planning to present me with a personal urn on permanent loan from the DeeDee collection and wondered how one disposed of funeral urns and whether they would take them at a recycling center. She was back in a flash with a cardboard box that had once held four gallon-sized jugs of Gallo Wine. Inside was a mind-bending array of more religious detritus. Rosaries, dashboard statues, holy cards, laminated holy cards with crucifixes, praying hands, mousepads with pictures of the Pope—it was an incredible testimony to humankind's ability to trivialize anything sacred for a buck.

"I have so many of these, and I get more and more every day. I think it started when I gave ten dollars to the Little Friends of the Destitute. My friend Mabel told me they sell your name after you donate to make more money. I suppose that's alright because it's all for a worthy cause. But the next thing you know, I have hundreds of these things."

"Why don't you just throw them away?" I asked.

She was aghast. "Oh no—I can't do that. They're religious! They were blessed by a priest or sprinkled with holy water or some such thing. I can't just throw them away."

Then what did you do when you didn't want them, shoot them into the sun?

"I know just what to do with these." I fully intended to do her and the rest of the world a favor by pitching them into the first dumpster I could find.

"I knew you'd know what to do, Grayson." Her eyes beamed.

I picked up the box and walked toward the front door. "It was nice to meet you…all." I opened the door to return to reality.

DeeDee waved goodbye from the front door. "Let's get together soon. We haven't even gotten to my mother's side of the family. I'll send you an email."

I waved back as I got into my car. "Sounds good. Looking forward to it."

A few minutes later, I pulled into a small lot behind a convenience store and deposited the box into a dumpster. Then I sent Dean a quick text. **Made it out alive.**

Dean texted back. **I was worried. ;-) How's DeeDee?**

She never asked about the letter. Definitely an acquired taste, absolutely not a killer. BTW James has a brother named Thomas who's a Catholic bishop.

Chapter Seven

Monday, April 3

I t always struck me as odd that police detectives on TV went to a suspect's home or office to interview them, which would seem to give away their home-field advantage. Wouldn't the potential suspect be more intimidated being called down to the police station? Then I read somewhere that, in real life, the cops never called someone down to the station because it gave the average person time to conjure up all manner of pretexts, excuses, and rationales for whatever foul deed they may or may not have committed.

In that spirit, I decided to visit Andy Murphy, Senior Partner of Murphy, Brennen, & Murphy, which was also the scene of the crime. I wanted to take another look at James's office to see if I missed anything. Law offices usually opened at nine, so I arrived at nine-thirty and reminded myself to act as if I'd never been there before. I brought James's portfolio along as an excuse for the visit.

I avoided the elevator and took the stairs to the third floor. The doors were open this time, and I walked in.

A striking lady was selecting files from a filing cabinet at the reception desk. She smiled at me. "Can I help you?" Blue eyes, blond hair, cute nose, two inches shorter than me, wearing a beige silk blouse, a black skirt, and black pumps.

The term svelte popped into my head, but I couldn't remember exactly what it meant, and I decided to look it up later. I was wondering if she smiled at everyone when she asked them that question.

"I'm looking for, um...." Who was I looking for, James or Andy? Did it even matter? "Andy Murphy."

"Is he expecting you?"

"No. I was in the neighborhood and thought I'd drop off James's portfolio." I held it up as I spoke.

"I can take that for you." She held out her hand. "How did you end up with it anyway?"

I handed her the portfolio as I couldn't dream up an excuse for giving it to Andy personally. "I had dinner with James recently, and he accidentally left it behind."

"Okay. Thanks for dropping it off."

This plan was running out of steam. I had to think of a reason to talk to Andy pronto, or she'd see me to the door. I couldn't back down now, as I'd really look dumb coming back later with some other sorry excuse for a visit. Besides, I wanted to spend more time with my new friend. I tried to look at the ring finger on her left hand, but the file folder she was holding blocked the view.

"Actually, I'm here to discuss a legal matter."

"You're here to discuss a legal matter?" She smiled.

Okay, maybe I was crazy, but there might have been just a hint of mutual attraction going on. Of course, guys tended to think this even when a lady was just being polite, so I didn't want to jump to any conclusions.

"Yes. I have a legal matter to discuss with Andy." I smiled back, hoping that didn't seem creepy.

"Wait here, please. I'll see if he's available."

I was proud of my decision not to check out her butt as she turned away when I noticed she was looking at me in the mirror behind the front desk. She was still smiling as she walked down the hall out of sight. I wondered if this was her desk and walked over to see what it held during working hours. It was bare except for a box of tissues and a phone. Maybe she wasn't the receptionist after all.

A couple of minutes later, she came back. "Andy will see you now. I can take you back to his office. Would you like some water or coffee?"

"No thanks."

"I'm Kate." She extended her hand to shake. Firm grasp—striking.

"Grayson Dyle. Nice to meet you."

She turned to walk back down the hall, talking over her shoulder. "Your resemblance to James is remarkable. Are you related to him?"

Didn't see that coming. "I'm trying to figure that out." Sometimes honesty was the best policy.

"Yeah, I'd go with that approach. You don't sound like someone with a legal matter to discuss." She dropped me off at Andy's office. Sometimes honesty could be a little too much.

Andy came around his desk to shake my hand. He had probably been six feet when he was younger but was now slightly stooped. His dark-blue suit and white shirt were showing signs of wear. It looked like forty-plus years of practicing family law had taken it out of him. Hearing some of his war stories over a few beers would probably be fascinating.

"What can I do for you, Grayson?"

"I'd like to inquire about James Brennen. I believe he and I are, or I guess were, related, and...." Wow, this plan was falling apart fast, too. Why was I here again? I wondered how much an online course on becoming a private investigator would cost.

Unbelievably, Andy came to my rescue. "You just want to talk to someone about him. It's no problem. It happens all the time. A client might be going through a terrible divorce, but that doesn't mean they hate their spouse twenty-four-seven. They often want to talk it through to make sure they're doing the right thing. Of course, a divorce is a much different loss than a death in the family, but it's still a loss nonetheless."

This guy was good. "Yes, that's it exactly." Until that moment, I hadn't realized that, despite the intense anger I displayed at the restaurant, I had been mourning this guy, my birth father, who I'd just met and barely knew. Maybe it would help to talk it out.

"Please, sit." He indicated either of two chairs set a couple of feet apart, between which there was a small table with a box of tissues. Family law offices must go through a ton of the stuff. "Would you like some coffee?"

"No thanks."

"It's a bit obvious that you're related to James in some way—there is a definite family resemblance. So, how can I help?"

I went through a brief version of recent events, ending with the visit to DeeDee's house.

Andy grinned. "You've met the infamous DeeDee? Does she still have one and a half husbands on her dining room table?"

"She does indeed. Sounds like you've visited her."

"James asked me to represent her when someone was threatening legal action. He said he had to recuse himself because she was family. After meeting her, I wondered if that was the real reason. Anyway, go on."

Andy seemed trustworthy, but only to a certain point. I decided to fudge on the whole fatherhood thing. "We know we're related to James but don't know how exactly. We agreed to stay in touch and try to figure it out. Then I read about him in the paper. Now it's too late, which is a real shame. He seemed like a good man."

"He was. It's been a real loss for all of us. James and I had worked together for many years. He was more than just a colleague. He was a good friend." After a brief pause, he made an offer. "I can recommend a grief counselor if you like. As you can imagine, in our business, the need often arises."

"Thanks, but I don't think that will be necessary. Do you think I can see his office? It might be consoling to see where he worked and learn more about his life."

The sudden pained look on Andy's face told me he didn't like the idea, but he agreed anyway. "I guess that would be okay. As you know, James suffered a horrible death. The office was cordoned off until the police finished processing it, and then we immediately had it cleaned and restored to avoid any additional trauma for the staff. It seemed like the right way to honor his memory."

We walked down to the end of the hall. Andy opened the door to James's office with a passkey, entered, and turned on the lights. Now that things were calm, I noted the office was nicely furnished with a traditional law office look of solid, reddish-brown mahogany. The bullet holes wall had been spackled over but not painted over yet. They were much larger now, probably because the forensic team had pulled out the slugs.

"It looks like they haven't had a chance to fix the wall yet. Sorry, you had to see that."

"No worries," I said as if I'd seen a dozen crime scenes before. I walked behind the desk, narrowly avoiding an involuntary reflex to step over the spot where James's blood had pooled, which might have given me away. I was surprised to see the bloodstains were gone. Even the bloody toe prints were gone. Someone had done an excellent job selecting a crime scene cleanup company.

There were two pictures on James's desk I hadn't noticed before. One was a studio photo of James and a woman, who must be his wife, Cathy, in a serious pose. The other was a candid shot of them at a lake cabin, embracing a cute kid with braces, who must be their daughter. It looked like an older picture, and they seemed happy. It was sad to think her father wouldn't be there for her. Or for me either, which drove home the point Dean and I now had a half-sister. Would we forge some more or less healthy family relationship with her, despite the secrecy and James's death? For that matter, how many other half-siblings were running around out there?

Andy was fidgeting and seemed to regret letting me see the office.

"I appreciate your doing this. It gives me a feeling for what James was like." As I scanned the desk from left to right, I noticed an outdated landline phone and a leather desk pad with leather side rails in front of the chair. Talk about old school. Light green blotter paper was tucked under the side rails and was heavily covered in detailed geometric patterns, doodles, and notes. James must have spent a lot of time on the phone. The display, mouse, and mouse pad were missing, presumably stowed for a future user.

"Did he have any unusual visitors during the day or two before the incident?"

Andy was silent for a moment, with a strained look. "Not that I can remember. Why do you ask?"

"Just curious."

It was obvious he wanted me to leave, and I was about to go when I noticed a few names scribbled in marker on top of some of the doodles. I was surprised to see the names included Grayson, Dean, Cathy, Frank, Jane, and Tom. If I were a real PI, this would be a clue. I took a mental snapshot of the blotter paper and followed Andy out.

We walked down the hall toward the front desk. "Is there anything else I can help you with?"

"My brother, Dean, and I would like to attend the funeral. Has it been scheduled?"

"I've been assisting James's wife, Cathy, with the arrangements. It will be held this Friday, April seventh, at St. Celestine in St. Paul. You may want to contact her if you'd like to learn more about James and your family history. Cathy is our office manager, and she's on bereavement leave for the next two weeks. I'm sure she'd be happy to speak with you after she returns."

"Thank you so much for meeting with me this morning."

We shook hands.

"It was good to speak with you. I'm sure I'll see you at the service."

As I turned to leave, Kate was walking down the hallway toward us. "It was nice to meet you." I waved to her.

"Nice to meet you, too." This time, I could have sworn she was smiling at me.

As soon as I returned to my office, I fired up my laptop and searched Facebook for any pages related to James, Cathy, or the law firm, wondering why I hadn't already checked them out. The personal pages were marked private, and virtually no information was available unless you were friends. I suspected most family law attorneys did this to avoid being stalked by any disgruntled former clients. The Murphy, Brennen, & Murphy page had some candid shots of a company picnic and a few endorsements but not much else. I clicked on the link to the company website, where I found the prerequisite picture of the partners on the home page. It still included James and didn't mention their loss, which wasn't surprising. It usually took non-techies a week or two to realize they should update their website and then another week to figure out who to call to get it done.

I clicked on the "office staff" link at the top of the home page, and the new page included pictures of Kate and Cathy, with their names and titles listed underneath. Kate had somehow forgotten to mention she was the Chief Financial Officer, and the omission intrigued me even more. How presumptuous of me to assume she was an admin, although, in my defense, she had been searching through files near the receptionist's deck when we met. Her bio also said she volunteered at St. Celestine Church. Of course, she did—James probably asked her to help with their books.

I didn't want to wait until next week to talk with Cathy and tried to think of an excuse to revisit the law office, where I might accidentally run into their charming CFO. I realized James's cell number was still stored in my phone, and I called it on the off-chance Cathy would pick up. She answered after a few rings. "Hello. Who is this?"

"Hi. My name is Grayson Dyle, and—"

"Grayson Dyle. I know that name. I saw it on my husband's schedule. You had dinner with him about a case on the night he was—the night he died. How can I help you?"

She seemed distracted, and I couldn't blame her for that. I didn't know where to start, and this call was quickly becoming another terrible idea.

"Did you say James was your husband? You must be Cathy Brennen."

"That's right. Are you calling about your case? If you are, I'll have to refer you to another one of the attorneys in the firm now that James is deceased."

"I noticed that in the news… I'm so sorry for your loss."

"Thank you. I'm afraid I don't have time to talk right now. Why are you calling?"

"I had been doing some research into my family tree, and it turns out that James and I are related, so—"

"You're related to James? How could that be?"

"I don't know. That's one of the things we were discussing over dinner."

"He never mentioned anything about you. I know all his relatives, and I don't see how you could fit in unless you're a distant cousin or something.

Why are you bothering me about this now? There must be other relatives you can talk to."

"None that I'm aware of, and that's part of the problem...." What to say, how much to reveal? I doubted James had confessed anything to his wife between the end of our dinner and the time he was killed. But certain facts would have to come out eventually, even if the whole truth never did. "My brother, Dean, and I recently found out we were adopted at birth, so I took a DNA test, which led us to a relative named DeeDee. She connected—"

Cathy jumped on the reference. "DeeDee, that lunatic? She told you that you're related to James, and you believed her? Have you met the woman? She's psychotic. She thinks she's related to the Queen of Sheba, for Pete's sake. She's caused more arguments among the partners than anyone else in the firm's history."

I just wanted this call to be over and thought it best to remain quiet.

"Look, Grayson, I can't talk about this right now. I have a husband to bury. What I can tell you is that anything that woman says is highly suspect. James seemed to have a soft spot for her, and I never understood why, but she knew it, and she took advantage of it. I can't allow that to happen again. I won't allow it. If you figure out how you're related to James, and if you truly are related, we can talk. Otherwise, I have nothing left to say." With that, she hung up.

What a lovely way to meet your stepmother. Why did things like that never happen to the amateur detectives on TV?

I tried to focus on company work for a change when an email from Dean arrived. I couldn't resist and opened it immediately. He discovered that James was originally from Rochester, Minnesota, and he had a brother named Tom who had entered the priesthood. He included a link to James's funeral notice, which said Bishop Thomas Brennen of the St. Paul Diocese would preside. That had to be the same guy. It was interesting to learn we had a notable uncle. He also had tried to hack the family-origin website but found it too well protected, so that idea was a non-starter. I was about to reply when Paul stopped by with a big grin.

"Alexa, Windows." Uh oh. Paul frosting the glass as he closed the office door was usually not a good sign, but maybe this was good news. He looked like a schoolboy as he sat down with his head down, back erect, legs together, and hands folded in his lap. Then he took a deep breath, looked up, and beamed at me. "You're not going to believe this, Grayson. I just got off the phone with Mike Wilson. He's the owner of Wilson Construction, and he called to see if we're interested in bidding on a project he's planning."

"That's fantastic, Paul!"

"I know!" he trilled. "Listen to this. Mike's company has been doing a lot of the redevelopment on Sheppard Road, across the river from Harriet Island. He's all excited about this new construction material that's made from carbon. It's supposed to be extremely lightweight and ten times stronger than steel. He's installing a park along the waterfront, and he wants to make some sculptures with this material. He wants them to look like they're floating in midair. It sounded like a fantastic opportunity, so I immediately said we'd love to work with him...."

I was confused. "We don't normally design sculptures. What part will we do?"

"I'll have you know I did a lot of sculpture design work in school, and I was thinking...."

I was still confused. "There are plenty of designers that do that for a living. Why would he hire us?"

Paul glared at me. "The design work would be a perk. He wants us to use our CAD people and 3-D printers to help him test this material. What was it called again, graphen, graphit, or something like that—"

"You mean graphene. Oh, now I get it. Mike wants us to create a computer model of the sculptures and then use our 3-D printers to make graphene prototypes to see if this material is as light and strong as they say. If they pass the test, we can print the full-sized version in pieces and assemble them into the finished product."

"That's what I just said. You weren't paying attention, were you?"

Whatever, Paul. "That's brilliant."

"Thanks, but we still have to win the business."

"Of course. How did he hear about us?"

"He found our website and liked our design work. It was our 'unique combination of engineering and design principles,' as he described it, so he rang us up. Good thing I put a blurb about our 3-D printer on the website."

"Agreed, but why didn't you send him over to me?" I usually handled new client opportunities.

"Are you really saying you don't trust me to handle a simple phone call? Do you think you're the only one that can drum up some new business? I'm not just a designer, you know."

"That's not what I meant. I was just trying to figure out how I missed the call. It sounds like you were fantastic talking to Mike. When did you say we're meeting with him?"

"Friday of this week. Ten A.M. Think you can make it? It's only our company on the line. No big deal or anything."

As a small, relatively unknown design firm, we continually prospected for new business. Carson Companies, one of our major clients, had recently been acquired by a Chinese firm, which had already taken their IT work in-house and moved it to China. If they moved the design work offshore next, we'd have a big hole in our revenue stream, and we'd have to lay off a few team members or, more likely, take big pay cuts ourselves. Paul and I were both stressed over the potential of losing so much business, but there wasn't much we could do other than continue to do the best work possible while simultaneously trying to land new clients.

"We're going to have to reschedule. I have a funeral on Friday I really must attend."

Paul got up and started pacing back and forth. "Whose funeral? You didn't tell me anyone died. Are you just making this up because you're mad I didn't consult with you before setting up a simple meeting? Why do we even work together if you don't trust me? You're just like Richard said."

Richard? Since when was his husband throwing me under the bus? I thought he liked me. "Paul, you've got to calm down. I haven't had a chance to tell you or anyone else, but a relative died late last week, someone from my birth family. I really need to...."

Paul's face was turning red. He stopped pacing and interrupted me. "Your birth family? I thought you said you didn't know any of them. Now I know you're making this up! What if Mike won't reschedule, and he blows us off altogether? Then what are we going to do for new clients? They don't just walk in the front door by themselves, you know."

After seven years of working together, we were just now finding out how the other person reacted under extreme pressure.

"Look, I can't explain this all right now. Don't you trust me?"

There was an awkward pause as Paul seemed to be considering this. "It's not about trust. I don't think I can keep doing this, Gray. Richard and I have been talking about moving to the west coast—Portland or Seattle, maybe—there are so many fun design shops popping up out there. This whole thing could be a sign it's time to make a change."

While I really didn't want to have to talk Paul down off the ledge right now, I couldn't lose him either. Paul was the yin to my yang. We were two parts that needed each other to make a whole. I trusted my design sense from an engineering standpoint, but the results could seem a bit sterile at times. They needed Paul's design sense to breathe life into them. It was the combination of the two that took our work to the next level. We both knew that which was why I figured he was talking more from frustration than intent.

"I know it's been rough going lately, but we'll get through this. We always do." I paused to ask myself the same question I had just asked him. Did I trust my partner? Of course, I did. I decided to tell him the whole story—okay, I skipped the part about finding the body, but I told him everything else—Ben's death, retrieving Maggie's letter, finding DeeDee, meeting James, losing James, visiting Andy, and meeting the stunning CFO, Kate. By the end, we were laughing over DeeDee's crazy urn collection.

"I have to meet this woman," he grinned. "She sounds like a hoot!"

"You two would be fast friends."

"Maybe things aren't so bad here. The Minneapolis design scene is just as much fun as the west coast." Paul paused to take a deep breath and slowly let it out between pursed lips. "But we still have to get this new client. I don't just want to do the 3-D printing either—I want to do the designs, too. You have to promise me we'll do everything we can on this one."

"I promise. We can always offer him a discount if he lets us bundle the printing and the design work."

Paul seemed relieved and nodded. "When are you going to call Kate?"

"Call Kate? Why would I do that? A relationship is the last thing I need right now."

"You should have seen the way your face lit up when you talked about her. You're so smitten, and you don't even know it. You should call her. You haven't had a girlfriend for, let's see, how long has it been?"

"Too long to think about."

Chapter Eight

Friday Morning, April 7

I met Dean in the church parking lot before James's funeral. He had done some research, and he wasn't about to let a memorial service get in the way of sharing it. "The St. Paul Diocese created St. Celestine Parish in 1929, despite the Depression, by acquiring a small bungalow from a couple who could no longer afford it. They turned it into a church and held services there for over twenty-five years, eventually adding a school and a gymnasium. During the fifties, they acquired an adjacent property, razed the church, and built a Rectory and a much larger church. Seating went from under a hundred to over seven hundred fifty."

I was impressed until I noticed a fountain near the front entrance, which had been shut down and planted with flowers, probably to cut costs.

"Should we sit in the back?" I asked Dean.

"Let's sit on the far left, about halfway back, so we can scan the crowd without seeming obvious." That was Dean—always thinking.

As we rounded the corner, a sandwich board sign informed us Bingo started at six pm each Wednesday. Over two thousand dollars in prizes could be won, including Amazon gift cards, toys, games, and a one-night stay at the St. Paul Hyatt. I wondered if the priests would require you to show your ID and stay with your spouse if you won that one. Bingo cards were only $2.50, and refreshments would be available for only a dollar. Did people still play Bingo?

From our seats on the far left of the church, we could see most of the attendees, which must have been well into the hundreds. In the front row, just right of the center aisle, sat Cathy Brennen, wearing a traditional black dress with sleeves that covered her shoulders, which looked like it only left her closet for funerals.

Next to Cathy sat a young woman, also dressed in black, who must have been her daughter. Having just occupied the front row at my adoptive father's funeral, I could relate to what she was going through. My mind flashed back to the picture on James's desk of the three of them enjoying life at the lake. I was sorry for James and especially sad for his daughter. I'd had an adult relationship with my dad for over twenty years. Their opportunity to have one disappeared in a cloud of gun smoke.

The rest of the Murphy, Brennen, & Murphy crowd were sitting a few rows back, including Andy Murphy, who was next to a lady that must be his wife and Kate Larson. My heart jumped at the sight of her, even if it was from the back. Maybe Dean and Paul were right, and I should ask her out.

The organ music started, and the procession began from the back of the church. As a former altar boy, I'd been through this routine many times. A casket proceeded slowly down the aisle with the deceased feet-first as if they were going toward God of their own volition. Incense lifted prayers to heaven. Family members softly wept. I'd witnessed these things many times without realizing the pain and grief of the participants.

Bishop Thomas Brennen solemnly followed immediately behind the casket. Seeing the bishop in his formal robes with a traditional miter hat and walking with a pastoral staff reminded me of a funeral I served many years ago for a popular parish priest. The presiding bishop took the time to explain how clergy members' caskets were walked down the aisle with the occupant's head first so they would still be facing their flock, even in death. It was one of those trivial things that somehow humanized the clergy and made you appreciate them more.

Bishop Brennen must have selected the bible readings specifically because of their connection with his brother because, during his sermon, he tied them into a number of stories about his brother's generous spirit. It was heartwarming to listen to a talented orator talk about his brother in such loving ways. He even got the congregation laughing at a few of his anecdotes, which is something that didn't happen at funerals very often.

Soon, the pallbearers were guiding the casket to the back of the church, followed by the bishop and altar boys, with the congregants trailing behind. Dean and I thought going to the service at the cemetery would seem intrusive, so we decided to wait at the back of the church until the motorcade left. Through the large vestibule windows, we saw the pallbearers loading the casket into the hearse. Then family and friends headed to their private cars to affix a small bright orange flag with a black funeral cross to their windshield and turn their headlights on for the trip to the final graveside service at the cemetery. We were about to head out when a short, stocky priest wearing a long black cassock with purple buttons up the front and a long purple sash running across his waist and hanging down one side approached and introduced himself.

"Hello, I'm Monsignor Scarpino."

The Monsignor tipped his head back and to one side when he spoke, which gave the appearance he was talking down to us even though he was much shorter. He held his hand out to shake with his palm facing the floor, which meant Dean and I had to take turns meeting his hand with our palms up. It was a subtle but effective form of showing dominance. We were in his dominion, and he was not going to let us forget that he was a ranking clergyman. Dean and I shook his hand, although it seemed like a bow would have been more appropriate.

"I noticed you two at the side of the church and thought I'd stop by. Did you know James Brennen well?"

"We'd only just met him," I said.

"He must have made quite an impression for you to attend the funeral of someone you just recently met."

"Yes." Why was I acting like a nervous altar boy again?

"Why was that?"

I looked at Dean, hoping he would bail me out.

"We recently found out we're related to James," Dean said.

That was not exactly what I had in mind.

"How are you related?" He seemed very insistent for someone we had just met.

"We're not one hundred percent sure," I said. "We were planning to discuss that with James when we heard about the unfortunate, um...turn of events. With that option no longer available, we're hoping to speak with the bishop."

"The bishop is a busy man and doesn't meet with just anyone. But I might be able to intercede on your behalf. How will a meeting help?" The monsignor seemed to consider himself the master gatekeeper. I wondered if the bishop would see it that way.

"It's simple. Since the bishop is James's brother, we'd simply like to ask him some questions about our family tree," I said.

The monsignor didn't try to deny James and Thomas were brothers—kudos to DeeDee for providing that intel. He seemed to be considering his options as he stared at us for a few moments. "I think we'll be more comfortable continuing our discussion in the Rectory." Apparently, he didn't want anyone overhearing us.

As he turned to lead the way, I gave Dean a quizzical look. He just shrugged his shoulders, so we both followed along.

The monsignor led us around the back of the church and entered the Rectory. Its small windows were made even smaller by the cross-hatched pattern of wood trim over them. This gave the exterior a formal look but made the interior inside seem dark, even on a bright and sunny morning. We paused by a small reception desk, where the day's mail was stacked. There was a leather writing pad and blotter set, which looked as old as the building. It reminded me of the one on James's desk.

"Would you like a cup of coffee?" the monsignor asked. "We usually have a pot going in the kitchen when there's an event in the church." There was a "Private Residence" sign pointing to the right and a similar sign that said "Offices" pointing to the left.

"No thanks," I said for both Dean and me as we walked down the corridor on the left to a small kitchen. "That was a moving service, especially the bishop's sermon. I didn't realize how many lives James had touched."

The monsignor poured himself a cup of coffee. "Yes. He was a good man and a dedicated servant of the community. We're still in shock he's gone and will miss him dearly. This way, please." He led us past the reception desk to the corridor on the right. A musty stench became apparent, then became nauseating. "My apologies for the smell. We've had some issues with water leaking into an old root cellar under the residence wing." We stood aside for a moment to let two construction workers walk by. They were both wearing bright blue jumpsuits with WC embroidered on their sleeve as they carried the tools of their trade toward the source of the smell.

I glanced into the room the workers had entered and noticed they were going down a ladder through a trap door into the root cellar, which must have been a holdover from the bungalow that had originally been on this spot. I could hear a sump pump draining water out of the cellar and saw bags of cement lined up along one wall, which would probably be used to reseal the cellar and eliminate the odor.

We reached a door with a diamond-shaped pane of stained glass in the center, which the monsignor opened to reveal a small library with bookshelves lining both sides and a larger diamond-shaped stained-glass window set into the back wall. The small coffee table in the back had four worn, overstuffed leather chairs around it. Dean and I sat across from the monsignor. You would have thought we were about to negotiate a nuclear arms non-proliferation treaty.

"What's this about discussing your family tree with Bishop Brennen?" he asked.

"Yes. Dean and I discovered we were adopted at birth after our adoptive father, Ben Dyle, passed. We've become interested in finding our biological family members before they're gone, too."

"How does that relate to James?"

I ignored the question for a moment. "Did you know him well, Monsignor?"

"I knew him quite well. He was more than just a brother to the bishop. He was a staunch supporter of the church and very generous with his time and donations to our organizations and charities. He frequently volunteered at events the bishop sponsored."

"Did he or the bishop ever mention a person named DeeDee?" I asked.

The monsignor's demeanor softened a bit. "He's mentioned her. Have you had the pleasure?"

"She's the reason Dean and I found James in the first place. I connected with DeeDee through a family origin website."

"What did you think of her?"

"A good deal of her heredity research is flawed, but she seems like a kindly person—"

The monsignor's stare sharpened. "You should know James disdained this person. He considered her to be a gold digger of sorts—a hanger-on looking for free lunches. I'm surprised you didn't see through her ruse immediately."

Where in the world was this coming from? "I thought DeeDee was fine—"

"Then you're a poor judge of character, aren't you?" The monsignor tried to burn a hole in my head with a menacing stare. "This woman is playing at some scheme to discredit the good name of people like James and Bishop Brennen. I wouldn't believe a word she said."

"You're missing the point." I was desperately trying to redirect the discussion. "I only mentioned DeeDee because she led us to James. Dean and I had dinner with him recently, and he—"

Dean straightened in his chair as he took the lead. "He was direct with us about our family relationship."

The monsignor leaned forward and turned his focus to Dean. "I thought you weren't sure of how you're related." It sounded like he was accusing us of trying to mislead him.

"James Brennen told us very directly that he was our biological father. Since James and Bishop Brennen are brothers, he must be our uncle. The family resemblance confirms it. Of course, James was single when he fathered two children, which means James and the bishop have been covering up this little scandal all these years." Dean was on a roll. "So, do you think the bishop will be interested in meeting his biological nephews to comfort them over the recent death of their biological father? Or perhaps you'd like to make us go away like all of the church's other scandals over the centuries."

Talk about speaking truth to power.

The monsignor sat back silently as he rubbed his eyes, giving the impression he was weary from fighting the good fight to save the name of the church. I got the sense he was also relieved. Being on-call twenty-four-seven, waiting for the next crisis to erupt, must be exhausting.

"If that's what he told you, then it must be true." He seemed to be mumbling, and I had to lean in to hear. "I didn't know James had children other than with his wife, Cathy. I'm certain she doesn't know, either. Assuming you're both in your forties, he must have been involved with someone before they met."

"That sounds right. James told us his wife had no idea he had children from a previous relationship," I said.

"Your family doesn't always turn out to be the people you want them to be, whether you know them or not."

I had no idea what that meant.

His sudden despondency was troubling, but he recovered quickly and sat up. "Cathy will have no idea she has stepchildren, and her daughter, who also just lost her father, will have no idea she has stepbrothers. It will be a shock to both of them. I strongly suggest you refrain from contacting them, at least until we can discuss this with the bishop."

"When will he be able to meet with us?" I asked.

"I'll see if I can find time on his schedule." His unspoken message implied he'd be doing us a big favor, which he would then expect us to return at a most inopportune time.

"What exactly is a monsignor, anyway?" asked Dean as he took out his phone while we debriefed in a pew in the back of the church.

"Don't you remember Monsignor Canning in Rochester? He was always walking around with that same purple sash looking like a senior statesman. I think it's an honorary title given to priests who have benefited the church with their virtuous deeds but aren't right for management positions like bishop or cardinal."

Dean, of course, had already Googled an answer. "According to Wikipedia,

'Monsignor is an honorific form of address for members of the clergy of the Roman Catholic Church, including bishops, honorary prelates, and canons. The title is granted to individuals who have rendered valuable service to the church, or who provide some special function in church governance.'"

"Rendered valuable service to the church? Holy crap, he's a fixer!"

"A 'fixer'? You've really got to stop watching those *Godfather* movies."

"No, seriously. It explains why he tried to discredit DeeDee before he'd even heard what she'd said. He was trying to deflect potential suspicion away from the bishop or his parish."

"Maybe you're right. How far do you think he'd go to save the good name of the church?" Dean gazed across the pew. "Could he have been involved in the murder somehow?"

"The monsignor silenced James to prevent him from telling the world there was a scandal in the bishop's family over forty years ago? Doesn't seem likely. Besides, don't fixers have some poor unwitting soul do their dirty deeds while they pull strings from a distance? If he was involved, we'd never be able to prove it."

"You might be giving him too much credit. Someone killed James. I say we put him at the top of the list of suspects."

"What list of suspects?" I asked.

He grinned. "The one we just created."

"Awesome. Who else is on it?"

"Andy Murphy? Business partners are always knocking each other off for embezzling funds or taking credit for smart business decisions or some such thing."

"I wonder if Paul knows about that?" I smiled. "Putting Andy on the list seems like a stretch. He had no motive I could see when I visited him."

"We can't rule him out, either. Let's put Andy on the list until we can confirm his innocence. What about Cathy, the grieving widow? Maybe James was having a fling with some client, and she found out and killed him in a jealous rage." I realized I had forgotten to tell Dean about my call to Cathy and quickly filled him in. "Then, she accused DeeDee of being psychotic, implied I was an idiot for listening to her, and hung up."

"I can't believe you called James's cell phone."

"You and me both. Anyway, that's what I call suspicious behavior. I'm adding her to the list."

We briefly toyed with the idea of adding DeeDee and Bishop Brennen to the list. But DeeDee seemed incapable of murder, and we decided to reserve judgment on the bishop until after we met him, considering we were related.

Twenty minutes later, we had four names and action items for each. Dean said he'd do more background research on James. I'd look at Cathy, and, oddly enough, Kate ended up on my to-do list as well.

"No fraternizing with the enemy," warned Dean with a smirk. "I'll research our family lineage and try to learn more about Maggie's family."

"Sounds great."

"Why didn't we think of doing this before?"

I just rolled my eyes. I didn't know how to investigate the monsignor. "Maybe I really will go to Bingo Night. I have a feeling he goes to all of the events at the church."

"Your funeral." Dean always liked gallows humor. "By the way, did you see DeeDee at the service?"

"No. I'm pretty sure I would have spotted her if she were there, which is a shame. I could have introduced you," I teased.

"Maybe she was upset they decided to bury James. No ashes to collect."

"Too soon." I smiled and considered sending her an email. Of course, that would only open me up to future communication with her. I decided to kick that can down the road.

Dean brought us back to the task at hand. "If we're going to get serious about this, we should set up the next meeting now."

"Good idea. Let's schedule a road trip."

"Road trip? To where?"

"Rochester, of course. Mom has got to know a lot more than she's letting on. We never asked her about the letter. No proper investigation would be complete—"

"She doesn't even know we have it!"

"No proper investigation would be complete without gathering all of the facts. Mom may have relevant information and not even know she has it."

"What about the letter? Are you going to admit to grave robbing, or should I tell her for you? Besides, she just lost Dad. Hasn't she been through enough?"

Dean liked to put on a gruff exterior, but he was really an old softy.

I figured it would be better to focus on consoling her versus grilling her about the letter. "It's been over a month since the funeral. Don't you think we should go see how she's doing?"

"Fine. When do you want to go?"

"Tomorrow. We can drive down in the morning and take Mom out for lunch."

"I'll call to see if she is free." While her social calendar was usually pretty open, she would drop everything to see her boys, so the odds of a road trip were excellent.

"How are you planning to ask her about the letter?" I asked.

"I haven't figured that one out yet. Let's talk about it on the way down."

I looked at my phone for the time. "The Mike Wilson meeting starts in less than an hour. I've got to get back to work before Paul has a good reason to kill me." I jumped up and headed toward the vestibule. "Text me about the road trip, and I'll text you about the next meeting. Bye."

As I hurried out, I noticed movement out of the corner of my eye and looked over to see the monsignor quietly exiting on the opposite side of the vestibule. Had he been listening in on our discussion? If so, I must have surprised him by running out so quickly. Maybe he really was a fixer.

Chapter Nine

Friday Afternoon, April 7

Paul and I could see Mike Wilson getting off the elevator, so we met him at the reception area. The Lake Street location in Uptown was perfect for Design By Dyle World Headquarters. But it was pricey, and I worried that first-time visitors would think we were overcharging them to support our extravagant lifestyle. So, while we walked through the office, I casually mentioned the deal I cut with the landlord who was rehabbing the building. I offered to do the façade design in exchange for a break on the lease rate. He agreed and liked the results so much that he gave me a deal on a second-floor apartment for more of the same. Of course, the unit he proffered had a partially obstructed view of the lake, but I didn't mind. The convenience alone made it an obvious choice. Besides, I liked to think of the view as partially unobstructed. I sold my duplex and moved in, along with the company.

In order to make a prospective client's visit to the office memorable, I'd asked Dean to figure out a way to automate some inanimate objects, whether they needed to be or not. The results were impressive.

When we entered the conference room, I said, "Alexa, table." The middle section of the conference tabletop immediately dropped a couple of inches and slid to one side, which allowed three high-definition displays, arranged in a triangle and displaying the Design By Dyle logo, to rise. The sideboard simultaneously opened up to reveal an assortment of warm and cold beverages. "Alexa, lights" simultaneously dimmed the overhead lights, illuminated the sideboard beverage selection, frosted the glass, and muted the spotlights on the artwork.

But then, a brief clip of Elvis singing "Welcome to My World" played, and the music switched to jazz. Dean must still have access to the office and too much time on his hands, as these were new additions to the conference-room schtick. There was even a slight aroma of vanilla. It was a good thing the menu included chocolate chip cookies for dessert.

Automation technology was fun until it wasn't, and then it got creepy very quickly. People saw inanimate objects being manipulated by hidden devices and then started to wonder if you'd done something weird in the bathrooms. I was relieved to see Mike smiling.

Paul brought the company presentation up on the three displays to start the meeting. "Design. Really Good Design. It reminds me of what that congressman once said about pornography. You know it when you see it, but it's almost impossible to define."

Paul talked about the company's history and some of the projects we had delivered. A few slides later, there was a quote from a press release about the design award. "That Grayson Dyle and Paul Cameron have an innate sense of design is readily apparent in this project. They propelled the medical device into an industry leader, simply by...."

I always got an internal chuckle out of the "innate sense of design" line and wondered what the article's author would think if he found out I had absolutely no innate sense of direction and was forever getting lost. Before Google Maps came into my life, I used to print out turn-by-turn driving instructions to each client and eventually had a thick stack of them in the car. I suspected some of my brain cells had accidentally been reassigned from direction to design at birth. I usually figured it was well worth the tradeoff, except when I got lost...in my own neighborhood...again.

Paul must have noticed I was daydreaming because he suddenly went off-script.

"Mike, I have to tell you a story. Last summer, we hired a great designer named Mary, who had recently graduated from the University of Wisconsin in Madison. She had three large pieces of IKEA furniture, a bookcase, a bureau, and an armoire, and she took them apart so they'd fit in the back of her truck. When she got to her new place in Minneapolis, she realized her friends had stacked all of the boards in one big pile when they loaded up the truck."

Mike's mouth dropped open. "Oh, my gosh!" He must have faced the challenge of assembling IKEA furniture before and understood that rooting through a pile of pieces was overwhelming.

"I know, right? But that's not all," said Paul. "She had put all of the connecting parts into the same plastic bag."

"So, you just used the directions to separate everything into three piles, right? They have pictures of all of the parts right at the beginning," said Mike.

"That's just it. She didn't have the directions, and she couldn't find them online because the furniture was so old. So, do you know what? My friend Grayson went over and set up all three pieces in about an hour."

Mike was astonished. "It takes most people two hours and a six-pack of beer to get even one piece put together."

"What's crazy is Mary eventually realized his builds were different than the original designs, and she liked them better. Unfortunately, he had one screw left over—he agonized about that for months."

I pulled a small Ziploc bag containing the screw out of my pocket. "I'm going to figure out where this goes one day." I meant it, too.

Mike got a laugh out of that.

Paul gave the rest of the presentation, which went well, as planned. Afterward, I used the app to reset the room so the three of us could discuss Mike's project.

Mike leaned back. "I like what you've done with this office, guys, and the work you've done is impressive. I thought your firm could do the computer work and the 3-D printing, but maybe you can do more than that. I don't have a designer lined up for the sculptures yet–can you help with that, too?"

Paul remained calm, but I could tell he was excited because his legs were vibrating under the table. Creative work was his reason for living. "Sure,

Mike. We'd love to help you with that."

"Okay, great. Would you look at the plans for the park and give me some ideas about how you'd approach this location?" Mike asked.

"Absolutely," I said. "We'd be happy to review them. Do you use Dropbox for online file sharing?"

Mike's face scrunched up.

We needed a different approach. "Or you can send them over on a flash drive."

"I think I'll send over a flash drive. I don't like to store important files online. You can't be too careful with internet security these days. Hey, I need you to look at the conference rooms, too. This place is great!"

It's always good to end a meeting like this on a high note. "We get that a lot. We can help you with that, too. It was good to meet you. Paul and I look forward to reviewing your plans."

We walked Mike to the door and thanked him for coming.

As suspected, Paul was giddy over the prospect of designing sculptures. But reality set in as we walked back to the conference room to clean up, and he was scrunching up his face again. "Have you heard back from Steve Hancock yet? I thought he was going to hire us to design the fixtures for his new retail outlet in Uptown. We need to close one of these deals soon, or we'll have to start laying people off."

"I know. No, Steve hasn't gotten back to me yet. He liked our conceptual layouts, though. We should be close to getting the deal."

"Great, but until we have ink on paper, we can't get paid."

"Yep. I know how it works." I hated to admit it, but I was worried too. "We'll get some new business soon. We always do."

"I've been running the numbers on our books. We only have about one month of reserves left. If we don't get a new client in the next few weeks, we may have to close our doors for good."

The scariest part was I was somewhat relieved. I thought we had only two weeks left.

I couldn't take any more of Paul's cheerfulness, so I decided to work from the home office that afternoon. After buzzing upstairs, I Googled Mike Wilson's company to get the street address, then wrote a thank you note in longhand. Snail mail letters were rare these days, so a personal, handwritten note always stood out.

Then I texted Dean about a meeting at our favorite Caribou on the following Wednesday, and he texted back to confirm. The Wilson website was still on my screen, so I browsed through a few examples of the company's work, which included an impressive number of landmark Twin Cities buildings. The current projects page portrayed efficient-looking workers wearing sparkling clean blue jumpsuits with WC embroidered on the arm.

Okay, that was odd. They were identical to the jumpsuits on the guys we passed in the Rectory. Wilson Construction was doing work for St. Celestine, and a few days after James died, Mike Wilson randomly called asking us to bid on one of his projects? That was either the mother of all coincidences, or someone had set it up, but who? Based on his suspicious behavior earlier in the day, the monsignor immediately sprang to mind. He had denied knowing James had children before his marriage to Cathy, but what if he was lying? Considering they were brothers, the bishop could easily have known James was our biological father, and he would probably have informed his fixer. Then, after James was killed, the monsignor asked his buddy Mike to infiltrate my company, probably to track us or for some other nefarious reason I couldn't even fathom. The timing would have been tight, but I could see the monsignor's fingerprints all over this. On the other hand, maybe I was giving him way too much credit. It was becoming obvious one of us was way too suspicious—either the monsignor for trying to plant someone in the company or me for thinking he was.

If it were the monsignor, and Paul found out, he'd be furious. He'd turn the work down if he believed we didn't earn it on our merits, and I'd be right there with him. This put even more pressure on finding other new clients in case this deal fell through. Just then, my cell phone chirped and brought me back to reality.

It was from an unknown caller, but I answered anyway. Anything for a distraction. "Hi, this is Grayson."

"Hello, Grayson. This is Monsignor Scarpino."

Speak of the devil.

I decided to keep my new suspicions to myself and sat at attention, ready for anything. "Monsignor, how nice to hear from you."

"Yes, I know. I'm calling to let you know I've spoken with Bishop Brennen. He will be pleased to meet with you and Dean. He's available next Saturday, April fifteenth, at two P.M. Is that a convenient time for the two of you?"

"That time works for me. I'll have to check with Dean, but I'm fairly certain he can make it."

"Please confirm Dean is available and let me know. My mobile number should be on your screen."

"I'll do that, Monsignor. By the way, Detective Copeland from the St. Paul Police visited me last Friday. He said he was leading the inquiry into James's death. Have you heard from him?"

"Yes. I arranged a meeting for the detective and Bishop Brennen. I'm sure he has spoken with all of James's family members. Why do you ask?"

"I was just wondering how the meeting went. Did the detective have any new information about the murder?"

"I'm not at liberty to say what they discussed."

I paused for a moment. "Did the bishop tell Detective Copeland that James is our biological father?"

"Did you mention this to the detective during your discussion?"

"Of course not. It would only cause unnecessary suspicion."

"You can rest assured the bishop will have taken the same approach."

I was relieved. "That's good to know."

"Goodbye, Grayson." With that, he hung up.

As I put down the phone, it occurred to me he didn't deny the bishop knew about our parentage. Copeland would have met with him right after James was killed and before we ran into the monsignor at the funeral. This seemed to confirm that the bishop, and likely the monsignor, knew we were James's sons. It also meant he probably lied to Dean and me about this. This from a man of the cloth, too. For shame.

An hour later, I was halfheartedly answering emails, wondering how the monsignor got away with being so rude, when a new message came in. It was from James Brennen's personal email account, and my heart sank. He was pretty busy emailing for a dead guy.

"You went to the funeral?! What part of stay away from the Brennen family do you not get? If you don't back off, I'll run you over. Then I'll back over you just for fun. Destroy that letter and STAY AWAY!"

Wow, what a drama queen. Even so, we needed to solve this thing before anyone else got killed, like Dean or me.

Chapter Ten

Saturday, April 8

As we were leaving the Twin Cities on our road trip to Rochester, I asked Dean if he could meet with the bishop on the following Saturday at two P.M. He said he could, so I texted Monsignor Scarpino to confirm the meeting. It was time to discuss more tender subjects. "I don't see how we can ask Mom about the adoptions without telling her I recovered the letter."

"You don't want to tell her the funeral director found it when she was making the final arrangements and gave it to you?" Dean suggested.

That was an idea I hadn't considered, and I was surprised to hear it from Dean. "Do you think that's wise?"

"No, you loser. I was just giving you crap. Of course, we have to tell her the truth."

"Fine. What about James? It might be a bit much to tell her— 'Mom, we've discovered we're adopted, found our birth father, met him for dinner, and, oh, by the way, he's dead.'"

"Yeah, that's not going to work. We'll just have to wait until more time passes to share that stuff."

Now that we had a consensus on two potentially explosive family issues, all in under five minutes, it was time to change the subject. I realized I had never razzed my brother for the conference-room stunt.

"By the way, 'Welcome to My World?' Really? Really? I mean, the jazz was a nice touch, but Elvis is a little passé, and what's with the vanilla?"

"Hey, the classics never go out of fashion, and everyone loves a little aromatherapy." Dean was snickering. He loved this stuff. "I was wondering how long it would take you to notice."

"It's a good thing the prospective client we had in there didn't run screaming from the room."

Dean became concerned because of how urgently we needed new business. "You mean there were clients with you?"

"A future client, hopefully. Okay, the show went over big, but check with me before you add anything else, okay? Or I might have to shut down your access card."

"Do you really think you can do that?" He was snickering again.

I decided to ignore his comment, mostly because he was right. "Tell you what, let's come up with one Alexa keyword for serious meetings and another keyword for the fun stuff. I have a feeling some of our clients won't appreciate Elvis or aromatherapy."

Dean sheepishly agreed, and soon we were pulling into the driveway of our childhood home again. It was a classic, single-story rambler with tan stucco and light brown trim. The landscaping was rough looking, and I figured I'd be back here in the spring armed with work clothes, clippers, fertilizer, and grass seed.

We greeted Mom at the door with big hugs. There was no doubt she had lost some weight, and her white sweater and light blue house dress seemed to hang from her frame.

"I must look terrible." Mom dabbed at her gray eyes with a handkerchief—still grieving the loss of her lifelong companion. I had to admit she did look frail, and I thought maybe we should postpone the discussion about the adoptions.

"You look great, Mom. Really," I said.

Dean nodded his agreement, and we followed her to the kitchen.

"I know you're lying, but thanks anyway. Would you boys like some coffee?"

Dean passed. I picked out a U of MN coffee mug, filled it, and took a sip.

It was exactly as I remembered—hot and strong enough to remove grease from the ball joint of a car. It was good to see some things never changed.

The pot of her famous chicken soup with the homemade, hand-cut noodles on the stove and the fixings for turkey sandwiches already laid out meant there was no point in asking where she wanted to go for lunch. Dean and I sat in our usual places. It was just like old times, and yet, it was completely different without Dad's master-of-ceremonies routine coming from the head of the table.

We kept the discussion light as we ate. Mom avoided asking if we were dating anyone, but I could tell she wanted to know. I almost mentioned Kate but decided against it in case things didn't pan out. Dean and I cleared the dishes and sat back down at the table. She must have known we weren't there for lunch as she waited patiently for one of us to speak, which was the opening I wanted.

"Mom, we have to talk."

"You can stop right there, Grayson. I'm not going to a nursing home or a senior care facility or whatever they call those places these days. I can get along just fine by myself. I've already got all the bills paid for April—"

I had to shout a bit to get her attention. "Mom. *Mom.* That's not why we're here—"

"I'm not moving to the Cities if that's what you're thinking. You boys don't want me there anyway, hanging around all the time. And all of my friends are here—"

"That's not it either, Mom. You're just making this harder."

"I'm sorry, but I know what happens when the two of you start conniving. If you think you can railroad me into moving out of this house, you've got another think coming." With that, she folded her arms, set her jaw, and stared out the kitchen window. She wasn't going to budge an inch.

"Mom...I have to tell you something."

Her face softened, and her brow furrowed with concern as she leaned forward. "What is it, Gray? What's happened? Are you okay?"

My face was burning as the shame of my indiscretion was hitting home for the first time. I had the same feeling every time I went to a Catholic confession. Sitting in a little box, declaring to someone else you are a miserable human being, was embarrassing and humiliating. It was one of the things I hated most about being raised Catholic. The official line claimed it would wash away your sins so you could emerge fresh and clean, ready to take on the challenges of life as a better human being. To me, the church designed the process to make damn well sure you knew who owned your soul and who would only get you into heaven if you toed their line.

Never having knocked over a grocery store or murdered anyone, the worse sin I ever confessed was fighting with my brother, something I did on a sometimes-daily basis when we were kids. Then, I left the confessional itching to pick a fight just to get that icky feeling out of my head. I had long ago decided I would never go through that ritual again, and yet here I was, about to plead guilty to something I'd done wrong.

"I saw you put the letter in Dad's casket. I'm sorry to say I went back after you left and took it out."

Nothing. Silence. Thirty seconds ago, I wanted her to stop talking. Now I was desperate for her to say something...anything.

"Mom...I'm sorry...."

She held up a finger to get me to stop, put her head down, and buried her face in her hands.

I was going to rot in hell. I should have known I'd eventually be sitting here in shame. Mom's shoulders started to shake, and I figured she must be crying. Maybe I should stop at a church on the way out of town. I finally had something meaty to confess.

"Did you read it?" she asked.

There was no getting out of this now. "Yes, I did. We both did."

Dean shot me a dirty look that surely meant "leave me out of your sin," but Mom didn't seem to notice.

Did I say I was going to rot in hell? I meant to say it would be on the level of hell reserved for thieves, cutthroats, and ungrateful sons. I was just gearing up to receive some kind of tirade when something completely unexpected came out.

"Maybe it's better this way. Maybe this is what God wanted." Even from across the table, it was easy to feel her embarrassment and grief. "I suppose you're wondering why we never told you about the adoptions or gave you that letter." She stole a quick glance at Dean and then looked down at the faded beige tablecloth.

"That did cross my mind," Dean said.

"Now that your father is gone, I feel like I can speak freely. It's not that I'm breaking any promise I ever made to him because I would never do that. I never promised him anything about the letter. It's just that…well, we never could agree on what to do with it or how much to tell you about the past. I wanted to tell you everything, but he didn't. After he passed, I didn't know what to do…."

As she trailed off, I realized her guilt over keeping the adoptions from us was deeper than my guilt over stealing the letter without her permission. I'd only had a few minutes to decide what to do, whereas she and Dad had had our whole lifetimes. I felt sorry for her. Maybe we should both make a quick stop at a confessional.

It seemed like she needed someone to give her permission to go on. "It's okay. You can tell us now."

She looked up and seemed anxious to finally unburden herself. "You must have figured out by now you were both adopted…." A wave of anguish washed over her face as she dabbed at the tears that were flowing freely. "Why didn't we tell you this when we were all together? When we still had the chance?"

I thought it might be easier if I asked a question. "Mom? Why didn't Dad want to tell us we were adopted? It's fairly common these days. I could see holding back when we were kids, but once we hit thirty, you'd have to think we could handle the situation."

"He was embarrassed, Gray. We tried to have children of our own for many years, but it wasn't happening. I went in to get tested, and everything was normal. I finally convinced your dad to get tested, and we found out he was infertile. It must have been from his diabetes. He didn't want to tell you about being adopted because he would have had to admit to his infertility. He thought it somehow questioned his masculinity."

I had to feel sorry for the guy. "Then what happened?"

"Once we realized we couldn't have children of our own, we contacted Catholic Charities right away. Back then, most of the adoptions went through them, and boy, did they put us through the wringer. They interviewed us, our neighbors, and your dad's coworkers. They did inspections. No one would put up with that crap today, but we didn't have a choice back then. They were quite invasive, but eventually, they gave us their approval and added us to the bottom of a lengthy list. We decided to wait for our turn, even if it meant dealing with all of their bureaucratic nonsense.

"One day, a friend of mine from the church.... What was her name again?" She put her head down, trying to remember. "Oh...um, Clara...and her husband...Roy. We used to talk after church since they had already adopted through Catholic Charities. She had even more horror stories about the inspections after they got to the top of the list. People dropped in without warning to inspect her home...to make sure it was neat and clean and ready to accept a new baby. Clara thought they were really inspecting her and Roy...making sure they'd be good parents. They gave them all sorts of instructions about how to raise a child and especially how to make sure their child would grow up to be a good Catholic."

Mom tended to overshare, and we were way off on a tangent. But she was skilled at layering three or four tangents together and always coming back to the original story. Dean and I usually sat and listened. Even though Rochester was only ninety minutes away, we didn't get down here often enough, and we had guilty feelings about that, too.

"Those people kept showing up, even after she adopted her little boy," Mom continued. "They just barged right in and said it was time for another inspection. If Clara tried to argue, they threatened to take her child away. Can you believe that?

"Anyway, Clara introduced us to a charming young priest named Father Tom. He was ministering to an unmarried young girl who was in a family way, and he had asked Clara if she and Roy were interested in another child. Well, one was enough for them, so she suggested he talk to us. Father Tom asked your dad and me if we'd be interested in adopting. He would handle it privately, so Catholic Charities wouldn't be involved. We were ecstatic, and we agreed immediately. It's funny. Your dad never did tell Father Tom why we couldn't conceive. He just said we couldn't and left it at that.

"Father Tom made the arrangements, and pretty soon, he brought Dean to us. It was like a miracle. He called the next day to check in and asked if he could stop by. I thought it would be another personal inspection, but that was when he gave us the letter. The only time I'd ever seen him upset was when he handed me that letter. He said giving it to me was against his better judgment, but your birth mom had made him promise, so he had no choice.

"It was the oddest thing. He said it was a matter of the utmost urgency to your birth parents that their identities remain secret. He told us to read it before giving it to you, and if there was any mention of the parents, we were to destroy it without letting you see it. That didn't seem right, but we figured we had plenty of time to decide, so your dad put it away for safekeeping.

"Then Father Tom called and said Dean's birth mother was expecting again. He asked if we wanted a second child, and we said yes immediately. A few months later, when Father Tom called to say you had been born, I could tell something was wrong. And there was no letter when he brought you to us, even though you had the same mother and father. I asked Father Tom about it, and he said it wouldn't be possible. Even though it was such a joyful day for us, he was downhearted because your birth mother had died from complications with the delivery. I'd always hoped to meet her one day, to thank her, even though it wasn't allowed, so I was overjoyed and heartbroken at the same time."

"Oh my gosh, that's terrible." Dean was sticking to our agreement to avoid letting Mom know we already had this information.

We both stared at the floor in mourning.

"When Dean turned twenty-one, I brought it up with your dad again. He wanted to open the letter before letting you see it like Father Tom said. I thought opening it first would go against your birth mother's wishes. We still couldn't agree, so we ended up just letting it sit. Your father must have filed it with his life insurance policy because I found them both in the same folder."

She must have agonized about this over the years. There was no point dragging her through the mud. Dean had brought the letter along, figuring Mom would want to read it, and this seemed like the most opportune moment. I gave him a slight nod in her direction, and he got the message.

"Mom, we discussed this on the way down, and we think you should read it." Dean offered it to her.

"Are you sure? It's your letter, Dean. I don't want to read it unless you approve."

Dean nodded. "I'm sure."

Mom accepted the envelope, took out the pages, and began to read aloud, which made it seem as if she was officially entering it into the Dyle family record. After she finished, we sat in silence while she dabbed at her eyes.

"I wish we would have opened it sooner," she said finally.

There were so many emotions going through me at that moment. I was furious they never told us about the adoptions, but my compassion for my mother's loss and her regrets about the past was overriding the anger, which seemed to be turning it into a sort of forgiveness. Well, forgiveness might be too much. It was more like understanding. Forgiveness would come later. "She sounds like a wonderful person. I'm sure she would have been thrilled at the way that you and Dad raised us."

Mom was wringing her hands and looking forlorn. "I'm sorry we didn't tell you the truth." Then she turned to Dean. "I'm sorry we never gave you the letter. We didn't know what to do. Father Tom was so insistent on how to handle it…."

Dean leaned over and put his arm around her. "It's okay, Mom. Don't worry about it. You honored Dad's wishes, and then you did what you thought was right."

I wanted to make one thing clear. "You know you and Dad will always be our real parents, right?"

She smiled gently, and relief passed over her face. "I know that, Gray."

My curiosity was killing me, and I couldn't wait any longer. "What else did Father Tom tell you? Did he say why Maggie gave us up for adoption?"

Even Dean seemed interested in her answer.

"No. He never said anything specific about your birth parents or why they gave you up. I never even knew the first name of your birth mother until just now. He did tell us how lucky we were to have two children from the same biological family, which must have been pretty unusual, especially in those days."

"What about Sister Anna?" Dean asked, to my surprise. That was going to be my next question, too. "Did Father Tom ever mention her?"

"This is the first time I've heard the name. It's good to know she had someone to help with her delivery. I heard those homes for unwed mothers were dreadful."

"Do you know Father Tom's last name?" I asked.

"I'm sure he told us, but I don't remember it anymore. We always just called him Father Tom. We lost track of him over time. He stopped by once or twice a year at first. 'Just to check in on the boys,' he always said. It's funny how nice he was, compared to what other people had gone through. After you both moved out, we sort of lost contact."

Recalling my reaction when I first learned the news, I took the conversation in a different direction. "Mom, who else knew? In the family, I mean. When a new baby suddenly appeared without you having been pregnant, they must have known Dean was adopted. Did everyone else know but Dean and me?"

"Only the adults knew. We swore them to secrecy because we wanted you to have a normal childhood. You know how cruel kids can be to anyone different."

Kids aren't the only ones who can be cruel, I thought. "I can't believe you managed to pull that off over all these years."

"We treated you as if you were our very own children, and I guess everyone else just went along with that."

Did they? "What about Aunt Phyllis, Mom? Every time we had a party, she was there treating us like crap while her perfect little angles terrorized us behind your back."

That really struck a nerve, and Mom started tearing up again.

"That's what I was afraid of, Grayson. I saw how my sister reacted to the two of you when you were just babies. She was even worse when no one else was around. The jealousy…the competition…the contempt. If that was how my family treated you, I couldn't imagine how the rest of the world would. I guess that's why I didn't push your dad to give Dean the letter. I didn't want you carrying that burden around your whole life. I didn't want you wondering if Dad and I loved you either."

As I'd thought about being adopted over the past few weeks, the idea that my mother had been carrying this burden to make her boys' lives that much easier had never occurred to me.

This seemed like the ideal time to move on to lighter topics, and Dean and I were soon reminiscing about growing up in Rochester. The statute of limitations on childhood offenses had long since expired, and we made Mom laugh by telling her how we used to sneak into the house through a basement window when we stayed out after curfew. It was good to see her happy again.

Soon Dean and I were back in the car, heading out of town. "Father Tom. Think there's any chance he's now known as Bishop Tom Brennen?"

Dean nodded. "I was thinking the same thing. Good thing you didn't ask her, or we would have had to admit we'd been researching things."

"I suppose we can just ask him next week. It seems odd to have our biological uncle acting as the broker for our adoptions."

Dean scrunched up his face. "Who knows? I'm sure there are loads of Father Toms in the church."

"Two of whom happened to be closely involved in our adoptions? That would be too much of a coincidence, and you know I don't believe in them."

Dean nodded. "Neither do I, but even if it's not a coincidence, that doesn't mean you can figure out how two events are related."

Chapter Eleven

Wednesday, April 12

I t was eight thirty Wednesday morning, and I was staring at a blank computer screen and the blank paper next to it. A flash drive containing the plans for Mike Wilson's park and building complex arrived via FedEx at our office on Tuesday morning, so Paul and I had driven out to the construction site on a scouting mission. We wanted to get a firsthand feel for the property, the riverfront, the neighborhood, and the community in general. Now, we were trying to decide how to approach this sculpture garden.

It had been easy to look up the history of the neighborhood and discover the rise and fall of gangsters and speakeasies in the twenties, followed by the rise and fall of supper clubs and gentlemen's clubs in the fifties and sixties, and then the general decline of the West Seventh Street area in the eighties and nineties. Now, a revival of sorts was occurring in fits and starts, and we had an opportunity to be part of it if we could come up with the right approach. Waiting for the muse to strike and deliver brilliant designs was the hard part. We'd tossed around ideas for most of the morning without much luck.

Paul was sitting across from me, staring out the window at the traffic on Lake Street, when he suddenly blurted out, "What is it you always say? 'If you need innovative ideas, do more research.' What else can we explore on this project?"

"Do I always say that?" I smiled. It was good to know people occasionally listened to my advice. "Good thinking. Maybe we should take a closer look at Mike to see what interests him. As much as we want the community to like the work, he'll be the guy paying the bills."

Paul did a quick Google search on Mike Wilson and found a bio on his construction company's website. "Born and raised in St. Paul. No wonder he wants to revitalize West Seventh."

I had also done a Google search and ended up on Mike's Facebook page. "He must be Catholic. He's married with three kids, all going to St. Celestine." I scrolled through the page. "He must have made a nice donation to the church because quite a few people thanked him for his generosity. That gives me an idea. How about something with a hint of Roman architecture to it? You know, columns, arches, patios with water features, that kind of thing. We can have sculptures of Roman gods like Neptune rising out of the waves. It should fit in with the vibe of the neighborhood and also appeal to Mike. People brought up in traditional religious settings usually love that kind of stuff."

"Works for me," Paul said. "I'll crank out a few sketches and see what happens. When would you like to get back together?"

"How about tomorrow afternoon?"

"Sounds good." With that, Paul headed to his office to work on the project.

I wanted to think more about the West Seventh Street project but had to meet with Dean. I grabbed my laptop and headed east down Lake Street to the Caribou Coffee. Dean liked this location because it got him out of his suburban existence. I liked it because it was only three short blocks from the office, and I could work on personal emails without having to worry about frosting the glass. I'd found employees start getting weird ideas if the owners spend too much time working in private, like thinking we were on the verge of laying people off, for example.

We usually met at ten, so Dean could avoid rush hour traffic. I got there early to think and ordered my usual large light roast with a splash of cream. I decided to send DeeDee an email to see if she was aware of James's passing and make sure she was still alive. I was just hitting send on the message when Dean walked in and ordered a cup.

"It seems like traffic in the Twin Cities is getting worse every day." He sat across the café table from me with a dark roast.

"No doubt. Have you had a chance to do some dark web research looking for buried secrets?"

I already knew the answer. Although Dean's primary focus was on automation consulting, he had to be up on the latest cybersecurity threats to keep his client's home networks safe, so you'd think he'd be tired of web searches. Quite the contrary. He seemed to relish each intensive investigation, and the higher the stakes, the better. So, I wasn't the least bit surprised to hear he had spent hours researching the past—our past.

"I managed to find some good intel. In general, James led a regular life. College, law school, law firms, marriage, one child. I think you know most of it. I needed more and broadened the search to some of the others on our suspect list."

"That's the Monsignor, Andy, Cathy, and Kate, right? What about DeeDee?" I asked since she was still on my mind.

"It sounds like it's all she can do to keep body and soul together. I don't see her getting up the nerve to kill anyone. Besides, what would her motive be?"

"No idea, never mind."

"Anyway, I didn't find anything else on Bishop Tom, but I'll keep trying. After that, I went through each person, but nothing unusual stuck out. Then I focused on the church staff and volunteers and tried to find anyone who was unusually close to James, the bishop, or the St. Celestine parish back in the time frame we were there, which covered 1978 through 1995."

"That's a pretty wide range. Wouldn't it have been easier to focus on the years we were born?"

"I didn't want to miss anyone. Besides, at small parishes, the staff doesn't turn over that fast. It was simple to find the ones that had been there for a long time. Their names and profiles are all listed on the website."

"Isn't that cheating?"

"Hardly. I had to dig around to find the staff members from the eighties and nineties using LinkedIn, Facebook, and social media. I went through all of the admin, building maintenance people, teachers, priests, outreach coordinators, music directors, IT people—you name it. I hit most of the staff but can't be sure about the volunteers. A lot of people don't bother to list that on social media unless it's fairly current or they made substantial time investment."

"What did you find?"

"A couple of things stuck out. First, before Tom became a bishop, he moved from one parish to another, as most priests do, but Frank Scarpino, James, and Cathy always seemed to end up in the same parish with him. After Tom moved, the others followed. Sometimes it took months, but they always caught up. James and Cathy eventually moved together, of course."

"They all hung out together, which is interesting but not incriminating."

"Agreed. Not sure what to make of that. I think our list of suspects is light by one. Do you remember Ms. Walsh from third grade?"

"Ms. Walsh. Wasn't she that really stern teacher who used to tell the boys they stunk after coming in from recess?"

"That's her. It turns out her full name is Jane Walsh, and she has been the principal at St. Celestine for many years now."

"Really?" Jane was a familiar name. I'd heard it sometime in the past few weeks, but where? "That's interesting, but how does that relate?"

"Once I found that connection, I did more research on her. She consistently ended up working in the same school district or the same parish as the others. I don't know what that means, except she must have known James and may have known him well. She could be a useful source of intel."

"Good point, but we can't just call her up unexpectedly and ask her about James's murder. She'd probably want some kind of proof he was our birth father, which we don't have."

"I know, so here's what I'm thinking. Jane is a heavy user of social media. Just yesterday, she posted a reminder about Bingo Night on the school's Facebook page. She even asked for volunteers. If you dropped by tonight, you could introduce yourself as a friend of James's. You could even volunteer if you wanted to make a good impression."

I shook my head. "Volunteering at Bingo Night. Have we really sunk to this level?"

Dean seemed to relish the idea. "Talk about your deep cover. It's a perfect way to cozy up to her. I went to the church website to see what kind of volunteers they needed. It turns out Bingo is big business for them. They use a large light board to keep track of the numbers called for each game. They must have over twenty volunteers, and they split them into two rotating crews each night, including callers, gate people, game card sellers, concession sellers, and kitchen staff. It runs from six to ten, and she's bound to be there to keep things running smoothly or sub in if they don't get enough volunteers."

"I'm not volunteering at Bingo Night. But I might go. Even if she doesn't show, I'll bet the monsignor will be there. You never know what I can find out from chatting him up."

"Maybe you should play. Local businesses and parishioners donate the prizes, so they don't cost the church anything. Between the Bingo cards, refreshments, and pull tabs, they must clear over ten thousand a night."

We kicked around a few other ideas but didn't come up with any better ways to chase down suspects, and soon it was time to get back to work.

What did people wear to Bingo Night? Did they dress up a bit since they held the event in the parish hall? Or was it strictly jeans and sweaters? After all, it was only Bingo. I finally decided on the old reliable—a light blue polo shirt, black jeans, and a sports jacket, which I chose to leave in the car at the last minute.

St. Celestine was just off Sibley Memorial Highway, right next to Cherokee Regional Park. Even though I arrived at about six-ten, a series of sawhorses blocked the parking lot entrance, and a sign said, "Lot Full." I ended up parking a few blocks away.

As I entered the hall, I had to admit it was impressive. The light board that showed the letter/number combinations was over six feet long, probably so it could be seen clearly from the back of the hall, which was quite large and must have been close to capacity.

The box holding the Bingo balls had a plexiglass viewing window so the players could watch the mixing action. A blower pushed one of the balls up a central tube when the caller hit a button. After calling it out, he placed the ball in the master board on top of the machine, which lit up the number on the light board. At the end of each game, he pulled a lever that released the balls back into the blower area. The machine looked sturdy and functional but was utterly devoid of style, which struck me as odd. Why draw the players' attention with a view of the ball chamber and then surround that chamber with cheap plastic and particle board? Good thing Paul wasn't here to see this thing—he would have had a fit. It made me wonder if there was an untapped market for creatively designed Bingo equipment.

The volunteers wore bright yellow button-down shirts as they roamed the hall, hawking Bingo cards and refreshments. Their most important job was verifying a card had a winning combination after someone called out, "Bingo!" It was oddly quiet for a room this size, holding this many people. Apparently, no one wanted to miss the next call because whoever shouted out "Bingo" first was deemed the winner if their card checked out. You did not want to be the pitiful soul who panicked and declared they had Bingo without actually having it.

"B-Seven, straight from heaven, B and seven, B-Seven," went the banter from the stage. A murmur rang out from the crowd. Some cards only needed one more number to fill a row, column, or diagonal, and some lucky person would likely score on the next ball. Exciting times!

I looked around and spotted a few seats in the back. Not optimal for scanning the crowd, but I'd be a lot less conspicuous sitting at a table versus loitering in the doorway. I passed a sea of fluffy heads, some with white hair and some with blue, with grandchildren and young families mixed in. Most of the players used a dauber filled with colored ink to mark each number/letter combination as the caller yelled them out, while a few of them used plastic chips. A lot of the players also had a backup dauber at the ready in case the primary unit failed at a pivotal moment. Some even had another one after that for tertiary protection.

"Psst, Grayson! Grayson, over here!" My name rang out from one of the fluffy white heads, sounding like a shotgun blast in the subdued room. So much for anonymity. I couldn't imagine who would know me and turned to see my old friend DeeDee. Yes, DeeDee, smiling and waving and moving over to make room for me at her table. Heads turned to watch my reaction, and people snickered. I must have looked like a deer in the headlights.

Fortunately, the next call rang out. "B-Thirteen, B-Thirteen, unlucky it seems, B and thirteen, B-Thirteen!" It seemed like a cruel irony to me, a feeling which spread to the rest of the room as one of the players yelled, "Bingo!" and a chorus of moaning was the response.

A gentleman who had been sitting nearby suddenly got up, ran around his table, and sat down in the same spot with a goofy smile on his face, probably trying to change his luck. The crowd forgot about me as I slunk over to DeeDee's table.

"Sit right here, Grayson. You can take Harry's cards. He never wins anyway." She moved Harry's urn out of the way.

Wait a minute. Harry was playing his own cards? Whose idea was that? Hers or the management? The thought of the Bingo police telling her Harry could only have a seat if DeeDee bought him cards made me smile. She must have been a regular, as no one else seemed to think it was odd.

I don't know what I was expecting from Bingo Night at St. Celestine's, but it wasn't this. I didn't see a way out and scanned the surrounding area to avoid any other urns that might be lurking nearby when I sat down. All of a sudden, the dark clouds parted, and an angel dressed in a bright yellow button-down shirt appeared. It was Kate—truly a vision from heaven. Hey, maybe there was something to this whole church thing after all.

"There you are, Grayson. I was wondering what happened to you. I thought we'd start you selling Bingo cards for your first shift. I've got your shirt at the volunteer sign-up table. It's right this way."

I couldn't believe my good fortune. Not only had I escaped from an evening playing Bingo using cards mooched off a dead person, but, as a volunteer, I would have carte blanche to roam around the room and investigate. Of course, the trifecta was hanging out with Kate.

"Hang on one second, Kate. I just want to say hi to a relative of mine.

DeeDee, thanks so much for the offer, but I wouldn't dream of playing Harry's cards. I'm sure his luck will turn around soon."

DeeDee looked crestfallen.

I hated to see her that way. "We should get back together soon and do some more family tree exploring."

Her smile regained its former location. "That will be great. I'll send you a message."

"Sounds good. Talk to you soon." I quickly followed Kate to the volunteer check-in table.

I would have hugged her right then if the opportunity had presented itself. "Thanks, Kate. You saved my life."

"DeeDee's not so bad. She's just a little eccentric." It was just like Kate to be charitable, even though I didn't know her that well. It was what I wanted her to be.

"You know DeeDee? I take it she's a regular."

"She and Harry are both regulars. At first, it seemed odd to have her bring Harry along. But everyone just got used to it, and besides, she plays twice as many cards when he's here, which means a bigger donation to the church."

"What do you mean 'when he's here?' Doesn't she always bring him?"

"Sometimes they're fighting, and she leaves the urn at home until they make up."

It was a perfect time to change the subject. "What do I do now?"

"Put this on over your polo." She grabbed a bright yellow shirt off the check-in table and handed it to me along with some Bingo cards. "Here is a stack of fifty cards. You sell them for two dollars and fifty cents each. The players use a new card for each game, which helps make it worthwhile for the church to hold these events. Some of the players using plastic markers may use the same card over and over again, and technically we're supposed to ask them to stop, but I just look the other way. I figure that's between them and their maker. Just return to this table when you sell out to exchange the money for a new set of cards. I can give you change if you need it."

I put the shirt on and fastened a few buttons. "Do you volunteer here every Wednesday night?"

"Do I come here often? Why, Grayson, are you hitting on me?" She smiled. "Tell you what, the first shift of volunteers gets off at eight. Let's talk then if we have enough replacements."

"Sounds great." I might have said that with a bit too much enthusiasm. I took the stack of Bingo cards, smiled at Kate, and began roaming between the tables, looking for anyone waving money. The demand for new cards was strong, and I made multiple trips for more cards during my two-hour stint. No wonder they did so well.

"You're a natural," Kate said.

I held back a smile as we passed the baton to the next set of volunteers. "I'll bet you say that to all the newbies to get them to come back."

"Maybe, but, in your case, I meant it. Volunteers get free refreshments. Would you like one?"

"Sure." Anything to get her talking. I followed her to a small kitchen area just off the main hall where we could talk in relative privacy, taking off the bright yellow shirt as I went. She took out two cans of Diet Coke and gave me one. I tried giving the shirt back to her, but she waived me off.

"Why don't you hang on to that? We let our repeat volunteers keep their shirts."

"Who said I'm coming back?"

"No one. It's just a hunch." The twinkle in her eye made my heart melt.

"Thanks. I had no idea this operation was so big and so well organized. You must clear, what, ten thousand a night?"

She seemed a bit surprised. "You're a quick study. Most people have no idea what we take in."

As much as I appreciated the admiration, it was time to get down to business.

"I'm just a small businessman." I was trying to be nonchalant. "You neglected to tell me you're the firm's CFO when we first met. I'm guessing that was some sort of test. How did I do?"

Kate flashed that brilliant smile. "I found I'm a lot more interested in guys that treat everyone the same regardless of their job or income."

"Thank God for that."

"If that's your plan, you've come to the right place."

"Andy may have told you my brother Dean and I are related to James, but we still haven't figured out how. Considering he's related to the bishop at this parish, is it safe to say James asked you to help out here? You're probably on the Finance Committee, right?"

"Yep. What about you? Andy told me you met James through DeeDee, but I know you're not here to meet with her."

"The truth is..." *Think fast, Gray.* I couldn't divulge that my original intention was to find Jane, as I would have had to explain that I wanted to ask her why she was following Tom and James around from parish to parish. I toyed with the idea of admitting that James was my biological father to see if she had any intel to share. I desperately wanted to confide in her, and while I believed in my heart-of-hearts she was trustworthy, it was too risky. The stakes were too high. If she told Cathy, even if it came out accidentally, it could ruin any chance Dean and I had to solve the murder.

You've got to say something. "I've been banned from playing Bingo at my regular place. The church ladies said I was winning too much and must be counting the Bingo balls somehow. Can you imagine me cheating at Bingo?"

Kate laughed, and the moment passed.

"To be honest, I was hoping to see you here." The words were out of my mouth before I realized it. That seemed like a design flaw. The brain should screen all comments before speaking them. Nonetheless, it was true, and I was glad I'd said it.

Kate smiled back, and that said it all. "I'm glad you're here, too."

If we were on a third date, this might have been an opportune moment to kiss her. Considering we were having our first real conversation while sitting at a butcher-block table in a small kitchen just off the main hall of a church, drinking Diet Coke, I thought it best to move on. I wanted to ask about James but didn't want her to think that was the only reason I was here, so I decided to try making her smile more. I told her about Dean's job as an automation engineer and the undercover work he was doing for a wealthy recluse named 'X' and his undoubtedly buxom girlfriend. Okay, I might have played it up a bit, but it did get her laughing.

"Dean has been working overtime to get the drones ready. X wants to write words over the lake for their maiden flight. He's planning a big show for the Fourth of July."

Kate smiled, then suddenly got serious. "Wait a minute, what words is he planning to spell?"

"I have no idea. Dean never told me."

"Oh, this is not good."

"No, it's fine. It shouldn't be that hard. Dean is very good at..."

"No, that's not it. I think X is going to propose to his girlfriend using the drones."

"Wow, I think you're right. How could Dean and I have both missed that?" It was my turn to smile. "That's going to be awesome."

"No, it's not. Most guys think it will be, but she doesn't want to be proposed to using any kind of technology. Most women don't, no matter what they might say." Kate grabbed my arm for emphasis. "You have to trust me on this. She wants something more romantic."

As I thought about it, I realized she was probably right. "But, it's too late now. Dean has been testing the drones, and they're going to be ready in a couple of weeks." Kate's eyes darted back and forth as she tried to think of a plan. I could just about hear the wheels spinning in her head.

"Okay, here's what should happen. Dean tells X that he has a way to make the proposal more romantic. X invites his girlfriend over for an elaborate candlelit dinner on an outside patio. It should be catered with formal waiters, the whole works. After dessert, X uses the drones to spell out a series of clues to locations around the estate where he has hidden small gifts for her. Flowers, jewelry, that sort of thing. She has to figure out the clues to find them. Tell X not to make them too hard. The last one leads to a room where he is waiting for her. When she arrives, he proposes in person, down on one knee." Kate smiles triumphantly. "That will really be awesome!"

The brilliance of her design was immediately obvious. X would use the drones multiple times, which he would appreciate, and his girlfriend would have a fun, romantic, adventuresome evening that she could brag about for years to come. "No doubt there should be a videographer there to capture the whole thing."

"Well, yea. Of course. You don't expect her to take selfies, do you?"

Damn, she was good. I quickly texted Dean to remind me to discuss the drones before we met with the bishop on Saturday. He texted something back, but I let it go.

"I have a feeling X is going to owe you one."

"He doesn't need to know about me. Just let me know how it turns out."

And have another opportunity to meet with her? "Absolutely." Then, it was time to get serious. "How well did you know James?"

A micro-expression of what might have been contempt flashed on her face. "I've worked with James and Cathy for many years, so I got to know them pretty well." The smile returned, but there was less joy in it.

"What was James like to work with?"

"He was fine. He was a good attorney, really knew his stuff."

"Anything else?"

"I know you're related to him somehow, so I probably shouldn't say anything else."

"You can't leave me hanging like that. We are related, but I only met the man once, so it's not like you'll tarnish his reputation with me. What are you holding back?"

She leaned in to speak quietly so no one else could hear, even though we were alone in the kitchen. "James used to hit on me when Cathy wasn't there. It wasn't just harmless office flirting, either. He made his intentions clear, and I made it clear nothing was going to happen." She stopped abruptly. "I don't know why I'm telling you all of this. We've only just met."

A brief scent of her perfume, which was something floral, wafted by, and I wanted her to stay close and keep talking. Even though she was telling me my father was a bad actor, I wanted to know the truth.

"That must have been horrible. Did Cathy know?"

Kate shifted, clearly uncomfortable. "She knew the kind of man he was and kept a close eye on him because of it. That's how she ended up being the office manager. Most people don't realize accomplished attorneys typically don't have the skills or the patience to run a business, and she had them in spades. James and I ended up in a kind of unspoken truce, which was uncomfortable, but it seemed to work.

"Then Cathy left for a few days to visit relatives, and James saw his chance. He cornered me in a conference room and said he'd tell the whole office some crazy story about catching me embezzling funds if I didn't sleep with him. I told him I'd cut off his boy parts if he ever touched me again."

Mental note—never grab Kate without her permission. "What happened?"

"He never touched me again. As far as I know, he died intact," Kate said with a joyless smile.

Chapter Twelve

D ean winced. "She threatened to do what?"

We were in St. Celestine's parking lot waiting for our two o'clock meeting with the bishop.

"I know. I couldn't believe she told me all that right there in the church kitchen."

"On your first date, too."

I ignored the cheap shot and told Dean about Kate's ideas for using the drones.

"That's genius," Dean said when I finished. "She's a keeper, you know."

"Agreed, on both fronts." I knew Dean would immediately start processing this new information and work out the best way to approach X, so we sat in silence for a few minutes.

"The bishop must have been very disappointed in James when you were born, but then to let it happen again, he would have been livid. Considering it was the mid-seventies, he must have been pressuring James to marry Maggie."

"Yeah. Why didn't James just marry Maggie? Based on her letter, they seemed to be madly in love. Then again, she said something about him being committed to someone else. Why was she even sleeping with him if she knew he wasn't available?"

I could only shake my head. "Do you think the bishop knows James was still a philanderer even after he married Cathy?"

"No idea, but we'd better not bring that up if we want to keep him talking." Dean suddenly started fidgeting and seemed to be getting cold feet, which was odd as I'd never known him to be nervous about meeting someone new. "Why are we seeing the bishop again? Our birth parents are already dead."

"Jeez, Lousie, Dean," I gave a hefty eye roll. "We're investigating a murder. Copeland doesn't know we're related, remember? Any of this ringing a bell for you?"

Dean looked a bit sheepish, but he'd never admit it was a dumb question. "Okay, but we can't just ask him about it directly. Let's just say we're looking for a family health history or something innocuous like that."

"That could be a big rathole. If one of them had a serious health issue, we could spend the whole time talking about visits to doctor's offices and treatment plans."

Dean threw up his hands. "What else do we do? I wonder if he's going to accuse us of trying to horn in on an inheritance."

"I doubt it. The bishop wants to keep his hands clean. He'll have his man do that."

"Do you think the monsignor will be there?" Dean asked.

"I'm sure the monsignor has fully briefed the bishop on our discussion, so he wouldn't need to be here. But he'll probably be lurking nearby in case we need fixing afterward."

A few more moments of silence passed as we waited for two.

"Did you bring the letter?" I asked.

Dean patted his sport coat pocket. "Got it right here. I even made a copy for him. But let's avoid showing it to him unless we need to get him talking. We can always mention it without showing it to him. We may need it as leverage to get a second meeting."

"Agreed."

At two exactly, we walked up to the main entrance and rang the buzzer. The bishop answered the door, wearing black dress pants and a black button-down shirt with the requisite white collar. Now that we were face-to-face, I could see he was a tall man with salt-and-pepper hair that gave him a distinguished look.

"You must be Dean and Grayson Dyle," Bishop Brennen said. "Very nice to meet you both. Please come in."

"It's a pleasure to meet you," Dean said.

We shook hands and followed the bishop down the hall.

"Can I offer you some water or a cup of coffee? How about a beer? Priests are allowed to have libations, you know."

"No thanks," I said for both of us.

"This is my office." The bishop opened the door to a well-appointed room at the end of the hall. It was much larger than I expected, with a thick Persian-style rug on the floor under the desk and two visitors' chairs. An imposing picture of the bishop shaking hands with the current pope hung on the wall behind the black leather chair. Just as in the rest of the Rectory, the dark paneling gave the room a reverential feeling, where speaking in hushed tones seemed oddly appropriate.

Dean and I sat in the visitors' chairs.

"We heard your sermon at James' funeral. It was inspiring," I said.

"Thank you, Grayson. That's kind of you. My brother was a good man. I was pleased to do one more small kindness for him." The bishop got a sudden twinkle in his eyes. "I should let you know I looked both of you up on the internet. They let us use that here, too. I'm privileged to have in my office two distinguished businessmen. One is a home automation, and IT security expert, and the other runs an engineering and design firm. It's good to see you're both doing well!"

"Thank you, Bishop," Dean said.

"Please, there's no need for formality. It's Tom."

"Okay, ah, Tom. I'm sure Monsignor Scarpino has filled you in on our discussion with him, so you're aware of the family relationship," Dean continued.

"Yes, Frank told me about Grayson's DNA test and the meeting with James. What did he tell you?"

"James clearly stated he was our biological father," said Dean.

"I don't know what would possess him to say that, but I can't see how that could be true. He's been married to Cathy for over twenty-five years, and they have a daughter together. Either Cathy or I would have known if he had other children."

"Are you saying he isn't our biological father? Why would he tell us he was?" Dean's face was getting red.

"I know he always wanted more children, especially boys, but Cathy said one girl was enough. Maybe he liked the idea of having two successful guys he could call his own?"

I was appalled by Tom's story. This flew in the face of previous events, and he seemed to be making it up as he went. "We have the DNA results to prove it."

"Monsignor Scarpino shared your evidence with me. I believe the DNA results show you are related to DeeDee Miller, not to James. Just because DeeDee is related to James doesn't mean he's your father. Besides, I'm sure you're both well aware DNA results from those internet lineage sites are notoriously inaccurate. They can't afford to create a full genetic profile based on the small fees they charge. They tell you that in the fine print right on their website. I don't doubt there is some kind of family connection, but you could easily be first or second cousins or the like."

Dean and I looked at each other in shock. Neither one of us expected this.

"Maybe we should collect samples and submit them to a qualified lab, so we'll know the results are conclusive," I said.

"That's ridiculous. I don't need any tests to know what is and is not true. I'm afraid you boys are mistaken. James isn't your biological father. Let's just leave it at that. I don't want you to contact Cathy about this, either. She's distraught enough from James's death, and she doesn't need you two bothering her about something that almost certainly didn't happen before she married James. If you want to have any further discussions about this, contact Monsignor Scarpino first. He'll intercede with the family on your behalf."

Dean reached into his coat pocket for the letter, and I realized it wouldn't help. There was no proof in it that we were James's sons, so I cut him off. "We're not members of your congregation, Tom. You can't sic your fixer on us and expect us to kowtow to him."

The bishop's face went from firm to stark in a split second as he tried to stare a hole through me. "You're very perceptive, Grayson. But don't think you can be impertinent with me because we might be related somehow."

Oh boy. Catholic guilt in its purest, most unrefined form. "Sorry, Bishop," was all I could muster.

Dean and I stared at the bishop—stalemated. I couldn't see a way out.

Then the bishop's face softened as he dismissed us. "Let's not end this on sour terms. Let's get back together in a few months. I understand you were at our Bingo Night this week, Grayson. Maybe I'll see you there in the future."

"Thanks for meeting with us," I said in a final attempt at graciousness.

"Thanks for stopping by, boys. I'm sure you can see yourselves out."

"What just happened?" I asked Dean as we sat in my car, still in shock. "I expected to have a friendly family unification of sorts. Instead, it was just denials, veiled threats, and stonewalling."

"James having children before he got married would have been a big deal when we were born, but would anybody care today? He must be hiding something else—something big."

"Tom does have a good point, though. We have no proof James is our father. What if he liked the idea of claiming he had two successful sons and lied to us? And Tom didn't ask about the letter, so he must not know about it."

"Or he wanted to remain above the fray. If he did know about the letter, he probably wouldn't have admitted it. He'd have Fixer Frank deal with it."

I just shook my head. "Where do we go from here?"

"I think you already know." No one told Dean he couldn't have information when he wanted it.

"It's good to see you're still onboard with the investigation." I grinned. "We know James and Tom are brothers. What if Tom wanted to keep the family's illegitimate children secret to avoid sullying the family and the church by proxy?"

Dean was silent for a minute. "Right after James told us he was our biological father, it seemed like he wanted to say more, but something stopped him. Then he asked us to stop digging around until he could figure out how to spin it with his wife. What if that was just a smokescreen, and he had to check with Tom instead? When you're related to a bishop, you can't just run around admitting to dirty deeds, or the wrath of God could strike you down. Or the wrath of Tom, in this case."

"Maybe, but that doesn't sound like a motive to kill James, so we're no closer to finding the killer."

"Okay. I'll do some more research—"

"Tell you what. You do the online research, and I'll do the field research."

"What do you mean?"

Dean wasn't going to like my new plan.

"I'll get a sample of Tom's DNA so we can have it tested and prove we're related. He'll have to talk to us after that."

"Are you crazy!? How are you going to do that? Even if you did get past the palace guards, how would you collect a sample?"

"Assuming he uses a water bottle like the rest of the free world, maybe he threw one out with some spit remaining at the bottom, and I can grab it. If it's in the garbage, it won't be stealing, right? If we can prove Tom is our uncle, he won't be able to brush us off anymore."

"I can't be involved in anything untoward. I'm supposed to be a trustworthy consultant, remember?"

"Maybe that is crazy." Okay—it was crazy. But that didn't make it dumb. I started mentally designing the approach. Dumpster diving wouldn't work as there was no way to tell which water bottle was his. I didn't relish the thought of breaking and entering at night, so it would have to be a daring daytime job when Tom's office would be accessible. From my altar boy days, I knew the main Rectory door was usually left open on Sunday morning, with all sorts of people coming and going—priests, ushers, altar boys. I could try to blend in and see how far I got. Since tomorrow was Sunday, I made a mental note to surveil the situation in the morning.

We sat in silence for a few minutes, and I realized the lot was filling up and crowds of people were walking toward the church. The kids in robes were pretending their parents weren't right behind them. "I suppose we should head out and free up the parking spaces."

Dean said, "That sign says there's a Choir Concert at the five-o'clock service. These kids are probably here for one more rehearsal before it's showtime. You know what that means?"

"We should get the hell out of Dodge before someone thinks we're stalking teenagers?"

"It means the Principal will likely be here to support the troops. You should introduce yourself. She's the one person we haven't nailed down yet."

"Under what pretext do I do that?"

"You're here for the five-o'clock mass and wanted to say hi. She'll probably recognize you based on your resemblance to James like everyone else has."

"Why don't you do it? I don't even know what she looks like."

Dean quickly brought up the school's website on his phone and handed it to me. "Here's a picture of her. Now you know as much as I do. Besides, she's the principal. She'll be the one that's acting like she owns the joint."

The picture showed a solid, smartly dressed woman wearing a plain but tasteful black dress. Her serious expression said she wasn't about to take any guff from a bunch of school kids. I handed him the phone back and realized we were at an impasse, which could only mean one thing. Odds or Evens. None of this silly Rock-Paper-Scissors stuff for us, where you could end up with a draw and have to replay. This was a man's game. High stakes. Single elimination. No ties possible. Of course, we'd been playing it since we were old enough to walk to the park and argue over who got to bat first. It also came in handy when deciding who got to choose the first piece of cake.

"Odds," I exclaimed.

Dean and I extended our fists, simultaneously waved them up and down three times, and then stuck out a random number of fingers. I put up three, and Dean put up three for a total of six—evens.

"I win," Dean smirked.

"Damn it." Why did I always pick Odds?

As Dean drove off and I walked into the church, I figured he was on to me. Next time, it was Evens, for sure. Or maybe we should switch to Rock-Paper-Scissors, like everyone else. A draw was better than a loss.

The choir was assembling in the first six pews on the right side of the church. Proud parents filled the rows behind them, doing their best to embarrass their offspring and elbowing each other for access to the best camera angles. The choir director was easy enough to pick out. She was the only adult wearing a robe. She was chatting with a lady that looked like she owned the joint and who resembled the picture Dean just showed me. 'Bingo,' as they said on Wednesday nights, that must be the principal.

The choir director soon walked off to try to regain control and prevent the hordes from killing each other.

I seized the opportunity to introduce myself. "Are you the principal? Hi, I'm Grayson Dyle." I extended my hand to shake.

She stared at me for a moment with a curious look. "Hi, Grayson. Yes, I'm Principal Jane. I don't remember seeing you here before. Are you one of the parents?"

"No, I just got here early for the service and wanted to meet you."

Jane was five-seven and wearing a simple but tasteful black dress with a black-and-white silk scarf draped around her neck. Her blond, shoulder-length hair was offset with pearl earrings and a matching bracelet. The same no-guff look was on her face. Maybe she did own the joint.

"I recently found out I'm related to James Brennen. I understand you were a friend of his, and I was just wondering if you'd be willing to share your memories of him with me. He seemed like such a nice man." I wouldn't have bought this story, but Jane didn't seem to have an issue with it.

"I thought you might be connected to James somehow. The resemblance is remarkable." She had a sad expression when she looked away. "How did you know I knew him?"

"I think his partner Andy mentioned it." Was it a bigger sin to fib inside a church? Maybe we should move this discussion outside in case I need to tell a few more whoppers. "I'm sorry to hear what happened. It must be difficult to deal with."

"The four of us have been friends for quite a long time, and we've been through a lot together." Jane seemed to be reminiscing for a moment and was absentmindedly fiddling with her scarf, which revealed a small swatch of cloth underneath. It looked like the brooch of a necklace and was being held around her neck by two thin cloth strips of fabric. There was a small picture of a saint on the swatch with the words "St. Scholastica Save Us" underneath. I remembered seeing some Holy Redeemer Church ladies wearing similar swatches, although they usually had images of St. Joseph or the Virgin Mary.

I just thought you rarely saw people wearing signs of devotion these days when she snapped out of her reverie. "Look, I've got a choir to introduce in a few minutes. Why don't you stop by the school sometime if you want to talk more?"

"Okay. Sure. Have a good night," I said as I turned to leave.

Jane furrowed her brow with a quizzical expression. "I thought you said you were here for the service?"

I enjoyed the concert a lot more than I thought I would.

Chapter Thirteen

Sunday, April 16

D ean and I met at our usual Caribou Coffee at nine on Sunday morning. It was his turn to buy, so I loaded up with a large Mint Condition and a Depth Charge, which was their name for an extra shot of espresso. It was my passive-aggressive way of getting back for my inglorious loss at Odds and Evens the day before.

As we sat at a two-person table by the windows along the parking lot, I tried rocking the top. As I suspected, it was wobbly. If one of us suddenly leaned on the table the wrong way, coffee would slosh all over. There was an entry on my bucket list, somewhere in the top ten, to design a sturdy, low-cost, easy-to-clean café table and wipe the scourge of tippy tables from the face of the earth.

I wanted to focus on the investigation and started right in. "Kate made it extremely clear she didn't like James. What if he kept hounding her for sex even after she threatened to turn him into a eunuch? Pretty soon, she couldn't take it anymore, and she plugged him."

"She just happened to have a gun on her?"

"That's a dodgy neighborhood. Maybe she has a concealed carry permit and always totes one for protection."

Dean scrunched up his face. "That seems like a stretch. Why wouldn't she just pull the gun and tell him to go screw himself instead of putting a couple of rounds into him?"

"It could have been a crime of passion, or there could be some other reason we haven't figured out yet. I'm adding Kate to the list of suspects, so we now have six, right?"

"Unless you'd rather keep your girlfriend off the list." It never gets old with him.

"I'm kind of hoping she did it. Then, after we start dating, I can sic her on you."

"Nice." Dean quickly got serious. "Here's what we've got. Cathy killed James when she discovered he had illegitimate children he'd forgotten to mention. Kate killed him because he wouldn't take no for an answer. The monsignor killed him because he'd already spilled his guts about being our bio father, and our mere existence would sully the good name of the bishop and the church. I suppose Tom could have killed him for the same reason—some things are too personal for a fixer to do. His partner, Andy, killed him because...he...found out James was hitting on Kate and couldn't get him to stop? That leaves Jane. We still don't have anything on her."

"Maybe she was going through some old records and discovered he lied about getting a thirty-six on his ACT? That would be pretty distressing for a principal," I joked.

"I don't think so. Are you going to call on her at the school?"

"Not sure. She seems pretty harmless. Maybe I'll give it a few weeks."

The barista called my name, and I retrieved my coffee, careful to steady the table as I sat down. "I wonder where Copeland is with his investigation."

"Maybe you should ask him to stop by your office at seven A.M. again. I know how much you enjoyed the first visit."

"I wonder how much time he has for this case now the first forty-eight hours are long gone."

"No idea."

I was frustrated and needed more than a sugary, highly caffeinated beverage to make me feel better. "What do fictional detectives do when they get stuck?"

"Put pictures of the suspects on a murder board and scribble a bunch of allegations and accusations next to each one. Then they wheel it around the set of the station to find the best camera angles. There's usually a timeline of the relevant events, too."

"I don't think the coffee shop staff would appreciate that."

We were silent for a few minutes.

I was thinking about the timeline when a similar idea took hold, just like on TV. "Let's start at the beginning."

"Which beginning—contacting James or the dinner meeting?"

"I mean the timeframe when all this seems to have started. Let's go back to when we were born. I mean, when you were born."

"I'm afraid I can't report much about my birth."

"No, but we do know a few things. We know Maggie was living in Rochester, Minnesota. She was having an affair with James, and they seemed to be in love. She got pregnant, and, after many months, she delivered a baby boy."

Dean chimed in. "Father Tom had arranged the adoption, and he brought the baby to an overjoyed Dyle couple who couldn't believe how incredibly fortunate they were to have an extremely bright and attractive child delivered directly to their doorstep."

"Right, whatever. Let's back up a minute. Let's say I'm James, and I'm already dating Cathy, but I'm having a fling with a young lady from the church. Then Maggie gets pregnant. I'm not willing to give up Cathy for her, and I'm pretty sure her religious beliefs mean she won't have an abortion, so what other choice is there but adoption? I call my brother, the priest, admit I have sinned, and ask for his help. He's probably helped a lot of other girls over the years, so he hooks them up with the home for unwed mothers."

"Yeah, I was thinking about that. Most of the maternity homes had closed by the time we were born because the social stigma of being a single mother was going away. Why didn't Maggie just keep the baby? It sure seemed like she wanted to."

"Good question. Rochester has always been a conservative town, and we're talking about a tight-knit religious community. Based on her letter, it sounds like James talked her into it. But her parents could have convinced her, too. I suppose we'll never know what really happened." Dean nodded.

I went back to the timeline. "Father Tom is now on the case. He arranges the adoption with a couple who can't have children of their own because of the guy's diabetes. He makes sure to find the right couple—two people who love each other, are devoted to the church, will raise their boy to be a good Catholic, and live nearby so he can keep an eye on things."

Dean picked up the thread. "What was the name of the nun that was helping Maggie? Oh yea, Sister Anna. This must be when they get her involved. Either she volunteers, or one of them enlists her to help this poor young girl in need. They convince Maggie to blame the pregnancy on a one-night stand with a local boy who she refuses to name, so Sister Anna doesn't know James is the birth father."

"The monsignor would probably be sticking his nose in right about now. Of course, he would have been known as Father Frank back then, but I'll bet he would have jumped at the chance to fix things. Maybe dealing with this mess was the reason the original group formed in the first place, and they've been together ever since."

"That's a scary thought," Dean said ruefully.

I just shook my head in disgust. "You've got to hand it to them for pulling it off, even if it was deceitful."

"But they were almost too good. James never gets caught and never learns his lesson, so Maggie gets pregnant again, and they have to run through the same drill a second time."

"Good thing, too, or I wouldn't be here. You know, this may be the strongest reason of all why Mom and Dad never told us about the adoptions. Father Tom must have put the fear of God and the church in them. It wasn't just embarrassment at being infertile that kept Dad's mouth shut—he wouldn't have wanted to go against a priest's directive." I realized I'd been holding some resentment toward my adoptive father about this and was just starting to let it go.

"So, what does all of this tell us about the investigation?"

"Hang on, think about the letter. There's still one person whose past we haven't looked at."

"Oh, right! I never gave Sister Anna another thought. She can probably tell us all kinds of things if we can find her." Dean appeared to be getting excited. "I'll get on that right away."

"We're not done yet. Let's fast forward fifteen months to the day I was born. What unusual event occurred at that time?"

"Maggie's death."

"Right. How did that happen? I know these homes for wayward girls weren't hospitals, but they delivered babies all the time. How did they let our birth mother die?"

Dean leaned back. "The people in the delivery room. I should have thought of them."

"You'll get the next one. We were probably delivered by midwives, right? If we can find them, maybe they can tell us what really happened."

"That's a bit thin, but we don't have much else to go on. I'll see what I can find online."

"Sounds good. I have an errand to run."

We headed out.

About forty minutes later, I parked my car a couple of blocks from the Rectory. My hands were vibrating on the steering wheel, and I wondered if maybe the Depth Charge had been a bad idea. *You don't have to go in,* I told myself. *You can just knock on the door, and if someone answers, just ask about volunteering at Bingo Night. Okay, that's good. That'll work. Here we go.*

The Rectory was usually empty after the service had begun on Sunday morning. The office staff had the weekend off, and the priests and deacons were either serving mass in the church next door or out and about in the community visiting shut-in parishioners. It was ten-fifteen, which meant the ten o'clock service would be well underway. It was now or never. I looked up the number to the Rectory on my phone, stored it, put the phone in silent mode, then walked the two blocks, taking deep breaths and trying to act natural.

I had stopped at home and changed into a white T-shirt, black dress shirt, and black dress pants to blend in. I pulled the white T-shirt up to my neck and left the top button of the black shirt open, hoping that, from a distance,

I'd look like a priest entering the Rectory. The black dress shirt also hid the sweat rings. I had tucked two sizes of Ziploc bags into my pocket in case I needed to collect evidence without cross-contaminating it.

As I neared the Rectory door, I dialed the main number. No answer. I ended the call and stowed the phone. No one was around outside, so I knocked on the solid oak door. No answer. I took a deep breath and tried the door. To my sudden relief and great apprehension, it was unlocked. "Hello?" Still no answer. I walked in and closed the heavy door as quickly as possible, hoping no one saw me enter. Panic quickly set in—what if the parish had surveillance cameras? A quick scan of the room revealed nothing, and the 1990s vintage push-button phone on the reception desk would surely have been replaced if they had installed a video system. I moved down the hall toward the bishop's office.

The door was slightly ajar. Good thing he was a trusting soul. I entered the office and returned the door to its original position. When we met here yesterday, I hadn't noticed Tom's desk was massive. It had wooden panels that went to the floor on three sides, finished in what would probably be called artisanal black with antique brass drawer pulls. It was solid oak—no simple veneers for our leading man.

Sitting on the desktop were notes from what appeared to be a sermon on the church's financial needs and the spiritual benefits of tithing. A brief image of St. Peter standing at heaven's pearly gates wearing a green accounting eyeshade and marking up a ledger book flashed in my head.

Walking behind the desk, I rolled out the worn leather desk chair and looked in the small trash can underneath—no water bottles or anything else that might harbor DNA. I tried the center drawer, which was unlocked. I stopped to check for any sounds in the hall but heard nothing beyond my heart pounding in my ears.

The drawer contained office supplies, a relatively new appointment book, a well-worn address book, and a stack of papers, which I rummaged through but found nothing of interest. There were deep drawers for hanging folders on both sides of the desk, and I quickly rifled through them, not sure exactly what I was looking for, but found nothing there either.

Then I noticed a hanging folder at the back that was a lot more faded than the others. I opened it up and found newspaper clippings about Tom that covered his ordainment, moving to new parishes, and finally being promoted to bishop. I had a similar file of clippings in my home office. It was nice to see the clergy cared about these earthly accomplishments as much as we commoners did.

I was about to close the file when I spotted the corner of an old sheet of notepaper sticking out from the back of the stack. It was old and yellowing and addressed to Tom, but there was no date at the top and no signature at the bottom. The author professed their devotion and promised to support him no matter what happened. I couldn't tell if they meant personally or professionally. Maybe the bishop was a rascal before he was ordained. It occurred to me that the Monsignor could have written the note just as easily as some college girl with a crush.

Just then, the main entrance door was yanked open was a loud bang. I jumped and dropped the file folder, which sent papers flying in all directions. As I crouched to gather them together, I heard two voices that sounded like the bishop and the monsignor coming down the hallway.

"Is there anyone there?" asked the bishop in a booming voice. He must have heard the file hitting the floor.

I was totally busted and needed to think of a cover story quickly. Maybe I'd decided to volunteer for custodial duties as well as Bingo? I gave up, dropped the papers, stood, and steeled myself to face the wrath of Tom. "I'm..."

The monsignor replied over the top of me. "No, I don't think so."

The bishop must have been asking his fixer if the coast was clear.

"Good, we can talk. What do you think those boys were really up to yesterday? I don't believe that crap about researching their family tree."

They were slowly coming down the hallway to the bishop's office, their shoes clicking louder with each step on the highly polished marble floor.

The monsignor said, "I'm not buying it either. I'll bet it has something to do with the rumors about Grayson's business."

"What rumors?"

119

My palms were sweaty, and I was in full-blown panic mode. The voices were two rooms away, and I was standing there in plain sight, just waiting to get busted. To make matters worse, they were talking about Dean and me, and I desperately wanted to hear this.

Just then, my cell phone vibrated, which sounded like a game show buzzer. I grabbed it before it buzzed again.

The men stopped in front of the room next door, and the bishop asked, "What was that?"

The monsignor was silent for a moment. "Probably the heating system—it's been acting up for months now—I'll ask Mike's crew to look at it after they finish the other repairs."

"Might as well, right?"

I took advantage of this delay to send the call to voicemail and scoot under the desk as silently as possible. This gave me an idea, and I quickly redialed the Rectory number. The phone in the foyer started ringing, and the two men stopped right outside of the bishop's office.

The monsignor started back down the hall. "I'll get it."

"Fine. I just need to grab my Capital Campaign sermon so I can head over to St. Timothy's. We'll have to talk about the boys later." He walked in, picked up the sermon, and left.

I breathed a heavy sigh of relief.

"Ah yes, the sermon asking for big money—loved by parishioners and clergy alike. Let me know how it goes," said Monsignor Scarpino as he picked up the phone. "Hello…hello?"

I'd already hung up. Good thing the phone was so old it didn't have Caller ID. He moved down the hall toward the residence as the bishop left.

I stayed hidden for a minute to make sure they were gone. As I began backing out, I noticed hairs on the floor in the corner under the desk where it would be difficult for a vacuum cleaner to reach. Figuring they must be the bishop's, I pulled out a small Ziploc bag, grabbed as many hairs as possible, sealed them up, and put the bag in my pocket. Then I swung out from under the desk, scooped up the papers, tried to put everything back where they had originally been, and peeked out of the room. The hallway was empty, so I quickly walked down and let myself out of the main entrance.

"Oh, hello, Father!" said a voice from a few steps down the walk.

Holy crap, now what? I turned around. "Excuse me?"

The ten o'clock service would be ending soon, and the parishioners who were leaving early had started filing out. An older lady in a Sunday hat and coat stopped to chat. "Are you the new priest at St. Celestine's?" she asked sweetly. Then a look of panic spread across her face as she noticed my wet shirt and unruly condition.

In for a penny. "Hello. I must look a mess—didn't set my alarm to ring at the right time, and I'm horribly late. Got to dash—nice to meet you!"

"Nice to meet you, too, Father." She seemed confused.

"Thanks for being a part of St. Celestine's," I called over my shoulder for good measure.

I couldn't believe I didn't get busted in there. So much for being a Master of Design—that plan sucked. Of course, now I had to find my car. In my caffeine and adrenaline-fueled buzz, I forgot to make a mental note of where I parked. At least it wasn't twenty below outside, which wasn't unheard of during April in Minnesota.

I walked down a few blocks, convinced I was getting closer to my car, and was about to step off a curb when a large black sedan cut the corner and roared by me. I jumped back and realized if I had taken one more step, it would have been my last. My heart was pounding furiously, and my hands were trembling. I wanted to run down the street, break open the driver's window with my bare hands, and throttle the guy for being so careless.

Wait a minute, wasn't a brush with death supposed to cause your life to flash before your eyes? Because there was a long weekend I'd spent with a certain lovely lady in a cabin up north that I wouldn't mind reliving. Nothing. I felt cheated and lucky at the same time.

As rational thinking returned, I looked up to see if I could get a license plate number, but the car had already turned the corner and disappeared. I thought about running after it but just didn't have it in me. It seemed odd someone would be driving so recklessly in the middle of the day. Then I realized—this was only a warning. If they'd waited another two seconds, I would have been spread out all over the street. Someone was trying to tell me, and probably Dean too, to stop doing whatever it was they thought we were doing. We needed to figure this out before someone got hurt—someone like me.

I looked down the street, spotted my car halfway down the block, and silently thanked the reckless driver for helping me find it. I got in and sat for a moment to catch my breath, then took out my cell phone and dialed up a former client who ran a medical lab testing facility.

"Hey, Toby, Grayson here. Do you remember that design work we did for your lab and how you said you owed me a favor? You do? Good."

Chapter Fourteen

Wednesday Morning, April 19

It was early Wednesday morning, and I was sitting at my desk, thinking it was good to be alive and feeling grateful no one had tried to run me over for nearly three days. The radio weatherman said we'd have freezing rain this morning, which would turn to snow by the afternoon. It seemed like a perfect time to stay in my warm and cozy office and write a blog post, having recently come across a perfect subject.

After Paul and I started Design By Dyle, I began a blog critiquing designs for products and services. I'd built up a small following of design enthusiasts who enjoyed the snarky comments. Some of them even posted reviews of their own, most of which described poorly designed products.

Sprayable Maple Syrup? I typed, hoping this would help return me to my regularly scheduled life.

Disclaimer—I haven't tried this product, but I'm going to give them the benefit of the doubt and assume they got the taste right.

I don't think "sprayable" is the right word for this. First off, is that even a word? Secondly, spraying something, to me, implies atomizing a liquid into a fine mist, like hairspray, for example. The can shoots a stream just like a can of Easy Cheese. Of course, they call that spray cheese, and I'm not crazy about that name, either. Stream cheese seems to be more accurate. "Streaming Maple Syrup," maybe? Of course, that could also mean listening to an indie, heavy metal band on Spotify.

Semantics aside, to me, this product is an SLFP (Solution Looking For a Problem).

One of the guys in the product video says he puts his regular bottle of maple syrup in the fridge between uses, and then he has to nuke it to use it, a problem that this new product solves. After weeks of detailed root-cause problem-solving, I have come up with a better solution — don't put your maple syrup in the fridge between uses in the first place! Room-temperature maple syrup will flow just fine, and it isn't a health hazard. I checked my bottle of maple syrup, and it clearly states on the back: "Refrigeration not required."

I suppose if you have small children who tend to spread maple syrup all over the table, this product may have some appeal. Then again, haven't you just upped the ante by weaponizing the problem? "Hey, Timmy, hold your plate toward me. INCOMING!"

I reread the blog, fixed a few typos, and posted it. It was a good thing I co-owned the company so I could spend time writing blog posts without anyone complaining. My cell phone rang, and I answered it without checking to see who was calling.

"Grayson Dyle," I said.

"This is Detective Copeland."

Just like that, three days of normal everyday life went down the tubes. "Yes?"

"I'd like to have another word with you about James Brennen today. I can come by to pick you up in thirty minutes."

Heavy sigh. "You want to pick me up and bring me down to the station?"

"That's right."

I tried to avoid being picked up by the police in front of the building as it attracted unwanted attention. Copeland would probably use an unmarked car, but they were so easy to spot it would be sure to get people talking. "I'd rather come to you. You're in St. Paul, right? Can you give me the address?" I brought up my schedule and started moving some internal meetings to free up the next few hours.

He rattled off the address. "Shall we say nine?"

"See you soon."

"Grayson, don't make me come over there and get you."

I guess the cops did call you in advance to tell you they wanted to talk. If

I'd known what this was about, I would have started conjuring up excuses immediately.

The twelve-mile trip to the St. Paul Police Station took forty-five minutes—freezing rain did that to the Twin Cities, despite the best efforts of the city's salt trucks. I walked into the station and stopped at the front desk.

"Detective Aaron Copeland, please," I said to the officer at the reception desk through a small metal voice port in the bulletproof glass.

"Is he expecting you?" asked the receptionist loudly enough to be heard over the police scanner in the background.

"Yes. My name is Grayson Dyle."

"I'll let him know you're here." She pointed her pen toward a beat-up wooden bench along the wall.

The three-inch-thick glass that separated the waiting room from the rest of the station created a sense of foreboding. There were large rivets in broad metal columns that held the sheets of bulletproof glass in place. It didn't have to be this creepy. They could have countersunk the rivets so they'd be flush with the columns, made the columns much thinner, and covered them with strips of natural wood, maybe put in another window for more sunlight, or added a dash of color to the walls. It would've been a much friendlier place.

Then I realized they probably wanted this room to be intimidating. I found myself wondering how to crank up the creepiness factor and figured some FBI Most Wanted posters would come in handy. Fortunately, my train of thought was soon interrupted.

"Grayson, thanks for coming down on short notice." The detective opened the security door, shook my hand, and showed me into the station. "Would you like some coffee?" Maybe he only had a few quick questions, and I'd be out of here pronto.

"Sure, that would be great."

We walked over to a small kitchen. "Don't believe everything you see on TV about crappy coffee in police stations. We don't mind spending a bit more for the good stuff." He handed me a cup of coffee with the logo of a well-known local chain on the side.

We both ignored the ironic half-empty box of donuts on the counter.

"Cream or sugar?"

"I can do that." I picked up a canister of powdered cream to add to the coffee. My hand was shaking slightly, and coffee sloshed onto the tile floor. "I'll get it."

"Don't bother." Copeland dropped some napkins on the floor and used his shoe to wipe up the coffee, all the while looking at me as if to say, "Do you have a reason to be nervous?"

He put the wet napkins in the trash and led me to a conference room in the back. His tone turned somber, and the relative friendliness of the previous meeting was gone. "Right this way."

I was surprised to find a nicely appointed, well-lit conference room with framed pictures of famous local buildings, including the state capitol and the St. Paul Landmark Center. Not a single sheet of one-way mirrored glass was in sight. "This is pleasant."

"Thanks. People always have a lot of preconceived ideas about police stations that we try to rectify."

"I assume you have some news about James's murder?"

"We recovered the slugs, and we know he was shot with a .22 caliber handgun. You don't see a lot of those on the street. It's the kind of gun people buy for personal protection. Do you own a gun, Grayson?"

How did I not see these things coming? Of course, he was going to ask me if I owned a gun. I didn't see any point in lying, although I wanted to just for spite. "Yes, I do. My father bought me a Ruger with a scope many years ago, and we used it for target practice. It's been sitting in a box in my closet ever since."

"Is it a .22 caliber?"

"Yes, it is."

"Have you shot it recently?"

"No. As I said, it's been in a box in my closet for years. I don't even know if it still works. The scope is still attached, which would make it almost impossible to conceal."

"Do you mind if I have it tested? I'd like to see if it matches the slugs we pulled from the wall."

"Not at all. I put a security lock on it, and I'm pretty sure I can find the key. Would you like me to bring it down to the station?"

"No. We'll send someone by to pick it up...today." He was staring a hole in my head and must have been trying to either intimidate me into confessing or read my mind directly from my brain cells.

"I have nothing to hide."

"Why didn't you tell me you owned a handgun the last time we met?"

My heart was pounding harder. "How was that relevant? I didn't even know the killer used a .22."

The detective backed off slightly. "Nothing seems to be missing from his office, so we're fairly certain it wasn't a robbery."

"Where does that leave you?"

"You're looking pretty good for it."

"What?! Why would you think that?" I ignored the urge to run screaming from the room.

"We saw your emails with James before your dinner. Why didn't you tell me you and Dean were related to James?"

"Again, how is that relevant? We don't even know how we're related exactly." I figured lies told in a police station wouldn't count as much as lies told in a church. "Just being related to someone isn't a motive for murder."

"The three of you got together..."

"As we've already discussed."

"You have dinner. He tells you how you're related. Maybe he says he's an older stepbrother, and you have the same father. Then he calls your mother a whore and says he'll sue you for defamation if you ever reveal you're related to him. He has a nondisclosure form, and he threatens to shut down your business and ruin Dean's reputation if you both don't sign it. You don't like what you're hearing, so you threaten to kill him."

My heart wasn't pounding quite so hard now as I listened to these lame theories. "That's ridiculous."

He seemed to process his thoughts better when he said them out loud, and he was on a roll.

"You both go home and stew. You talk to Dean, and he's just as pissed off as you. Who the hell does James think he is? He can't treat you that way. Pretty soon, you're furious. You decide you're going to do something about it. So, you take your gun out of the box, take off the scope, load a few rounds, and drive over to his office. You sit in the parking lot and watch. Other people are leaving, but not him, so you decide to go in and scare him a little. Make him sorry he threatened you. But he doesn't scare that easily. The next thing you know, there are two slugs in his chest, and you're holding the murder weapon."

"That story has so many flaws in it. No one would be that stupid."

"You're right. You wouldn't use the gun from your house. You're too smart for that. So, you took the one you had stashed in your office because Lake Street is a scary place, right? Then you waited for the right time, and you shot him—twice."

I could tell he was trying to make me angry enough to say something incriminating. "That's a load of crap. You know I didn't kill James, and I won't admit that I did, no matter how much you bully me. After James left, Dean and I hung out in the parking lot, talking about what had happened. People were coming and going the whole time, so I should have quite a few alibis for the time of the murder." I stared at him with a smirk.

We both knew this wasn't true, and Copeland didn't seem impressed.

"Then what did you do?"

"I went home and answered some emails. No, I didn't stop at a gas station to wave at their security camera, nor did I see anyone who'd remember me. But the timestamps on my computer log will show what time I was there."

The detective leaned in. "You're a smart guy. You could have signed into your computer from your car before or after you killed him to change the logs. Or, you could have set up the emails to auto-send while you were out doing the deed. You're our primary suspect. You had dinner with the guy and threatened to kill him in front of a few dozen people. You two are the only new people in his life, and you have no good alibi for the time of the murder. Unless you want to throw your brother under the bus and tell me he did it—he doesn't have an alibi either."

"This is nuts. Neither Dean nor I have a motive. We both wanted to learn more about our family tree from James. Why would we kill him?" Then, I got it. "You don't have any other suspects, do you? That's why you're hitting me up with these crazy accusations—to see if I accidentally divulge something that gives you a new direction for the case."

Copeland frowned. Apparently, he didn't like me calling him out. "Where were you last Sunday morning at about ten-fifteen?"

Whoa. Didn't see that coming. "I went to St. Celestine to go to the ten o'clock mass."

"You didn't go into the church, did you?"

"No, I like the design of the church grounds, so I decided to take a walk around. It helps clear my head. Why do you ask?"

"Someone reported a suspicious person loitering near the Rectory on Sunday morning. The description is a perfect match for you, Grayson."

Damn, it must have been that lady who spotted me leaving the building. "I don't know if you're aware of this, but James told Dean and me he is related to the bishop. I wanted to ask him about that, and I figured if I called for an appointment, he wouldn't see me. I thought I'd see if the bishop was available after the service."

"You broke in."

"No, the door was open. I stuck my head in and didn't see anyone, so I left. Was anything missing?"

"The Rectory staff said nothing was missing. But the bishop doesn't like members of the public being in the Rectory without an invitation. You can certainly understand that."

"Of course. By the way, now that you've confirmed Dean and I are members of James's family, what else can you tell me about his death?" I tried to turn the tables.

Copeland stared at me for a moment as if considering how much to say. "I've already told you most of what we have. He was shot twice between eight and nine P.M. in his office at the law firm. His wife told us they didn't keep a gun in the office, so the killer must have brought one with them, which implies premeditation. The slugs we pulled from his office wall don't match any online records. It looks like he was killed by someone he knew, which makes it personal."

James's office flashed through my mind as he was talking. "What about his computer? Was that taken?"

"Yes, but it was pretty old and not worth much. James was left-handed and used his mouse on the left side of his laptop, but it was on the right side when we arrived. Maybe the killer wanted to find something."

"Or erase something."

"We thought of that, too. We've looked at the emails in the cloud and didn't find anything. The laptop had been backed up about six weeks before the event, and there was nothing in the backup files either. If someone wanted to erase something, it must have been entered after the most recent backup."

Maybe the murderer stole the laptop so they could send threatening messages to me, I thought but managed to avoid blurting out. "A six-week-old backup? That's pretty good for a law firm. But how did they get into the laptop without the password, which they probably didn't have?"

"The staff was good at backing up data because one of the partners lost some critical files a few years back. But they didn't require passwords on their system. Most of their work is paper-based, so they relied on locked doors for protection."

"It could have been a disgruntled client or former employee then."

"We're looking into all possibilities."

"Other than me or possibly Dean, who do you suspect?"

"I'm not at liberty to discuss that."

Copeland probably eliminated James's clients and couldn't find a meth addict to blame, so he had nothing. He wouldn't disclose this much intel if he thought I did it, and he was trying to work the family tree angle to see if he could generate a new lead or two. His question from our previous discussion popped into my head. "Why did you ask about bloody shoes the last time we met?"

"We found bloody footprints on the floor next to James. We think the killer may have been looking for something other than the laptop, or they wanted to make sure he was dead."

I guess that would make sense, but it wasn't what happened. For a moment, I considered telling him what I'd learned so he could sweat actual suspects instead of me. Then I realized he'd take the intel Dean and I had developed and block us from any further investigating. Worse yet, we'd still be suspects. I said nothing.

He got up to show me to the door. "I've got a case to solve. I'll send an officer around to collect your gun. And, Grayson, unless you have an appointment, stay away from the Rectory."

As predicted, the freezing rain was slowly changing into snow, and traffic into Minneapolis was crawling along, giving me plenty of time to think. It was obvious Copeland had nothing substantial, and he'd been grilling me to help develop a new angle on the case. That was why he didn't stop by unannounced and didn't argue when I said I'd meet him at the station. He didn't want to waste that much time on a fishing expedition. I was simultaneously pissed at him for trying to play me and glad I avoided the trap.

Had there been something on that laptop worth someone's life? Dean's plan to place a backdoor on James's laptop had worked, and he had been able to search through the files, but he hadn't found anything relevant. Then again, he didn't know what to look for, so he might have missed something. Maybe a former client with a grudge disclosed something to James and regretted it later. Perhaps their court records were sealed, and they wanted to eliminate the data on the laptop, too. Maybe they deleted their data before Dean searched it, then saw the emails I'd sent to him about DeeDee and the letter and decided to send some threatening emails to divert attention from them to James's family members. There was no way Dean and I could find a suspect like that.

I drove slowly through Uptown, parked underground, and made my way to the office, deep in thought and discouraged by the lousy weather. Then I realized it was Wednesday, and tonight was Bingo Night. I decided to drop by the church to see if Kate was there despite the crazy weather. I could grill her about James's other clients to see if any of them might have had a reason to kill him. I was sure Copeland had already asked her that, but at least it was a reasonable excuse to see her again, not that I needed one.

I checked emails when I reached the office, and the one from Steve Hancock stood out. The subject was "Decision," and I crossed my fingers as I clicked on it. *Hi Grayson. We were impressed with your proposal and your office, but I regret to inform you we've decided to use another firm for the design work because they have more experience in this area. We plan to ask you to bid on new work in the future. Best of luck, Steve.*

Damn it. To make matters worse, our contacts at Carson Companies had just given us some difficult news. Their new owners directed them to start sending any future design work to their offshore subsidiaries in China. The local managers were extremely apologetic, saying they would much rather work with us, but their hands were tied. There was no way we could turn down Mike Wilson's business now. We'd just have to watch him closely. Of course, we still had to win it first.

I sent a text to Paul and asked him to stop by my office. He arrived a few minutes later, and I turned my screen toward him without saying a word. When he finished reading the email, he sank deep into the chair across from my desk and stared at the ceiling.

"Paul, it's okay. Mike Wilson will hire us. We'll be okay. I know we will. We might have to take a smaller paycheck for a month or two while we recover, so we don't have to lay anyone off, but we'll make it through this."

"This is the last straw, Gray. I had a feeling this was going to happen. I told Richard last night I was going to leave the firm if we didn't get both deals, and he said he'd stand by me." Tears were forming in his eyes. "I'm sorry to do this to you, but I quit."

"Paul, hang on—"

"Gray. Stop. Don't try to talk me out of it. We're down to our last few dollars, and I can't take the stress anymore. I must not be the business owner type. All I've ever wanted to do was good, solid design work. I'm going to find a new job where I can focus on interesting projects and not lay awake at night, wondering how we're going to make payroll." He got up and walked to the door. "At least now you'll have a few more weeks to drum up some new business before you have to lay people off." Just like that, he was gone.

Dammit. My nerves were on edge already, and this definitely wasn't helping. There was no point in chasing after him. He just needed some time to process things. He'd be okay in a few days, I tried to convince myself. In the meantime, what else could go wrong?

Chapter Fifteen

Wednesday Night, April 19

I was in a gloomy mood as I drove to the church for Bingo Night. I was looking forward to seeing Kate again but couldn't stop worrying about losing the business. So, I kept reassuring myself the monsignor would make sure we won the Wilson business, which we would have to accept, even if it meant letting Mike into our offices for meetings. Then I could use that to entice Paul to come back. It was unsettling to think I was relying on my number one murder suspect to help save my company. I had stopped at my apartment to grab my bright yellow shirt but wasn't wearing it yet. I wasn't going to volunteer unless Kate was there.

I parked a block away from the church and noticed a white panel van with a large Wilson Construction logo on the side access door as I walked past the parking lot. Standing beside it, seemingly impervious to the snow, were Monsignor Scarpino and Mike Wilson. I quickly crossed the street to make sure they wouldn't see me. No point in tipping my hand that I knew they were in cahoots. I found a Suburban to hide behind and watched through its windows as Mike was relating something that involved multiple facial expressions and aggressive arm waving. The monsignor's grin grew wider as he listened, and they both laughed heartily when the story ended, looking like old semi-drunken buddies in a bar.

Just then, they shook hands and went off in opposite directions. Mike got into the panel van and drove off. The monsignor walked over to a far corner of the church lot, got into a large black sedan in a reserved parking spot, and started it up. I was shocked to see it was a Crown Vic, and it looked exactly like the one that nearly separated my body and soul. I memorized the license number in case it tried to sideswipe me again. Then I realized there was another identical Crown Vic next to the one the monsignor was driving. Maybe he wasn't the one who tried to kill me after all.

I decided to see what my friend was up to, so I walked over and knocked on the driver's window.

The Monsignor looked a bit startled as he lowered the window. "Grayson, how can I help you? If you're here for Bingo Night, it's in the church hall, which is right down the stairs."

"No, I wanted to talk to you, Monsignor. Is this your car?"

His face snarled up. "No, it's part of the rectory's carpool. Why do you ask?"

"A car exactly like this one nearly ran me over last Sunday. Would that have been you driving?"

"What?! What did you say?"

"I said a car exactly like this one nearly ran me over after church on Sunday. Would you know anything about that?"

"Are you accusing me of reckless driving? Are you nuts? Maybe you should watch where you're walking." As he raised the window and shook his head, I got the distinct feeling he would have flipped me off if he wasn't in uniform and on church grounds.

I decided not to worry about it and walked into the church hall just in time for the start of the second shift. I scanned the volunteers as I headed toward the back of the room, looking for Kate but didn't see her. Maybe she was in the kitchen. Then I heard my name ring out.

"Grayson! Over here." I recognized the honeyed voice and headed in her direction.

"DeeDee, how nice to see you again. I see the weather didn't stop you from coming down."

"Oh, we never miss it." She moved Harry aside to give me a place to sit. "I thought I might see you here tonight. Probably looking for Kate, if I'm not mistaken?" She wore a knowing smile.

I sat next to her. "DeeDee, you know I'm just here for the thrill of playing the game."

"That's good because you just missed her." DeeDee looked around to see if anyone was listening, then leaned in conspiratorially. "She kept watching the door. It looked like she only braved the weather, thinking you'd be here, then left when she didn't see you."

I hoped it wasn't as evident to everyone else as it was to DeeDee that Kate and I were interested in each other. She might not be as dotty as she first appeared.

"I'm not one to talk, but you might want to think twice before dating that girl." Having delivered her message, she sat upright again to play the next game.

"Everyone ready? Good, here we go," announced the caller. "The first ball is...I-Twenty-nine. Twenty-nine, and we're doing fine. Two and nine, twenty-nine."

"Here. Use Harry's cards. He doesn't mind."

"Thanks, DeeDee." As we were doing fine looking for I-29, I waited for her to continue. But she seemed unaware I wanted more information. Finally, I asked in a hushed voice, "Why do I want to think twice about dating Kate?"

"Well, I'm not one to talk, but rumors were flying around about her last year. Something about the church books being off."

Hmm. Now we were getting somewhere. "What was the problem?"

"G-Fifty-seven. Fifty-seven Heinz Varieties. Five and seven, Fifty-seven."

No luck for me, but DeeDee had that one.

"I never did hear anything more about it. Kate seems like such a nice girl, too. She's in tight with the bishop and probably the monsignor, too, so I was surprised to hear those rumors. But they must have worked it out because she's still here."

"B-Five. B-Five, man alive. All on its own, number five," said the caller.

"Do the bishop and the monsignor come here often?"

"Oh, sure. They stop by. But they don't stay too long—don't want to spoil the fun, they always say. Now, let's play—it's just getting good."

Soon the second round was over, the players were filing out, and the volunteers were cleaning up. I had to admit. I'd had more fun than I thought I would. DeeDee was quite entertaining with her crazy stories of working at the crematorium. Some were a bit gruesome, such as the eight-hundred-pound corpse they had to cut into two pieces to fit in the cremator, which generated so much heat the building caught fire. Others were gross, such as the kids that thought they'd stolen cocaine only to discover they were snorting someone's ashes. She was a real character. It didn't hurt I won one of the games, and I selected the Popcorn Lover's Gift Basket. It was either that or the Gift Basket for Babies. I thought I chose wisely.

DeeDee agreed to let me walk her to her car for safety, so when I offered to help clean up, she did, too. We cleared the used Bingo cards and other trash into large garbage bags, folded the tables, and stacked them alongside the chairs. I was taking two full garbage bags through the kitchen to throw in the dumpster out back when I noticed the cash box sitting on the butcher block table, unattended. Despite the harsh weather, it had been a busy night, and I figured they cleared more than their usual ten grand. Maybe this was one way to keep the company going.

I threw the bag in the dumpster and came back into the kitchen. The cashbox was still there unattended, and the temptation was getting the better of me. I peeked into the parish hall. Most everyone was gone except for DeeDee, who was chatting up another volunteer. I figured he must be responsible for taking the cash to the Rectory. I walked back and opened the box. I had no idea how much money was there, but it looked like a lot, and even a few thousand would help. *Am I really going to do this? Is this how low I've sunk?* My heart was pounding wildly as I reached toward the stack of twenties. Maybe Aunt Phyllis was right when she said, "those boys were just born bad" all those years ago.

"Ready to go?"

I whipped around to see DeeDee standing there, eyeing me suspiciously.

"I'm sorry for startling you."

"I didn't hear you walk up."

As we left the building, just as my heart rate was returning to normal,

I heard a muffled sound, which sounded like someone had just opened a bottle of champagne. Then there was another one, followed by a loud ping, and I realized what was happening.

"Get down, DeeDee! Someone's shooting at us."

DeeDee went face down in a fit of panic. Without thinking, I threw the Gift Basket aside and jumped on top to shield her from more bullets. Then I heard an engine turn over, and I jumped up to see a car fishtailing down the street, with a blurred figure wearing a hoodie and something across their face behind the wheel. I remembered to look for the license plate this time but couldn't see it around the parked cars.

I figured the danger was over and asked DeeDee if she was okay as I helped her up. She nodded, but tears were forming in her eyes. I guessed Winston Churchill got it right when he said, "Nothing in life is so exhilarating as to be shot at without result."

She retrieved the urn from the sidewalk, inspected it, then showed it to me. "He took a bullet for me."

I looked down to see Harry's urn had a hole in the side, and ashes were leaking out. If she had been holding the urn differently or if the gun had been of a higher caliber, she might have joined her ex in the great beyond.

"Oh, Harry, you took a bullet for me." She let out a happy sigh and, regaining her composure, put her thumb over the hole to stop any more ashes from spilling out. "He was always like that. Watching out for me, taking care of me. I know you're that way, too. I can tell by the way you look at Kate."

I wanted to get off this subject quickly and realized there was only one hole in the urn. "I think the bullet is still in there with Harry. Would it be okay for the police to retrieve it? I'm sure they'll be careful with the ashes."

"Here, put your finger over the hole." She handed Harry to me, unscrewed the top, fished around, found the bullet, and gave it to me in exchange for the urn. "Scooping up the ashes after a cremation is more of an art than an exact science. They never get it all, so a few ashes plus or minus doesn't much matter."

I accepted it with an open palm and called 911 with my other hand. I wondered if Detective Copeland would show up and made a mental note to add him to my favorites list so I could call him more quickly if any new shootings occurred. When DeeDee wasn't looking, I wiped the bullet down to obscure any fingerprints. There was no point in having Copeland snooping around since this was obviously a family matter. Dean and I needed to crank this investigation in high gear, though. What the bloody hell was in that letter that was worth killing over?

Gun violence in the Twin Cities had been skyrocketing over the past few years, and "shots fired" calls to the police were off the charts. The dispatcher answered quickly and said they had already received other calls on this incident, so the police were on their way.

Two uniformed officers drove up in a squad car within a few minutes. They collected the slug in an evidence bag while they took our statements concerning the description and location of the shooter. They assumed the shots were gang or drug-related, and I didn't see any reason to disabuse them of this idea. If the police thought this was a random shooting, maybe they'd be too busy with actual murders to test the rifling on the bullet, which could potentially match the shots that killed James.

Another squad soon arrived. The officer we had spoken with directed the two new arrivals to the shooter's location to recover any shell casings that might have been left behind. Since no one was hurt, and neither DeeDee nor I could identify the shooter, we were soon allowed to go about our business.

Despite her initial shock, DeeDee was recovering nicely. She assured me she would be fine, which was good enough for me. I walked her to her car and held the passenger door open while she gingerly tucked Harry in behind the seat belt. Despite her protests, I put the Popcorn Lover's Gift Basket on the seat next to him to stop any more ashes from spilling out. She gave me one of her trademark mischievous smiles as she said thanks and drove off.

Chapter Sixteen

I n a product design review meeting at nine on Friday morning, one of our designers was displaying her preliminary analysis of a new corkscrew on the three flat screens in the middle of the conference room.

A local entrepreneur I'd gone to college with had ordered a bottle of wine at a trendy restaurant and sat there helplessly as a server struggled to open it using the standard-issue corkscrew-on-a-stick. He called me the next day, asking if we could create a better one. It was a small project, but we needed the work, so I told him we could, and we started immediately.

After doing some market research, my team discovered most restaurants only invested in high-end corkscrews if they had a wine steward or sommelier who needed to open a bottle with a flourish, which helped justify higher wine prices. This meant we needed an innovative design with a high-end look that was inexpensive to make and easy to use. Good thing there was no pressure.

A large design firm would do a detailed stress analysis on a high-powered computer with sophisticated physics software. We didn't have the time or the budget for that. After a preliminary stress analysis, we created physical prototypes using a 3-D printer, cranked them out quickly, tested them, and tweaked the design until it worked.

I told the designer I liked the design aesthetics but was concerned it would be too costly to manufacture. We talked through a few changes, and the team went back to their desks to revise the design and start printing 3-D models.

I was reminded again we had a talented crew, and it pained me to think we might have to downsize if we didn't land some new business soon. Assuming Paul came back, of course. It had only been two days since he'd left, so I didn't want to panic. But now, I'd have to do both the physical and esthetic design work, and I hoped I was up to it. I decided to text Paul to check in.

Hey - how about a cup of Joe sometime soon?

Ten seconds later, the pinging sound of a text message arriving on my cell phone made me jump. I started thinking about where to have coffee with Paul when I realized I didn't recognize the new text's number.

If you want to know who killed James Brennen, bring the letter to the Rectory at 1:00 today

I reread the text, sat back, closed my eyes, and took a deep breath. This had the hallmark of every slasher movie ever made. The hapless teen victim walks directly into the trap while the audience warns them not to, then dies a bloody death. Was I really this desperate? Yes. Yes, I was. I would just have to be smarter than them. Then I realized I couldn't be at the Rectory at one due to the critical, save-the-company meeting with Mike at two in Roseville. There was no point in trying to identify the texter. They were probably using a cheap burner phone to remain anonymous. Maybe I could get them to change the time.

I can't make it at 1:00. I texted in reply. **How about 3:30?**

This isn't a dentist appointment. Be there at 1:00. This is a one-time offer. Bring the damn letter.

As we were texting, I found the address for Mike's office in my email system and did a quick Google Map search. It was just off Fairview Avenue, across from Rosedale Center, which would be about twenty minutes from the Rectory. Whatever this person had to say couldn't take more than thirty minutes. **Fine 1:00** I texted back.

Hiring a fixer who could also serve as a bodyguard seemed like a brilliant idea at the moment, not that we could afford it. I saved the presentation on a memory stick, put the stick in my pants pocket, threw the letter and a few sketches into my folder, and headed out.

Fortunately, traffic was light this time of day. I arrived at twelve fifty-five and parked on the street, a quarter block away.

I dialed the main Rectory number, but there was no answer. From my car, I could see both Crown Vics were gone, and the parking lot was empty, except for a large utility trailer, with the Wilson Construction logo emblazoned on its side, hitched up in a far corner. I figured that was where they would be hiding.

It was time to stop this insanity, identify the killer, call Copeland, and have them taken away. I thought about calling Dean for backup, but he would never get here in time. It was now or never. I would just have to be cautious and outsmart them.

A surprise attack seemed promising, so I hid the letter under the car seat and snuck out of the vehicle toward the trailer. A big pile of melting remnants from a previous snowstorm made me realize there were some makeshift weapons handy as I ruminated about the time Dean hit me with a slush ball from just such a pile. I quickly turned the corner of the trailer, ready to pounce, only no one was there, and a heavy-duty padlock secured the back door.

I decided the main entrance would be safer and tried that first. It was locked, and no one answered my knocking. I went back to the side entrance, which was unlocked, and walked in. Technically, I wasn't disobeying Copeland's order to stay away from the Rectory because I did have an appointment...of sorts. I half expected to find someone pointing a gun at me, but the corridor was empty. "Hello?" No answer.

The jitters returned as I slowly moved down the hall toward the main entrance, making sure the doors I passed were locked so no one could jump me from behind. As I passed the library, I noticed a familiar odor and saw light coming from the next room, where Mike's team had been working on the root cellar. I slowly crept forward, trying to be stealthy. I glanced at my phone. It was already eight minutes after the hour.

I quickly turned the corner and took two steps into the room in a weak attempt at a shock-and-awe move—nothing except for a truly disgusting smell, which seemed to be coming from an open trapdoor. A drain hose and the top few rungs of a ladder were sticking out of the opening. If someone thought I was climbing down there, then they didn't know me very well. But no one else was around, and I was running out of time, so I threw caution out with the baby and the bathwater and leaned over the hole to say, "Hello?"

My first sensation was pain. The back of my head was throbbing as I sat up. The killer must have hit me with something and pushed me into the hole. The ladder probably helped break my fall, but it also did a number on my legs. I ran my hands along each one. Nothing seemed broken, but I had no doubt they were severely bruised. Good thing the floor was dirt, or the damage would have been much worse.

Then I noticed the overwhelming stench. I was trying not to retch when I realized the room was almost totally dark. That jackass must have pulled up the ladder and closed the trapdoor. There was a small sliver of light coming through the semicircular cut out along one edge of the door, where someone could insert their fingers and lift it open, but it was blocked by a hose. I clenched my fists and slammed them into the dirt floor, which only caused more pain. I had to calm down and think.

Why did the parish keep the root cellar open when they purchased the bungalow? Maybe the priests stored their church wine down here, which I could break into if I got desperate for something to drink. Having stolen sips of church wine many times over the years, I didn't know if that would be a blessing or a curse.

How long had I been out? I checked my coat pocket for my cell phone but found it had been turned out, along with all my other pockets. The killer must have climbed down here and searched me for the letter. Blindly feeling around the ground revealed my car keys and cell phone, which must have been tossed aside. The phone had a cracked screen, no bars on the cell signal indicator, and a battery charge of eight percent. I was relieved to see it still worked, so I would at least have a source of light down here.

Then I noticed the sound of gushing water, turned on the phone's flashlight, and pointed it at the noise. The killer must have connected the other end of the drain hose to a faucet and was dumping water into the hole. The water level was rising fast. I was getting the distinct impression someone didn't like me.

I used the phone's light to examine the rest of the room. It had whitewashed stone walls and was about six feet wide by eight feet long and about nine feet high. The mason that laid these stones must have been talented as they were closely matched with very little grout required to seal them in place. There was no way to scale these walls without making hand and toeholds, which would take many hours using tools I didn't have.

There was a stack of boards, a few cement bags, and some drainage tiles along one wall. The construction crew must be planning to install the drain tiles to eliminate the smell. The water was now covering the entire dirt floor, which was quickly turning into mud. I was pretty sure some small scurrying sounds were coming from behind the drain tiles, but I decided not to investigate.

I grabbed one of the wooden planks, put it up to the bottom of the trap door, and pushed hard. It didn't budge. My captor must have put something heavy on top of the door—probably a few of the bags of cement I noticed the last time I was here. How the hell was I going to get out?

It was Friday afternoon, and the Rectory was deserted, so there was no point in screaming for help. I wondered if my body would be at the bottom of the room or floating at the top by the time the workers arrived on Monday morning and noticed I was dead. Either way, it wouldn't be a pretty sight. I checked my phone, which said 1:25 and six percent power. I had to get out of here so I could still get to that meeting. Oh yeah, and avoid drowning, too.

I took a few of the boards and laid them out on the floor in a crisscross pattern, which gave me a reasonably firm surface to stand on. It also gave me an idea. If I positioned them right, I could use two boards to force open the heavy trapdoor, the same way a small scissors jack could lift a heavy car. It was all a matter of leverage.

Using the phone for light, I took one of the longest boards and stood it up on the makeshift platform at about a thirty-degree angle to the floor. I took a second long board and put one end against the bottom of the trap door, then lined up the other end against the end of the first board. They formed a very wide-open, sideways letter V. All I had to do now was push at the tip of the V, where the two boards met, moving them into a straight line. The lower board would force the upper board upward, thereby opening the trapdoor. This turned out to be more challenging than it sounded.

During my first attempt, the wet ends of the two boards slipped past each other and went crashing down. The water was now covering the platform I was standing on, so I put down another layer. This would be the last one, as I needed the rest of the boards to make my escape.

On the second attempt, the first longboard slipped just as the trapdoor started moving, and it knocked my phone into the water, killing the light. "Damn it!" I said in the direction of the scurrying sound I'd heard earlier. Fortunately, nothing answered back. I really hoped I'd been mistaken before and there were no furry friends who wanted to join me on the platform.

Even though I was working in the dark, I managed to align the boards properly on the third try, and the trapdoor opened by a crack. At least I had some light back. I inserted a different board into the gap and used it to make the opening bigger, which sent a powdery mix of cement cascading down. Continuing this process, the door was soon open over a foot, enough for me to shimmy through if I could only reach it.

My final building project was to take a few of the platform boards of progressively longer lengths and lean them against each other and then against the wall to form a makeshift ladder whose rungs were the width of a board. I set up two such sets of boards and figured I better get to the opening on the first try, or I'd really get hurt. As I started up the boards, there was enough light coming in to see my cell phone on one of the remaining boards in the corner. It wasn't in the water after all, so the battery must have finally worn out. At least, that was some good news. I dropped down, put it in my pocket, then carefully used the toes of my shoes to step up on the top edges of the boards to the opening, where I finally hoisted myself out of the cellar.

I crept down the hall to the restroom and looked in the mirror to see a complete wreck staring back. The crusty gray cement mix covering my hair and face made me look about ten years older, and I felt every bit of it. I brushed off my clothes and washed my face in the sink, then headed back toward the main entrance to see the time. It was eight minutes after two. I was late, and I looked like a construction worker who had been paving a sidewalk. Perfect time to see Mike Wilson. I raced over to my car, took the letter out from under the seat so it wouldn't be ruined, and took off, not caring that the seats would need a deep cleaning after this.

The dashboard clock read two forty-two as I pulled into the lot. The charging cord had been out of reach during my wild ride here, so my phone was still dead. The rearview mirror confirmed I still looked like hell, but I went in anyway.

The receptionist must have been used to workers coming in straight from their job sites because she didn't give me a second glance as she showed me into Mike Wilson's office. He wasn't there, and I figured I was doomed. At three ten, Mike walked in—also looking like hell. As we shook hands, he started apologizing for being late and then realized I looked just as bad as he did. We both laughed.

He explained that a couple of his contract workers had put away a few too many beers over lunch and weren't allowed to return to the job site, so he had to pitch in to help keep the job on schedule. That sounded like something I would do, and I liked this guy. Maybe I could trust him after all.

I reached into my pocket for the memory stick with the presentation on it, only to find nothing. It must have been stolen in the cellar or tossed aside along with my car keys and phone without me realizing it. I was seriously thinking about screaming when it occurred to me I had saved a backup copy on my Dropbox site, and I asked Mike if we could use his computer for the discussion.

In the end, Mike liked our concepts for the project, but I could tell he wasn't as delighted as I was hoping. I told Mike we would have new and improved designs for him in a few weeks, and he agreed to give us another chance. Dammit. If Paul had done more of the design work instead of me, we would have knocked his socks off. I had to get my partner back, or I might as well fold the company.

As soon as I got back to the car, I plugged in my phone and checked for new messages, but there was nothing from Paul. It seemed like days since I'd texted him about going for coffee, but it had only been a few hours. Paul could be a bit volatile, and he sometimes stormed out of the office when we disagreed about something important. He'd never gone quiet for this long before, and it was making me very nervous. I texted him again, saying Mike thought the design work was good but not great, and we really needed to work together to win this new business and keep the company alive. Paul hated substandard work more than the devil himself, and I hoped he would be outraged enough by Mike's reaction to at least text me back. I waited for about ten minutes, but there was no reply. As I sat there, I couldn't help wondering why Mike was giving Design By Dyle another shot. Did he really believe in our potential? Or had the monsignor compelled him to work with us so he'd have the leverage to stop me from investigating any further?

Chapter Seventeen

Saturday, April 22

The sky was dark and overcast as I drove to St. Celestine's for the five o'clock Saturday night service. It was threatening to rain any minute, but I didn't care. I was on a mission. I had been thinking about Kate all day and recalled her saying she usually attended the Saturday night service. So, there I sat, cheerfully driving to the church on a gloomy evening, hoping to see her.

I parked in the half-full church parking lot and realized once I was in, I'd have to hang around for the entire service, whether Kate was there or not. I wondered where she usually sat and if I had twenty bucks on me for the collection plate as I took a seat about halfway back. I studied the crowd carefully but no Kate.

The service was about to begin when she swooped in, blond hair flying, wearing a bright red sweater with black slacks. Her shiny red high heels clicked against the marble floor as she walked up the center aisle. It occurred to me that she might have gotten dressed up for a hot date later this evening. This was turning into another of my famous terrible ideas.

She sat a few rows behind me on the other side of the center aisle and shed her raincoat with a flourish, her focus darting about the church as she scanned the crowd. It finally landed on me, and she smiled and gave me a quick wave. She had the unique ability to look classy and alluring all at the same time. If she could figure out how to put that in a bottle, she'd be a rich girl. I'd love to blog about that product. I returned the wave in a hopefully discrete manner and bowed my head, trying to look like I was praying but really just wanted to hide the smile I couldn't seem to shake.

Soon, the organist began playing, and the priest and two altar boys started up the center aisle from the rear of the church. I stole a glance at Kate, who began mouthing words at me.

"See...you...after...the...service," she seemed to be saying, silently exaggerating each word.

I was staring at her lips long after she was done and wondered what it would be like to kiss them. Just then, the procession moved between us and broke my eye contact. Or eye-lip contact. I glanced at the priest, who was glaring back at me. It was just like old times, although getting a nasty look from the priest before the service even began might have been a new personal best.

After the trio reached the altar, the congregation sat back in their pews, and I did, too, hoping I wasn't too out of practice to look reverential. I was reminiscing about the crazy number of masses that Dean and I had served together and the many times we got busted doing something dumb, like sampling the church wine in the sacristy when we thought the priest wasn't looking.

The sound of the congregation praying brought me back to reality, where I discovered everyone else was kneeling, and I was still sitting. I stole a glance at Kate, who was kneeling and paying attention to the service. A sudden motion behind her caught my attention. It was Monsignor Scarpino, who was sitting a few rows behind her, motioning for me to kneel with a scornful look. Yep—just like old times. I crept forward to the kneeler.

The service proceeded as usual, and the priest and altar boys were soon heading down the center aisle toward the rear of the church. As Kate and I started moving toward each other, I wondered which of us was smiling the hardest.

"Grayson Dyle, how are you?" she asked as we met in the center aisle.

I was expecting to shake hands, but she moved in for a big hug, which I had to admit felt pretty good. Over her shoulder, the monsignor frowned at us with contempt, then turned to leave via the side aisle without a backward glance.

"Kate, good to see you again." I was still being hugged and thought this would be a good time for her to let go.

She finally released me. "Would you like a cup of coffee?"

I had been thinking about asking her out for something a bit stronger. "Coffee? Um, sure."

"I mean at the back of the church. We serve coffee and juice after the Saturday night service so people will stay and get to know each other." The wicked smile was back in full effect. "I don't bite, you know."

My face was warming, and I hoped the church was dark enough so she wouldn't notice. "Coffee, in the back...um, sure, why not?" Why did I suddenly sound like I was still in high school?

We joined the other parishioners who were sipping beverages and chatting. It had finally started raining, which was probably keeping some of them from making a mad dash to their cars.

"What brings you to St. Celestine's?" She had a look of angelic innocence. "They have churches in the Uptown area, you know."

"Those modern churches aren't the same. There's something about the classic, old-school design of St. Celestine that's uniquely compelling."

"I'm glad you're here."

"Me too." I leaned in conspiratorially. "I couldn't help but notice the good monsignor sitting a few rows behind you."

Her face threw away the smile like a losing Bingo card. "I noticed, too. I try to avoid him when I can. Too many issues to deal with."

"I've only spoken with him a few times, but he seems a little smarmy to me. Why does the bishop put up with him?"

"Smarmy is an understatement, but he does get results. He's navigated the church through a few tight spots in the past."

"Really? What could happen in a sleepy little church like this?"

Fortunately, she didn't take offense. "Uh-uh. I'd better not say anything."

"Kate, come on. We're within fifty feet of a confessional booth. Anything you tell me will be in the strictest confidence. Besides, who would I tell?"

Kate seemed to consider me for a minute, then must have decided she could trust me. "You'd be surprised what happens around here. Last summer, the monsignor thought he found some discrepancies in the books. One of the account balances was lower than it should have been, and he accused me of either mishandling the account entries or just plain theft. Somehow, a rumor started that I was embezzling the church's money, which is just crazy as I don't even have access to the checkbook. Don't most people know the person who does the accounting is never the same person who writes the checks? That's a basic separation of duties. I would've had to collude with someone to steal anything." Kate leaned in as she lowered her voice. "Anyway, Scarpino said he'd been following the trail, and he knows who took the funds. I've seen him operate. He'll get them to return the money, and then they'll quit working for the church. The police will never know, so there will be no scandal. He'll fix it like it never happened."

"Which will be a happy ending for you, right? The fixer wins again, but so does the church, and so do you. What's wrong with that?"

"It's just that he hasn't done it yet. He keeps making up excuses saying he needs more time to catch the real thief in the act. It's been months now. I'm pretty sure he's stalling because he thinks he can use it to control me. Even if he does get this person to quit, he'll keep all of the evidence, and I won't be able to prove I'm innocent. He's a devious little son...."

"But you're still here?"

"Don't remind me."

"Why do you stick around? I thought you were a volunteer. You don't have to put up with that."

"I've asked myself that a thousand times since this whole thing began. I guess I like the rest of the team, and I like working with the bishop. He's a good man. Scarpino doesn't have as much control over me as he thinks. He can't prove it was me, and I can't prove it wasn't me, so it's more of a stalemate. As long as he stays at arm's length, I can deal with him." Her lips turned into a devious little smile, and I desperately wanted to kiss them.

"Have you ever wondered what the bishop thinks?" As soon as the words left me, I realized I'd missed the opportune moment to do some serious flirting and then ask her out for dinner or a drink. No wonder I was still single.

"Of course, but how would I find out? I can't just ask him."

"Why not? You've always had a good relationship. He would probably tell you."

Kate frowned and looked down dejectedly. "I'm not sure I want to know. Besides, his favorite is Jane, the grade school Principal. He seems to spend every free minute with her."

"What's that about?"

She leaned in again. "Well, they've been spending Sunday afternoons together after the services are over, supposedly discussing 'the proper teaching of Catholicism' or some such thing. So, you tell me. What is that about?"

I had no idea and wanted to change the subject to James. The crowd was thinning as the rain settled into a mild drizzle. I figured I only had a few more minutes to grill her, so I decided to go for it. "Do you ever wonder what happened to James Brennen? I mean, doesn't it seem odd the police have made so little progress to this point?"

Kate's eyes squinted, and her face turned dark. It was a good thing we were in a church, or I'd have been wearing her drink.

"Is that what this is all about, Grayson? You're fishing for information, trying to figure out who killed James because he's some relative of yours? I thought you were here to see me. Boy, was I delusional."

"I am here to see you. I've been thinking about you all week. I even went to Bingo on Wednesday to see if you were there." Did I really just say that out loud? Yet, I didn't regret it. "DeeDee told me you were there, too, but then you left. I had to spend the whole night talking to her. She's quite a hoot. She told me this one story...."

Kate turned and waved me away. "I'm sorry, Grayson. I've got to start cleaning up. Maybe I'll see you at Bingo next week."

Just like that, I'd been dismissed. It had been going so well, too. Okay, maybe not that well, but at least we were talking. "Sure. See you at Bingo." Dammit—why didn't I ask her out when I had the chance?

As I left the church, I thought someone was skulking in the shadows of the vestibule. I was mad and didn't care, so I pretended not to notice and left. But when I reached my car and realized the lot was almost empty, I became concerned for Kate's safety. I snuck around the church, slipped past the double doors as silently as possible, and peered in from the vestibule.

Kate and another volunteer had almost finished cleaning up. She hefted a tray of coffee pots and plastic juice bottles so he could stow the final table away.

"If you throw the garbage in the dumpster, I'll take the tray back to the kitchen, Pete. I've got to head over to the Rectory to work on some financial reports anyway," Kate said to the volunteer.

"You sure you've got that?" asked Pete.

"Yep. No worries."

"Okay. Thanks, Kate." Pete grabbed the garbage and looked out. "The rain is finally letting up a bit. Have a good night."

"Night." Kate awkwardly maneuvered the tray toward the side door that led to the Rectory and tried pushing it open with her hip.

"WHAT was that all about?" someone cried out behind her.

Kate jumped, and the tray went flying with coffee pots and juice bottles going in every direction, sounding like machine-gun fire as they clanged against the marble floor of the empty church.

The racket had provided the cover I needed to creep closer.

"Oh my gosh, you startled me!" She turned and came face-to-face with Monsignor Scarpino, who was wearing a nasty grin.

"Oh, it's you. What do you want?" She bent over to put the containers back on the tray. "You could help me, you know."

The monsignor ignored her. "What's going on between you and Grayson Dyle? I thought you'd sworn off men."

"Nothing is going on. Grayson is related to James Brennen, and we were discussing him."

"Did he tell you how they're related?"

"No. What's it to me? Or to you, for that matter?" Then her curiosity must have kicked in. "Why, what did he tell you?

"He said James was his father."

Kate was about to lift the tray off the floor but left it there and stood up instead. "His father?"

"Forgot to mention that, didn't he?"

"Shut up, Scarpino. It still doesn't make any difference."

"It's monsignor to you, Larson."

"With all of the dirt I have on you? I don't think so."

Watching the monsignor getting rattled wasn't a pretty sight. "You... WILL...keep your mouth shut...if I tell you to. Besides, you're the last person who should be threatening anyone. I know what else you did."

"What the bloody hell are you talking about now?" Kate shouted.

"You killed your boyfriend's father."

I honestly thought she was about to slug him and wondered if I should jump in before she did something dumb.

"What?! Why would I kill James Brennen?" Kate moved toward the door. "I don't have to put up with this crap."

"I know you were there that night. I don't know why you killed him, but I'm going to find out."

Kate stopped in her tracks, her face turning bright red.

"I'll bet you were stealing money from the law firm, just like you were stealing money from the church. James found out, and you had to do something. You probably offered to have sex with him to keep him quiet. It must have been a real letdown when he said no."

"You bastard..." Kate lunged at him, but he quickly warded her off.

"It's true then, isn't it? You're turning out to be a real piece of work, aren't you?" He twisted the knife with a grin. "Wait until your boyfriend finds out you're a murderer."

Kate was breathing heavily. Her eyes had narrowed to slits. "One more word, and I'm going to kill you, Scarpino. I'll say it was self-defense that you attacked me. Then I'll tell them about the pedophilia lawsuit."

The monsignor moved in fast and stood nose-to-nose with her, his face an evil sneer. "How did you find out about that? Where have you been snooping, Larson?"

"People talk, Scarpino. I listen, and I remember."

The monsignor scowled. "It will be best for you to forget you ever heard about that little incident. We settled it out of court, and no one ever admitted any wrongdoing."

"That's not the only thing I know. I know a lot about you. Always skulking around and fixing things. You may fool everyone else, but I know some of the things you've done and some of the things you've covered up...."

"If that truly is the case," he said slowly, menacingly, "then that is the best reason of all to shut...up. Don't forget I still have the evidence you need, Larson, and I'll have more as soon as I figure out why you killed James Brennen."

I was amazed at how quickly she composed herself.

"That's ridiculous. I didn't kill James. Search around all you want. You'll have to manufacture the evidence, and Tom won't let you do that, will he?"

After pausing for a moment, he backed up and said, almost too calmly, "Let's focus on the present, shall we? You will keep Grayson Dyle in line and get him to stop asking questions, right?"

"What do I get out of it?"

"I may just clear you of those pesky embezzlement charges, even if you did take the money."

Kate's eyes widened, and her brow creased with anger, but then she seemed to cave. "Fine."

The monsignor quickly drew closer again, his voice so low I could barely hear him. "Don't you ever mention that lawsuit again." Whispered threats were the worst kind. "It doesn't matter anymore. We settled out of court. That suit should never have been brought against a man of the cloth in the first place."

"You can take those back to the kitchen yourself." She left the tray on the floor and stormed off toward the exit.

"Talk to your boyfriend, Larson. Tell him to stop snooping around," the monsignor called after her. "Or I will go to the police."

She left and made sure the door slammed behind her. I waited until her car cleared the parking lot and headed out, too.

As I drove home, I didn't know who to believe. Was Scarpino threatening her solely to prevent her from helping me solve the murder he committed? Or did Kate take the money from the church and possibly from the law firm, too? Maybe James hit on her again, and she finally snapped, shooting him twice instead of just cutting off boy parts. She didn't seem like the gun-toting type, but who knew these days?

I doubted the monsignor would involve the police in any of this, just like I wasn't going to contact them about the attempted murder. These were matters that needed to be settled without outside interference, but I figured it was time to make myself scarce so I could try to figure it out. One thing was apparent. Despite what I'd told Dean, I didn't want to be dating a murderess.

Chapter Eighteen

Sunday, April 23

"Hello, Grayson Dyle. Welcome to my world," said Stephen Hawking. Well, it was his voice anyway.

Now I knew why Dean wanted to meet at his home. He had a new toy and wanted me to come out and play.

Dean came out from his home office, laughing so hard he was staggering. "That was awesome. You should have seen the look on your face."

I was used to this by now and shook my head. Next, he'd proudly explain his latest invention, and I'd be amazed.

"I hid a sensor in that plant that scans the face of anyone walking in the front door. It feeds the image into that facial recognition app I downloaded a few weeks ago. When the app finds a match, it sends the person's name to the Stephen Hawking voice simulator, which welcomes you to his world."

"Okay, pretty cool stuff. Will it work on anyone's face?"

"Not yet. Right now, it has to be someone whose picture I've scanned into the app so it has something to compare to the new image. But I'm going to connect it with Google Images, so it should be able to identify just about anyone. By the way, nice blog post on weaponizing maple syrup. You're getting pretty good at those."

"Thanks."

"Do you want some coffee? I've already got a pot going."

I nodded. We headed to the kitchen, and he poured us both a cup.

"Any luck on finding the midwives?"

"No. I've been crazy busy on a big work project."

But you had time to build a Steven Hawking machine. "What project is that?" I asked him automatically before realizing I didn't want to know.

"My company is developing a fingerprint scanner that will lock and unlock your car door. Most modern cars use a wireless fob key that hackers can access because carmakers don't bother encrypting the signals between the fob and the car. If we can get the scanner to work, you won't need the fob anymore. The only problem is the scanner gets a little wonky after being exposed to the elements for a few months. I'm running some tests on a beta version in my car." Dean was getting a faraway look, which meant he was going into problem-solving mode. "I think there's a layer of grit forming on the sensor after it rains—"

I quickly regained his attention by changing the subject and filling him in on the past few days' events, ending with the bizarre argument between Kate and the monsignor. "We finally have proof he's a fixer. I'm more convinced than ever he did it or was involved somehow."

"It's too bad about Kate. I thought you had a chance with her. Maybe, if you take her out on a proper date, instead of meeting at the church all the time, you'll still—"

"As crazy as it sounds, I'm still willing to believe she had nothing to do with James's death, no matter how many times he hit on her. Scarpino only accused her of murder to scare her into keeping me away from the case."

Dean seemed skeptical. "She may not be as innocent as you think. What if she did take money from the church? Doesn't it seem odd DeeDee told you there were rumors about Kate and the books being off? Then Kate gives you this big story about how she's the victim?"

"What's odd about that? You know how petty people can be, especially if they see an attractive lady hanging around with the top brass all the time. I'm sure a lot of them would have been happy to see her get knocked down a peg or two."

Dean must have realized I wasn't going to let him badmouth her because he didn't say anything, so I changed the subject. "It was interesting to hear

Tom and Jane have been running around together on Sunday afternoons. I'm thinking about following them to see where they go."

"It must be nice to have that kind of time on your hands. I did make some progress on the investigation, though. I found an online newspaper archive that had an obit for a Margaret Fitzgerald. She died at a home for unwed mothers in St. Paul on the day you were born. It said she was from Rochester, Minnesota, and was an employee of the Holy Redeemer Church, so it must be our Maggie. It turns out James gave us her real last name after all."

"Did it say how she died?"

"No, but it did say Father Thomas Brennen presided over the funeral. How convenient is that?"

"A little too convenient. Did it mention the name of the home?"

"Nope. I'm still working on that. I've been through all of the online archives I can find. I'm going to have to head down to Rochester to check the physical newspaper copies. Remember the *Post Bulletin*? Their website says they digitized about thirty years of microfiche and print clippings, but anything older is in their paper files, which go back to the eighteen hundreds."

"Better you than me. When are you heading down?"

"Wednesday night. I'm going to check in on Mom, too." Dean motioned toward my coffee cup inquisitively.

I shook my head, so he scooped up our cups and put them in the sink.

"Where does that leave us?"

"Reconnecting with our suspects seems like the only option. I think I'll start with Cathy. We haven't connected with her yet."

"The cops always look at immediate family members first. Copeland will have interviewed her three times already."

"Probably. But I think I'll mention the letter in passing to see how she reacts. We can learn a lot about her involvement if she already knows about it or demands to read it. Copeland can't do that."

"Good idea. I suppose you'll want to reconnect with Kate, too."

"It all depends on if she wants to reconnect with me." I thought about that pensively for a moment and hoped I hadn't permanently damaged that relationship. "Well, I'd better run."

Dean looked at his phone. "Why so soon? It's not even noon. Wait, let me guess. You're going to hang out at the church and surveil Tom and Jane, right? Just to see what you can see?"

"I can neither confirm nor deny the existence of any surveillance plans. However, if there was such a plan, you could drive separately, and we could use the two-car version of the FBI's floating box vehicle surveillance system to tail them."

"This is why they have warnings on TV not to try these things at home. You need at least three cars to run a floating box team." Dean's company recently sponsored him to attend a six-week Minneapolis FBI Citizens' Academy, which included a trip to the FBI Headquarters in Quantico, Virginia. He was now the self-appointed expert on all matters of spycraft, whether they had been covered in the course or not. "Besides, you only need one car to tail someone if you know what you're doing."

Whatever you say, big guy. "I have a couple of suspects to surveil, so I'd better run."

"Good luck with that."

I couldn't be sure, but it sounded like he meant it.

Traffic was light, and I made the trip from Eagan to St. Celestine's in under fifteen minutes, early enough to catch them if they headed out for lunch together. I found the optimal parking spot, providing both visual access to the targets and stealthiness, about a quarter of a block down from the church. Dean wasn't the only one who knew spycraft.

At first, any movement caught my attention...every bird, squirrel, and dog walker. After fifteen minutes, I was grateful I had never ordered that private detective correspondence school course. My head was drooping when a sudden BAM-BAM-BAM lit up the back window of the car. It sounded like shooting again, and my heart was pounding as I ducked under the steering wheel. Funny, I couldn't feel any broken glass raining down.

Then Dean's ugly grinning mug appeared at the front passenger window.

"Open the door, will you?"

I considered which part of him to hurt first as I sat up and unlocked the door for him.

"You should have seen the look on your face. Here, I filmed it." He held up his iPhone.

"You scared the hell out of me." I caught my breath. "I'm going to kill you."

He put the iPhone away but was still grinning like a Cheshire Cat. "Maybe I'll show this to you later."

"How did you find me?"

He gave me a fake punch in the arm. "I followed you the whole way here. You had no idea, did you?"

This was why family members killed each other. "You followed me the whole way here." It wasn't a question.

"Yep. Why did you drive around the block a few times? You looked like a dog circling a spot before deciding where to lie down."

Now I really was going to kill him.

Dean was smugly informing me that trained professionals used techniques you wouldn't find on the internet when I glanced over at the church grounds and noticed Tom and Jane walking out of the Rectory, each carrying what appeared to be a suitcase.

"Shhh. Stay low."

Dean looked over, and we both slowly sank into our seats as they got into one of the Crown Vics and drove away.

"Is that the same car that nearly ran you over?"

"It's one of the two Crown Vics in the church's pool." I was about to pull out when the monsignor left the Rectory, got into the other Crown Vic, and drove off in the opposite direction.

"Who do you want to follow?"

I thought for a moment and finally decided. "Tom and Jane."

"I'll go with you. I can show you how to do a one-car tail."

I shot him a withering glance and drove off. We didn't have time to practice vehicle tailing techniques because Tom pulled into a parking lot about five minutes down the road. The marquee read Harriet Island Motel.

I drove past the lot to avoid suspicion and did a quick U-turn after we were out of sight. I slowly went by again in time to see Tom holding the motel door for Jane. She was carrying a medium-sized suitcase, and he followed her in with a large suitcase, still exuding an air of importance.

I turned the corner and pulled into the parking lot. To call the place seedy would have been charitable. There were large holes in the stucco siding where chunks had fallen off. Someone must have tried to chuck an overstuffed garbage bag into the dumpster at the end of the building but missed because it was split open on the ground.

There was a reddish-brown substance slowly oozing out from beneath one of the wall-mounted air conditioners, which was probably rusty water from an old condenser, but could just as easily have been blood. I thought about pulling out my cell phone and entering 911 in case one of the fistfights that were undoubtedly occurring in a few of the rooms at this very moment spilled out into the parking lot.

"Holy crap, they're checking into a sleazy motel. It looks like they're having an affair!" Dean looked more excited than I'd seen him in a long time.

"It sure does."

We both looked at each other incredulously.

"What is it about the men in this family?"

"I know, you'd think a classy guy like the bishop would spring for a nicer place than this," Dean mused.

"No, I mean, I can't believe he's having an affair after everything that happened with James. So close to the Rectory, too. They didn't seem too concerned about anyone seeing them walk in together."

"Gray, this kind of place is inhabited nightly by bleary-eyed truckers, adulterers on a budget, and down-on-their-luck parolees. No one looks anyone else in the eye for fear of being shivved. Those two are about as anonymous as they can get."

I hated it when he was right. "Still, they shouldn't get away with this so easily."

"Agreed. Let's get out of here. Those two are probably not coming out anytime soon, and this place is giving me the creeps. Can bedbugs get into a car all by themselves, or do they need to ride on your clothes?"

I didn't even want to think about that. I drove around the corner of the building and snapped a few pictures of the motel and the Crown Vic, making sure to include the license plate to eliminate any plausible deniability.

"What are you going to do with those?" asked Dean.

"No idea, but we may need some leverage in getting the bishop to talk." I drove back to the Rectory to take Dean back to his car. He only had to tell me where to turn once. Maybe I wasn't so directionally challenged after all.

I pulled up behind Dean's car, and he was just about to get out when a black Crown Vic drove by. The monsignor was returning, and we both automatically slumped in our seats to avoid being seen.

"Does that seem odd to you?" I asked Dean.

"Not really. Maybe he went to the quickie mart for a gallon of milk."

The monsignor got out and walked into the Rectory empty-handed.

"Maybe he was buying lottery tickets," Dean offered.

"Maybe he was leaning on someone to do a job for him," I countered.

"I suppose he left his grinder in the trunk. Gray, you've got to stop watching those gangster movies. You sound like Jimmy Cagney."

Chapter Nineteen

Thursday, April 27

The following week flew by. Without Paul onboard, I was left to shore up the design team for the work we already had in-house. The last thing the company needed now was to lose another client. While I was no Paul, a couple of our other designers, whom he had been mentoring, were stepping into the breach and showing some real promise.

It was Thursday morning before I had a chance to consider calling Cathy, which might have had something to do with me procrastinating for fear of being rejected again. I picked up my cell and found James's cell number in the directory. If I tried her at that number, maybe she wouldn't answer, and I could put this off until next week. I kept hoping Dean would call me with an update from his Rochester trip, but no matter how long I stared at the phone, it didn't ring.

I was about to hit the call button when there was a commotion in the office, and I thought I heard a familiar voice coming from down the hall—one I hadn't heard for what seemed like ages. I jumped up and stuck my head out the door to check. Sure enough, Paul was back, walking down the hall toward my office, fist-bumping the design staff as he went. I tried not to get my hopes up. Maybe he had just come in to clear out his office.

The look on his face as he walked into my office told me he was back for good. It was a strange combination of concern, affection, and righteous indignation. I guess I had earned that last part.

"Don't you ever do that to me again," I said as we did a bro-hug.

Paul laughed. "You sound like my partner. I saw the text about your meeting with Mike Wilson. What happened?"

"I did the best I could on the design work, but it wasn't the same without you. Now that you're back, we're going to nail this."

As he sat in my guest chair, I studied his face. He seemed older somehow, both in years and maturity, which seemed to say he'd done a lot of soul-searching and realized this was where he belonged. Professionally, of course.

"But you're not back because Mike Wilson didn't appreciate our work, are you?" I asked.

"No."

We both knew it wasn't about any one deal—his heart and soul were in the design business. This business. Our business. No need to say it aloud.

"What's the latest?" he asked.

I updated him on my Rectory adventure and the subsequent meeting with Mike. I thought he'd laugh at us both showing up late and covered in dirt, but his face turned quizzical.

"You don't think his clothes were dirty because he was the one who set the trap, do you?"

Realizing this was a strong possibility hit me like a bag of cement. Maybe Mike accidentally broke open one of the bags as he moved them onto the cellar door, which was why he was so dirty. But then I reconsidered.

"No way. Why would Mike try to kill me one minute and then give us another opportunity to prove ourselves the next? It was just a weird coincidence." But I still didn't believe in coincidences. The monsignor must have coerced Mike into doing his dirty work. Or maybe Mike was just plain psycho and willing to kill in exchange for a credit on his account of favors rendered for the monsignor. I needed to think about this, but now was not the time.

"Mike is fairly booked over the next few weeks since this is his busy season, so the soonest I could get on his schedule is mid-May. This will give us time to crank out a few prototypes, which should close the deal." I figured this business would give us enough working capital for a few more months. But that was it. We still needed more work, and we both knew it.

"Any new prospects on the horizon?" asked Paul.

I considered reminding him I had been doing both of our jobs for the past few weeks, which left little time to drum up new work, but why spoil a good reunion? Besides, it went without saying.

"Nope. I'm planning to call Carson Companies next week to see how happy they are with the offshore design work. Maybe we can win part of the work back."

We both knew this was a long shot, but we still had to try.

My phone pinged, which Paul took as his cue to get back to work.

"It's good to have you back," I said as he turned to go.

"Good to be back. Thanks for understanding."

The text was from Dean saying he would return from Rochester around sixish and asked if I wanted to grab a bite. It was supposed to be a warm summer evening, so he probably wanted to walk around the lake afterward. I think it had something to do with meeting women. I half expected him to borrow a dog from some neighbor to seem more approachable. We planned to meet at my place for dinner and head out from there.

I stared at the phone. It was time to try James's cell number. I decided to make the call, then reward my bravery by taking Paul to lunch. I texted Paul, and he agreed to head out with me shortly. Nothing left to do but call. Cathy picked up almost immediately.

I said "Hello" and started explaining who I was in case she didn't recall our last delightful call.

She cut me off. "I know who you are, Grayson. Andy told me you stopped by the office a few weeks ago. Why are you calling James's cell number? What do you want?"

"Cathy, I'm sorry to bother you, but I'm working with Detective Copeland on James's death, and we need to talk."

"You're working with Detective Copeland?" To say she was skeptical was putting it mildly.

"Yes, I am. He's working with the community, and I'm contacting family members to get to the bottom of this situation." I figured she knew about

James's history by now. "You probably know Dean and I are related to James. Wouldn't it be nice to get to know each other better? It doesn't have to be adversarial."

There was a long pause, and I almost said something, but then I recalled reading somewhere never to be the one to speak first in these situations.

"Fine. Where would you like to meet?"

"Why don't we meet at The Concord? That was where my brother Dean and I had dinner with James. How does next Tuesday sound?" I was trying to sound soothing and thankful at the same time.

"Fine. I can be there by seven."

"Great. I'll make a reservation." I started to say, "I appreciate your..." but she had already hung up.

Dean texted as he was leaving Rochester, saying he'd be at my place in about ninety minutes. I texted back, asking him to pick up an order from the organic Poke Bowl place on the first floor of my building, then called the restaurant to place the order. They didn't have burgers on the menu, and Dean wasn't a big seafood fan, but I brought clients there all the time and knew the chef enjoyed the occasional burger, so he agreed to make one for me.

Just after six, I buzzed him up, food in hand. I had laid out the plates and drinks on the kitchen counter, and he gave me the update as we dug in.

"Mom's doing pretty well. Still grieving Dad, of course."

"That's about the best we can expect. Has she been losing any more weight?"

"It didn't look like it. But she's pretty good at hiding these things."

"I'll call her later today to check in. Anything new on the investigation?"

"I started at the Olmsted County Vital Records Office. I'll give you the bad news first. They only store the amended versions of birth certificates for adoptees, which lists the adoptive parents but not the birth parents. We already have copies of these. The court automatically seals the original birth certificates that list the names of the birth mother and father. We'd have to file a petition and convince a judge to unseal them to get a copy. Just getting a court date would take weeks, and the clerk said the judges turn down these requests unless there's strong justification, like a medical necessity. That seemed like a waste of time, so that was a dead end."

"That's frustrating."

Dean didn't seem to be bothered by this. "Yes, but you'll never guess what I found on our suspects. I was digging through the *Post Bulletin* archives and found a local interest story about the Holy Redeemer Church. Guess who two of their priests were during the years we were born—the good Reverends Tom and Frank. I also found out that Tom and Frank attended the same seminary school near Kansas City. No wonder those two are so tight. They've known each other for at least forty years."

"Why am I not surprised?"

"Right? After being ordained, Tom was stationed in Rochester, and Frank was assigned to a parish in northern Minnesota but was eventually moved to Rochester, too. James attended law school in the Cities, then moved back and became an attorney at a family law firm. They've moved around together ever since. That must have been where James met Maggie. Remember how her obit said she was an employee at Holy Redeemer? James must have been having an affair right under their collective noses."

"That must be the same Father Tom who Mom told us brokered the adoptions."

"Agreed, but how does that help us find the killer?"

No brilliant insights or conspiracy theories popped into my head, so I cleared the dinner and headed out for a walk. It was a warm, clear night, and quite a few walkers and bikers were on the paths, getting an early start on a Minnesota summer.

"What about Maggie's death?" I asked.

"That's the weird part. Other than the obit, I can't find anything on Maggie. If the home had called in the police or a medical examiner for a suspected homicide, you'd think the paper would have written it up, but there was nothing. I haven't even figured out where she was from, and the last name Fitzgerald is too common to narrow it down much."

"That is weird. Maggie died in childbirth, and no one was suspicious? How often did girls die in these places? They must have been able to handle birth complications. Okay, this is just a hunch, but what if someone murdered her, too? Once Father Tom realized his brother couldn't stay away from her, maybe he had his fixer arrange things, so the birth mother 'died in childbirth.' Then he had James whacked to stop him from telling us all of this."

Dean stopped dead in his tracks and almost got taken out by a biker who really should have been on the biking path. "My gosh, you're losing it. You're saying Tom had Frank murder Maggie, the mother of his nephews, the woman James was sleeping with, merely to stop them from having more children? Who would do that? Even if it were true, how would we ever prove it?"

I started walking again to avoid any other near misses. "That's just my point. Depending on how Maggie died, it might have been impossible to prove it was murder."

"Then he had his brother murdered forty-odd years later to keep him quiet, too?"

"It was just a theory. We still want to find out more about Maggie, right? Why don't we investigate her life and her death at the same time?"

"I'm worried about you, Gray. We're not getting any closer to the truth about James, and you're suddenly seeing killers lurking around every corner. Let's not add another murder into the mix."

"Fine."

We both knew I wouldn't let it go. What was that old saying? Just because you're paranoid doesn't mean they're not out to get you. We still had nothing tangible, but I had a gut feeling we were getting closer to the truth about Maggie. We just had to keep digging.

We walked in silence until we got back to Lake Street.

Dean said, "Since we need to find the midwives, I'll try to find the home where she delivered. It's likely to be within driving distance of Rochester, and she probably delivered us both at the same place."

"Fine. I'll follow up with some of our suspects to see what they have to say. Have a good night."

Thirty minutes later, Dean called my cell. "That bastard Scarpino broke into my house," he screamed when I answered.

"What?"

"He broke in and rooted through all of my stuff."

"I thought you had every security device known to man monitoring your house. How did he get in?"

"The house is fully protected. Or I thought it was. He found the one vulnerability I hadn't fixed yet."

For my brother to admit he'd left himself open to an attack, he must be upset. "What did he do?"

"He broke into the back door of the garage and killed the power on the main electrical panel. I have a small auxiliary power supply on my computers but not on the surveillance cameras. Never thought I'd need one for the whole house. Now I want to kill that bastard myself."

"Was he able to hack into your systems?"

"You're kidding, right? No freakin' way is that going to happen. I don't even think he tried. He tossed my office and most of the rest of the house. Must have been looking for the letter."

"How do you know it was him? Maybe it was a neighborhood kid."

"It was him. The garage door camera caught him coming up to the house from between the neighbors' houses. He was wearing a hoodie, mask, and gloves, so none of his skin was exposed, and he wouldn't leave any DNA. He used a pry bar to get into the garage and then killed the power, so there's no camera footage after that."

"What about your facial recognition app? Will that work?"

"Nope. It won't work off of an image. It has to scan the face in person."

"Did you call the police? Did he take anything?"

"The police are on their way. It doesn't look like anything is missing, but he had the audacity to leave me a note."

"What!? What did it say?"

"It said, 'I will get that letter.'"

"Maybe you can trace the handwriting."

"I doubt it. It's scrawled in big block letters on the wall of my bedroom.

It's a good thing he's not here, or I would shoot him on sight."

Chapter Twenty

Tuesday, May 2

Tuesday soon rolled around, and I was at The Concord waiting for Cathy to arrive, hoping she wasn't going to stand me up. The maître d' eyed me suspiciously for a moment, probably trying to remember why he associated my face with trouble. But he must have decided to let it go and offered to seat me right away. I declined so I wouldn't have to be that guy sitting uncomfortably alone at a table in a fancy restaurant. I preferred to be the guy sitting uncomfortably alone in the lounge area, thank you very much.

Cathy arrived in a bit of a huff, twenty minutes late. I decided not to let it bother me and brushed away her mumbled apologies. She was smartly turned out in a dark blue tapered waist dress, a tasteful pearl necklace, and blue pumps. I hoped my sport coat, dress shirt, and black jeans were living up to the occasion but doubted it. The Concord was busy, especially on a Tuesday night. I was glad to see they hadn't given our table away yet.

We spent a few minutes chitchatting about the Minnesota weather, and wasn't it great someone reopened The Concord? When the server stopped by to take our drink orders, I was relieved to find it wasn't the same person that waited on James, Dean, and me just a few weeks ago. I suggested we order dinner at the same time to keep the evening short if necessary.

"Thanks again for meeting with me. It must be difficult losing a loved one so suddenly."

"Yes, it has been. We may not have had the most idyllic marriage, but we did love each other. It's been especially hard on my daughter. After her father died, she received approval from the university to take the rest of the semester off and make it up during the summer. She had to cancel the trip to Europe she'd been planning with her friends."

"How old is she?"

"Shannon turned twenty-three in February. She's going for her master's in biology and doing well."

"That's great. I hope you don't mind me asking these questions. It's just that—"

"I know, Grayson, I know. I read the messages. I know you connected through DeeDee, and you are related somehow, which isn't that surprising considering the family resemblance."

"Did he ever tell you about us and how we're related?"

"No. James told me you were a potential new client that wanted to talk about a lawsuit. I only learned you were family afterward."

"From the emails?"

"Yes." Tears were forming in the corner of her eyes, and she looked at the table nervously, smoothing out wrinkles that weren't there. "Tom told me, too. He told me everything."

I was relieved I wouldn't have to be the one to break the news. "Tom told you James is our biological father?"

"Yes." It was almost a whisper. I didn't know what to say. I was shocked by the amount of grief and guilt she must have been feeling. Having two of your late husband's heretofore unknown biological sons appear right after his death must have compounded her misery many times over.

After a few moments, Cathy used her napkin to wipe her tears. "After James died, Tom thought it would be best if he told me. I wasn't that surprised. I knew what kind of man he was, especially after so many years of marriage. What I don't understand is why he never said anything to me." She looked up and seemed to realize for the first time I had lost a father, too. "I'm sorry, Grayson. I'm sure this must be hard on you and Dean. You find your biological father, and then, before you have a chance to get to know

173

him, he's gone."

A lump formed in my throat, and I almost mentioned it was, in fact, much worse than that. We had just lost the father who raised us and had only recently found out we were adopted. But I wasn't that good at emotional scenes, and I didn't want to make this about me. I was relieved to see the server arrive with our dinners. We ate in silence for a few minutes.

"I still don't understand why there needed to be all this secrecy." Then I realized I was throwing James under the bus and took a different approach. "I got the impression from James and Tom they had been keeping an eye on Dean and me. They knew where we were, what we each did for a living, everything you can find on the internet."

"That sounds more like Tom to me. It was always about politics for him. I suppose that's why they made him a bishop. He and Frank were constantly working the angles. By the way, I dropped off some of James's things at the Rectory last week. I won't need them, and Tom is always looking for donations to the charities he supports. I never thought to ask if you or Dean would want any of his things as keepsakes."

"Do you mind if I ask what sorts of things they were?"

"Quite a few books, especially law books, watches he hadn't used in years, some clothes, that sort of thing. I should let Tom know soon if you want to look at them. He doesn't like to have the Rectory cluttered up."

I doubted I would want any of these things, but it could be a way to get back in front of the bishop. "I'd like to take a look, and I'm pretty sure Dean will, too. Would you mind letting Tom know I'll be in touch?"

"Not at all. I'll send him an email, but you should call the monsignor to set up a time to visit. Tom can be difficult to get a hold of."

"Thanks for thinking of us."

"It's the least I can do."

I asked Cathy what James was like, and she reminisced a bit. I studied her as she spoke and realized the grief was hiding an attractive and resilient lady. James had been a lucky man, and it was hard to see why he would have needed to stray. I struggled to remind myself she was one of the top suspects on our murder board, although it seemed impossible to think the person sitting before me could be a cold-blooded killer.

After the wait staff had cleared the dinner plates, our server asked about dessert. I ordered the first thing he recommended with coffee before Cathy could say no. Since the evening was good well, I wanted to buy more time to discuss our other suspects without revealing that Dean and I had been doing our own investigating.

"Cathy, do you mind if I ask you a few questions? I know it may be painful, but Dean and I are trying to learn more about our family."

"That's okay, Grayson. I figured that's why you asked me to dinner." She seemed to be steeling herself for whatever was coming next.

"You probably know Dean and I were born in Rochester. We believe our birth mother was a young girl named Maggie, who worked for Holy Redeemer."

"Yes, I've heard."

"Did you know Maggie?"

"No."

"We know Maggie would have been sent away to a home for unwed mothers, but we don't know which one. Do you have any idea where that might have been?"

"My guess is the Wilkes Hospital in St. Paul. It was one of the charities Tom supported. They had hundreds of unwed mothers up there over the years. James must have gone to Tom for help after Maggie told him she was pregnant. Tom would have seen to it that Wilkes took her in. A lot of the young ladies from Rochester went there to deliver because it was far enough away to avoid a scandal."

"Did Tom tell you Maggie died right after I was born?"

"Yes." That was all she said as she looked down again, nervously fiddling with her coffee cup.

"Did you ever hear Tom and James talking about what happened back then?"

Cathy seemed to be putting the pieces together in her head. "Not Tom and James, but now that you mention it, I recall Tom and Frank loudly arguing many years ago. I was in the next room and couldn't help overhearing them.

Frank was reminding Tom he knew what had happened in Rochester. It didn't mean anything to me at the time, but he might have been referring to Maggie's death. The odd part was, soon after that, Tom put in a request for the church authorities in Rome to consider Father Frank for the role of monsignor. I never realized James had been involved in that situation or involved with her."

I wondered if she knew how sharply she spat out the word "her."

Still, she seemed to be handling the discussion well, so I decided it was time to gauge her reaction to Maggie's letter. "Cathy, did you know Maggie smuggled out a letter to Dean and asked his adoptive parents to deliver it on his twenty-first birthday? But Dean just received it two months ago."

Cathy's face was a series of micro-expressions—surprise, fear, anger, uncertainty—and then curiosity seemed to win out. If she was the killer and already knew about the letter, she was doing a fabulous job of hiding it.

"I didn't know that. Why do you ask?" It didn't sound like the voice of a killer.

I decided to go for broke. "I brought it with me if you'd like to read it."

She hesitated, then nodded. I handed the envelope to her. A furrow formed in her brow as she read. Maybe this was a big mistake.

Cathy's face turned red, and she seemed to be processing what she had read as she sat back in her chair. "Already committed. Was she talking about me?" she muttered, almost to herself. Then she exploded and threw the pages back at me. "You bastard, why would you show me that? You invite me to a nice dinner, and you act like a nice guy, and then you show me a letter that says my late husband was a philanderer who was manipulating this young girl into giving up her child while he was cheating on me. What the hell is wrong with you?"

I was slowly sinking into my chair as the other diners stared at us. "I'm sorry. I just thought you would see how caring she was...."

Cathy leaned in and cut me off, her face so close to mine that I smelled her perfume. "I want you and Dean to stop this craziness for my sake and Shannon's sake. For James's sake, too." She got up, threw her napkin on the table, and stormed out of the restaurant.

Heads turned like spectators at a tennis match, first to see the embarrassment on my face, then to watch her leave, then to see what I would do next.

The server was sharp enough to bring the dessert in a box, drop off the check, and start clearing the table. Still in shock, I put away the letter and gave him a credit card. How could this have gone so horribly wrong? They weren't going to let me back in here anytime soon. Apparently, the only thing worse than my sense of direction was my ability to figure out how women thought. No wonder I was still single. At least I'd learned she had no previous knowledge of the letter.

I signed the credit card receipt, left the restaurant, and texted **Wilkes Hospital in St. Paul** to Dean from the car. He texted back he would try to get to it soon, but he was tied up on an urgent job for Mr. X. The mansion's wine cellar automation system had stopped automatically recalculating the value of X's wine collection when he added or removed a bottle from the racks. Clearly, this crisis needed Dean's immediate, undivided attention.

I sat in the car, feeling sorry for myself. What was it with people getting pissed and storming off? It seemed like ages since I'd walked from The Concord to James's law office in an attempt to return his leather portfolio. So, with nowhere else to go, I decided to retrace my steps. It was a pleasant May evening, and crowds of rowdy people filled the restaurant patios on Grand Avenue, which only made me feel worse.

Soon, James's building was looming large. I considered launching a lifelong addiction to alcohol at a local bar when my phone buzzed. Cathy was probably texting that she was filing a restraining order in the morning, and I was about to chuck the phone into traffic when I glanced down. It was from Kate.

Hi, Grayson! How are you?' In a flash, the exquisite beauty of the balmy summer evening became apparent. As I stared at the message, considering how to respond, a second message came in. **Turn around. I'm right behind you.**

I turned around but didn't see anyone. *She's pranking me.* Then I noticed someone waving through the window of the bar across the street. She looked down to text again.

I'll meet you out front.

I was so distracted I ran right into traffic. A small, crappy car swerved and narrowly missed my shins. After dodging a huge Crown Vic, how ironic it would have been to be accidentally run over by a purple Scion.

Kate came out to meet me, as ravishing as ever in a light blue sleeveless summer dress and thousand-watt smile. We hugged awkwardly for a moment, and I took a step back to look at her quizzically.

"I thought you were miffed at me?"

"Miffed? No. I was furious with you. Then, someone at the church told me about Bingo Night, how you rushed in to protect DeeDee without regard to your own safety. That was one of the sweetest things I'd ever heard. I figured maybe I'd misjudged you."

"Thanks, Kate." There was a long pause as I looked into her eyes and found what I hoped to see. "It's really good to see you again."

"Good to see you too, Grayson."

"How'd you like to go out for a drink? I know this great bar called the um…." I looked at the name on the sign behind her. "…Chester's. I hear the cocktails are great."

She laughed. "I really need to get back to my Finance Committee meeting. It's at this great bar called The Chester's. Maybe you've heard of it?"

"Okay. How about Saturday?"

"Saturday night sounds great."

"Great! I know this trendy new restaurant I know you're going to love."

"I'm looking forward to it, Grayson."

"Me, too."

With that, she went back into the restaurant. I wanted to turn cartwheels of joy down the middle of the street but decided not to in case the Scion was making a return trip. Now all I had to do was score a reservation at a trendy new restaurant with three days' notice.

The following day, I picked out ten of the trendier places in the Minneapolis North Loop and checked each of them on the Free Table website every thirty minutes for the next few hours, hoping there would be a cancellation, in between trying to save my business, of course.

While I waited, I received a text from the monsignor inviting me to look through James's personal effects. Tom had already donated the clothes, but his books and other personal items were still there. I silently thanked Cathy for keeping her promise, despite the scene from last night. I replied that Dean and I would be happy to drop by and asked if we could speak with the bishop as well. The monsignor texted back I was the only one invited, which sounded suspicious. I wondered if he had an ulterior motive, but I agreed to meet him the next day.

My persistence with the Free Table app eventually paid off, and I finally scored a table for seven thirty at a place on Washington Avenue. I texted Kate to let her know, and she texted right back, saying she looked forward to it. It was just a date, but I was still excited to be seeing her again.

Chapter Twenty-One

Thursday, May 4

"Right this way." The monsignor led me to one of the Rectory's small residence rooms.

Considering Cathy was getting rid of this stuff, I doubted there would be anything worth keeping. Then I spotted the two suitcases Tom and Jane had been carrying into the motel.

"Did these suitcases belong to James?"

"Those are Tom's. He uses them to drop off clothing donated by the parishioners at one of his favorite charities."

"I have some clothes I've been meaning to donate to the Goodwill. But if the bishop has a favorite charity, I'd be happy to drop them off there instead."

"I'm sure Tom would appreciate that. The drop-off location is the Harriet Island Motel. It's a bit seedy, but the owner is working to bring the area back. You can Google the address. Be sure to mention Tom's name if you go."

"Thanks." Damn. That explained why Tom and Jane were there last Sunday, suitcases in hand. That blew out the whole having an affair theory.

James must have liked a good whodunit as they made up over half of his collection, along with older books on a wide variety of topics. Murder mysteries were a passion of mine too, so I was pleased to see books by local Minnesota authors like John Sandford, David Housewright, and William Kent Krueger. As I picked up one of the books, I noticed a corner of what looked like a picture sticking out from the pages. "Monsignor, would you have a box or bag I can use for the books? It looks like James and I have the same taste in authors, and there are quite a few I'd like to read."

"I'll be right back."

As he turned to leave the room, I opened the book to find a few candid shots of Tom, Frank, and the rest of their friends. I didn't want to get busted, and I figured the monsignor might want to keep the pictures if he realized they were there, so I quickly stuffed them back in, making sure none of the corners were visible. I began shaking the other books to see if any pictures would fall out but soon had to quit as the monsignor returned with a cardboard box. He stayed to watch me load the books, along with an award from *Super Lawyers Magazine*, recognizing James as one of the top lawyers in the state. Cathy must truly be disillusioned with her late husband to give that away.

The monsignor lingered way closer than necessary, especially in such a small room.

"Tom knows you're here and agreed to meet with you, although it was against my better judgment."

"Thank you."

He moved in even closer and lowered his voice. "You need to be more careful about who you associate with."

I was exceedingly uncomfortable for so many reasons. "You don't say."

"You wouldn't want to ruin your reputation as an honest businessman by consorting with the wrong sort of person. It might scare off any prospective new clients." He glared at me for a moment, then backed up abruptly. "The bishop will see you now."

He dropped me off outside Tom's office and left. My mind was still reeling. Did he just threaten to have Mike Wilson pull his business if I start dating Kate? Did he somehow figure out we were planning to go out on Saturday? Just how extensive was this guy's network of spies?

"Hello, Grayson. I heard you wanted some of James's things," said Tom as I entered his office with my cardboard box.

I had to get my head back in the present. There would be time to deal with Scarpino later. "I picked up a few of his books and awards. Thanks for letting me look."

"I'm glad you're here. I've been thinking about our last meeting. I wasn't very forthcoming, and I thought this would be an appropriate time to set things right."

"Okay." I wasn't exactly sure where he was going.

"I was wondering if there's anything you'd like to discuss."

I didn't know where to start. The first thing that popped into my head was the relationship between Tom and James. "What was he like? James, I mean."

Tom sat back and got a faraway look in his eyes. "My brother and I grew up in a good Catholic home in Rochester. He was known as Jim back then. We got into scrapes together as young boys do, and, as his older brother, I made sure he didn't get into too much trouble. Eventually, I got the calling to become a priest, and Jim decided to attend law school. We went our separate ways for a few years, but soon, we were both back in Rochester. I was assigned to Holy Redeemer Church, and James was a freshly minted attorney who joined a family law firm. It's been interesting to see how close you are to Dean. It reminds me so much of James and myself."

I sat in rapt attention, trying hard to imagine what Tom and James were like as boys.

"I hired a lovely young lady named Margaret, or Maggie as she preferred. She was the most kind and thoughtful person, who was so full of life that everyone took a liking to her almost immediately. She had strawberry-blond hair and the bluest eyes. Anyway, Jim was becoming more involved in church activities, which I did my best to encourage. He became infatuated with Maggie, and the next thing I knew, she was pregnant. Back then, if word had gotten out, it would have disgraced my brother and harmed his legal practice. The church might have punished me, too, so I did what seemed best. I arranged for her to leave town for a few months to 'tend to a sick aunt' and have the baby. After she delivered your brother, I had him placed into a respectable home. I knew Ben and Linda would raise him right—the way James would have raised him if the circumstances had been different."

"Then it happened all over again," I said.

"Yes. As you can imagine, I was infuriated with James…and with Maggie, of course, but especially with James. I scolded him many times after it happened the first time. I even suggested they marry, but he wouldn't hear of it. He never really said why. By then, he had already met Cathy, and it seemed he preferred someone closer to his age. I don't know."

That didn't sound quite right, but I thought it best not to say anything.

"I tried to keep them apart as much as possible while maintaining James's role in the church, which was important to his redemption. But it wasn't enough. Maggie became pregnant with you, and I realized one of them would have to leave. I checked with Ben and Linda—they were overjoyed at the thought of having another child, especially Dean's brother, so I placed you with them. I think you already know Maggie passed right after you were born. It was regrettable…." As he paused, I realized sadness and fatigue were creeping over Tom's face. He seemed to be aging right before my eyes. "I know she would have been so proud of you two, even if she would have had to watch from a distance."

He paused again, and I thought about the bizarre events that had led up to this meeting. "I understand that you met my adoptive parents through a lady at the church named Clara."

"That's right. They were members of the congregation, so I had met them but didn't know them well. Clara told me they had been trying to have children, but Linda was having difficulty conceiving. You've got to remember, this was over forty years ago, and there weren't many medical options available, so they applied to Catholic Charities. I knew by their ages they had waited too long, and the agency would pass them over when their names got close to the top of the list."

Picturing my adoptive parents struggling to deal with infertility made me appreciate them all the more.

"I was looking for the right home for Dean. I knew they were just about perfect from the first time we spoke. I met with them a few more times to be certain, then offered to arrange an adoption. They were overjoyed. Placing Dean and you with them were two of the most gratifying things I've done in all my years in the priesthood." Tom's voice was thick with emotion.

"What was it about them that convinced you they were the right ones?"

"They were good Catholics, of course, but that was a given. Beyond that, they were good people. Ben worked hard. He didn't make much money, but he knew how to make do with what he had. Linda was always cheerful, and they adored each other. It seemed like the perfect place to raise a young man, so I pulled a few strings and made it happen."

"My mother already told me you kept tabs on us over the years. I suppose you would have intervened if there had ever been any issues."

A smile slowly crept across Tom's face, and he looked like himself again. "There was never any need, so I must have made the right call. Remember the ten-speed bikes that showed up one summer when you guys were thirteen and fourteen?"

"Oh my gosh. We loved those bikes. I always wondered how our parents bought them, with money being so tight…." I suddenly realized what he was saying. "Wait a minute, that was you! You bought those bikes for us?"

The bishop was so full of pride I thought the buttons were going to pop off his shirt. "I've been waiting to tell someone for years. I heard Ben's company had moved to another state, and he had gotten laid off. He found a new job soon enough, but the pay was less, so I put together a care package for them and got the bikes for the two of you."

"It probably sounds crazy now, but you have no idea what those bikes meant to us. We had been riding these old secondhand bikes, which we were happy to donate to less fortunate kids. We rode those ten speeds for years. All I can say is thank you!"

"Glad to have done it, Gray."

As much as I was enjoying the history lesson, I wanted to get back to the original reason for the meeting.

"Do you mind if I ask who you think is responsible for James's death?" I was trying to catch him off guard, but it was no good.

"I'm sure I don't know. That is a matter for Detective Copeland and the police to determine."

"You were interviewed by the detective, though."

"I spoke with Aaron. We go way back. He's a good man. I have every confidence he will solve this crime."

Was there anyone in a position of authority in St. Paul this guy didn't know? "I can't help but think James was killed by someone close to him... someone he knew."

"This isn't a puzzle for you to solve, Grayson." Tom's tone was grave. "This is serious business—police business. You would be well advised to stay out of it."

"I don't think I can do that."

Tom sighed. "I suppose you have a theory."

I decided to just come out with it. "I believe Monsignor Scarpino is involved in all of this."

"Monsignor Scarpino. Frank. You think Frank killed James. That is a serious accusation. Why on God's green earth would he do that?"

"I think the monsignor figured James would tell us everything, that he would be happy to meet his offspring instead of being ashamed for having an illicit relationship and for getting some poor girl pregnant—twice. So, he had to stop James from telling us to save the good name of this parish and the church in general. Think of the scandal if this had hit the newspapers." I tried to gauge his reaction, but Tom's face was a wall of stone.

"I don't think anyone would even notice nowadays, with so many bigger scandals hitting the news. It certainly wouldn't be worth killing for."

"But it would have been much different back then. Besides, someone killed him, and they're still out there trying to clean up a couple of loose ends. I've been shot at and nearly run over, too. Dean's house was broken into, probably by someone who would have killed him if he'd been home."

"I heard about the shooting at the church, but that or the break-in may have nothing to do with James. It could easily be related to your jobs. It sounds to me like you both need to screen your clients more carefully. Look, if you've come here to accuse my staff of some crazy conspiracy theory, I'm going to have to ask you to leave."

"I could be wrong about Frank killing James, but there's something about the relationship between the two of you I can't figure out."

Tom looked down and sighed heavily. "Since you're part of the family, I'll tell you something I'd never tell anyone else. Frank was a young priest when the incidents with James and Maggie were happening. I thought I'd managed to keep everything secret, but somehow he figured it out. We've had an 'understanding' ever since."

"He keeps quiet, and you bring him along as you move up the chain of command. I knew it must be something like that for you to keep him around."

"That's not quite how I would have characterized it, but I suppose it's true enough. You'd be surprised at how handy he has been to me over the years."

"Then you became a bishop and convinced Rome to make him a monsignor as a way of saying thank you for his years of loyal service."

"It's not that simple. Frank had to spend time in Rome and be approved by the Vatican to carry that title. But he is a very resourceful individual, and he soon had their full endorsement."

Fixing things at headquarters, too—how resourceful indeed.

"Tom, I hate to sound like a broken record or a scratched CD, but Monsignor Scarpino must have been involved in James's death."

"Look, Frank has gotten me out of a few jams, but he wouldn't kill anyone."

"Wouldn't he? How do you know that?"

"Grayson, we may have a few skeletons in the closet—most organizations do—but they're not human remains."

"I thought the church was supposed to be different than most organizations."

"That's what everyone thinks," said the bishop. "That's what we want them to think. But human nature is human nature. What makes you think the church is any different than any other large institution like the federal government, Tesla, or Facebook? They're run by people with all the virtues and faults human beings bring to the table. Some are truly righteous, some are not, and most are somewhere in the middle trying to do the best they can."

"Wait a minute. Shouldn't the members of the clergy be held to a higher standard? Don't you screen out the bad eggs during seminary school? If not, what's the point of having a church?"

"Of course, they're being held to a higher standard, but so should the other people that have a fiduciary responsibility for parts of society, like politicians and business executives. And I think you know how successful we've been in screening out the bad ones. The church has had its share of scandals, like all of these other groups."

"You make it sound like you condone that kind of behavior or at least look the other way."

"I certainly don't, but some of the church leadership may have looked the other way, I'm afraid."

"But not you."

There was a long awkward pause. "People are flawed, Grayson. Of course, I'd call out the people doing things that are immoral or harmful to others. But I have to pick my battles, and being in a position of authority makes that even more important. 'Let he who is without sin cast the first stone,' remember? I can't go around calling out every sin and every sinner—there wouldn't be anyone left standing."

What about you? I wondered. *Would you be left standing?*

Chapter Twenty-Two

Friday, May 5

I called Dean on the way back from my meeting with the bishop to give him an update. He was a bit surprised I'd been so blunt in sharing my suspicions regarding the monsignor. I told him about Scarpino's threat, which proved, in my humble opinion, that he'd been involved in the murder. He countered that it merely proved Frank was a fixer, not a murderer. But we already knew that.

What the bloody hell had I been trying to accomplish by warning Tom I thought one of his inner circle members might be deranged? I was pretty sure he knew all about Frank, and if it turned out Scarpino wasn't the killer, I looked like the deranged one. I hoped this issue hadn't permanently damaged my relationship with the bishop, not that it would stop me from continuing the investigation.

Dean told me he had fixed Mr. X's wine cellar tracking system by Wednesday night and had even added a new feature that would recommend dinner pairings for each bottle using an artificial intelligence system. He had slept most of Thursday and hadn't had a chance to research the home for unwed mothers, which was fine with me as I secretly wanted to do it myself. When I arrived at my desk, I frosted the windows, opened a browser session, and typed "Wilkes Hospital St. Paul" to start the search.

I quickly learned the Salvation Army operated the John Wilkes Maternity Hospital and Home for Unwed Mothers in St. Paul for over fifty years and had served over eighty-five hundred unwed mothers. It was repurposed in 1982 due to "the changes in the political climate and in the way the public is now viewing unwed mothers," and nowadays, it served as a residential treatment program and emergency shelter for homeless youth.

The website listed a phone number to call and request hospital records. But doing so was sure to result in a long, drawn-out bureaucratic nightmare that would involve filling out request-for-information forms, filing them in triplicate via snail mail, having them rejected for no good reason, writing sternly worded letters threatening legal action, being referred to the hospital's legal counsel, and so on. I decided to stop by in person to see what I could accomplish.

I had the whole thing worked out in my head. Arrive around 11:40, which would give me twenty minutes to charm some low-level bureaucrat before their lunch break—enough time to start looking through files but not enough to finish. Precisely at noon, this minimum-wage earner would decide I was harmless enough to be left unsupervised and head out for lunch, which would give me unfettered access to their entire file system.

As planned, I arrived at The Wilkes House, as it was now called, at exactly 11:40. From the street, it was an imposing structure. The lower-level exterior was constructed of massive gray rough-hewn stone, and the upper floors were reddish-brown brick. The main entrance was located within a central tower that stood between the two wings of the building. I strolled onto the grounds, wondering how far I could get before setting off a silent alarm system, and someone would release the hounds. I moved past the unkempt lawn and tall pines, which shrouded the house from the street and added to its air of mystery. I thought I noticed some movement at a window near the top of the tower but looked up and saw nothing. I managed to enter the building unscathed.

The two wings were set farther back from the street. According to the website, one of them had been a full-blown maternity hospital that served unwed mothers, and the other had been a school where the girls were taught domestic skills like sewing, cooking, and cleaning. It was sad to think some of these girls would be rejected by their families for having a baby out of wedlock and would need this training to be hired as domestic help after they delivered. The expensive rooms were a financial burden on top of the social strain their families were already experiencing. Over seventy-five percent of the girls left within a day or two of childbirth.

The front desk sat on a raised platform that gave the receptionist a commanding presence over the whole area and the distinct advantage of looking down at visitors. I imagined unfortunate young girls, some with family members or boyfriends in tow and some without, withering, embarrassed, and exposed beneath the stern eye of an overbearing administrator. This place was forcing me into a deep depression, and I hadn't even made it past the atrium yet. Why didn't school principals give their young girls tours of this facility? It would be a much more practical form of birth control versus the esoteric wrath of God stuff they probably had been using.

Despite its current mission as a homeless youth shelter, there were no young people in sight. An older man in a worn, dark-green janitor jumpsuit was pushing a damp mop around the marble floor, and a middle-aged lady was sitting at a computer behind the counter. She seemed to be on the verge of dozing off as she slowly keyed data into the system. Good. Maybe she'd let me penetrate the bureaucracy just to get me out of her hair.

"Excuse me," I said to the lady with what I hoped was a warm smile.

The janitor was hovering nearby and seemed to be mopping the same spot over and over. I preferred a private conversation and stared at him for a minute, hoping he'd get the hint, but it had no effect.

After a few moments, with what seemed like an enormous effort, she spoke. "Yes?"

I decided to ignore her crappy attitude and the janitor. "Hi, I'm looking for the Archives Department."

"We don't have an Archives Department." Her voice dripped with disdain. She reached down, opened one of the drawers, and pulled out a form, all without an upward glance. "If you're looking for information about a specific birth that may have happened at this facility when it was a home for unwed mothers, you have to fill this out and send it in. The mailing address and instructions are at the top. You can also fill out this form online. The website address is at the bottom."

"I was hoping to talk to someone because of the circumstances—"

Disdain went to contempt, which she used like a knife to cut me off. "Regardless of the circumstances, there's no one here who will talk with you, and unless you have a substantial grant from the Historical Society, you can't go digging through our files either." She finally looked up, only to squint at me in an annoying fashion.

"What's your name?"

"Grayson Dyle," I said before I could stop myself, wondering what possible difference my name would make.

With that, I was dismissed. She pulled over a small notepad and wrote something down, then went back to entering data.

At least I discovered they still had files of some kind. "You must get people like me in here all the time."

"You have no idea." Apparently, she was too bored to look up again.

As I turned to go, the janitor suddenly stopped trying to wear a hole in the tile and looked directly at me while pointing at a sign that read "Restroom." Did I look like I needed to pee? Then I realized he was trying to get me away from the reception area so we could talk privately.

"Sorry to bother you again, but I wonder if I might use your restroom."

"We're open to the public." She jerked her head in the same direction as the sign.

The janitor used his mop to slowly wheel his bucket down the hall and into the men's room, the keys on the ring at his waist jangling as he went. I followed him in, and when he turned to speak to me, I noticed the nameplate on his jumpsuit read Karl.

"Heard you talking with Betty."

"Yes, is there some way you can help me out?"

"Could be."

Here was a man of few words who knew how to coax the value out of each one. After a few moments of silence, it was clear I would have to make the next move. What else would a janitor have but keys? And keys meant access to rooms. Rooms contained files. Files provided information. Karl was quickly becoming my new best friend.

"Is it safe to say one of the keys on that ring will open the door to a certain file room?"

He smiled and patted the key ring without a word.

"If I were to make a small donation, such a key might turn in a certain lock?"

"Might be so."

Silly me. I thought the shakedowns in this neighborhood would occur on the street in the middle of the night.

"Interesting. What kind of a donation would be required?"

"What's it worth?"

The information was invaluable, of course, and he knew it. "How about fifty bucks?" I was pretty sure I had that much on me.

Karl's gaze dropped to the bucket, which he pushed toward the door. Too low.

"Look, I don't have any more than that on me. I'll have to stop at an ATM."

His expressionless face looked back up at me as he shrugged.

"How about two hundred?"

"East door, fifteen minutes."

We both left the restroom and went in opposite directions. I thanked the receptionist on my way out, but she seemed not to notice.

I headed back to my car, Googled the nearest ATM, and considered the janitor. He must have realized the steady stream of birth mothers, fathers, and adoptees visiting Wilkes would pay dearly for immediate access to adoption records. He was sitting on a treasure trove. I'd bet he made the motion in the tower I noticed earlier while he was scanning the street for his next patsy. I also marveled at his negotiating style. He hardly spoke, and what he did say wasn't incriminating. I could have played a recording of his comments to his supervisor, and he would have plausible deniability for all of it.

I hit the ATM at a gas station a few blocks away and soon returned. I peeked inside the east door at the appointed time but didn't see anyone and decided to wait without knocking. After five minutes, I wondered if he'd been playing me. Then I took out my cell and brought up Google Maps. Sure enough, I was at the west entrance. I cursed under my breath and headed over to the east side, hoping he would still be there. I turned my phone to vibrate mode as I pocketed it just to be safe. Karl was just inside the east door, which he held open for me. I followed him down a nearby staircase to the basement.

He led me to the end of a dimly lit corridor, held up his hand for me to stop, and looked around the corner. He simultaneously put his key ring in one of his jumpsuit pockets, probably so it wouldn't jingle. Karl seemed to think of everything.

The coast must have been clear as he turned the corner and motioned for me to follow. He led me to a set of large double doors and paused. He held out his hand into which I deposited ten twenty-dollar bills, which he put in his jumpsuit pocket without counting. Karl opened one of the doors with a key, followed me into the room, closed the door behind us, and turned on the overhead fluorescent lights to reveal row after row of five-drawer filing cabinets. It turned out eighty-five hundred case records took up a lot of space. It looked like the endless rows of crates in the *Raiders of the Lost Ark* warehouse. The smell was probably just as musty, too.

"Birth year?"

"Nineteen seventy-eight." I started with Dean's records first.

"This way." I'll bet this guy was a riot at a party.

He led the way down the central corridor to a row marked "1975—1980" and then pointed to the row on the right. "Only photos," was the stern warning.

Okay—don't take any of the records. Got it. My heart was beating faster in the hope the documents would include a list of everyone in attendance at each birth. I walked down the row until I found the right filing cabinet and began the search while the janitor stood near the door, presumably as a lookout.

The folders were ordered by delivery date, and I quickly found the file covering Dean's birth date. The papers inside had been stapled together into three sets, and Dean's was in the middle. The birth card indicated a baby boy had been born via a routine delivery, and both the baby and mother were doing well. There was a line at the bottom that read, "Attending physician/midwife." It must have been the midwife who had crossed out the word physician and signed it, but the signature was illegible. Maybe Dean had software that could decipher the name.

There was also a birth certificate listing the live birth of a baby named Kieran, with the mother listed as Margaret Fitzgerald. A thick black line redacted the father's name. Someone had made sure Dean's father couldn't be traced. A third page called 'Certificate of Adoption' listed Ben and Linda Dyle of Rochester, MN, as the adoptive parents. I took pictures of the fronts and backs of all three and texted them to Dean. If anyone else had attended the birth, they weren't listed in the file.

Just then, there was a knock on the door. We had gotten busted. I quickly put the folder back as I found it. I expected to see Betty standing next to Karl as I rounded the filing cabinets, but it was just Karl pointing to the large clock on the wall. I held up my hand with digits extended to say five more minutes, then realized I could have just said that. Karl was already rubbing off on me.

I looked for my records next and found the file in a lower drawer. There must have been a lot more babies born that day, as the folder was much thicker than Dean's. I rifled through the stack, scanning the pages for my name, then realized I wasn't "Grayson" yet. I went through the pile again more slowly and found a set with only two sheets stapled together. There was a birth certificate with "Baby Boy" written in for the baby's name and "Margaret Fitzgerald" written in for the mother's. The father's name had been written in and then redacted. The second page was a 'Certificate of Adoption' with Ben and Linda Dyle of Rochester, MN, listed as the adoptive parents. The birth card was missing, and there was no indication anyone else had attended the birth. Why was I not surprised? I took pictures of both sides of both documents and put them back in the filing cabinet.

I realized I had a golden opportunity to access more files but didn't know any other adoptees. I walked back toward Karl, who checked to make sure the hallway was empty before letting me leave the room.

As we started back toward the east entrance, I asked, "I didn't see any information about the hospital staff members who were on duty during the birth. Was that information recorded somewhere else?"

Karl stopped up short and shook his head vigorously. It looked like none of his previous co-conspirators had asked that.

"Employment records room...too risky."

I turned around to look back down the corridor and noticed the lights were much brighter at the end, where the main hall turned to the left wing. That must have been where the administrative staff worked.

Karl cocked his head to one side. "Why?"

I figured the wrong answer would get me booted immediately. "I just want to thank the people that took such loving care of me when I was born." That sounded lame even to me, so I quickly followed up with, "How does another hundred bucks sound?"

Karl looked down and shook his head.

"Two hundred?" I was pretty sure I would have to endure an expensive, protracted lawsuit if Karl didn't come through with access to the files, and I was willing to pay just about any amount.

There was a long pause. Then more head shaking. I figured I was getting close.

"Three hundred, final offer." It had to be final as it was most of my cash on hand. Maybe I shouldn't have spent my original fifty bucks on gas and lottery tickets when I used the ATM.

This time, there was a longer pause, after which Karl held out his hand. Since I had withdrawn five hundred dollars from the ATM, it was a simple matter to hand him the rest of the twenties, which he pocketed again without counting, bless his conniving little soul. He surprised me by heading back down to the east wing of the building.

"Wait here," he said after we turned the corner, then he went up the stairs. A few minutes later, I heard an elevator door open down the hall. I wanted to peek around the corner to see if it was Karl but decided not to in case it was a staff person. Then I heard jingling keys and a short whistle, and I knew it was him. He had brought his mop and bucket for a cover story. I didn't know how he would use short choppy sentences to explain my presence. I just hoped it wouldn't come to that.

He started toward the west end of the building, so I turned the corner and quickly caught up. We stopped at the end so he could peek around the corner again. I looked at my phone and noticed it was 12:40, which I hoped meant everyone was at lunch. We entered the office area, which was brightly lit and even had windows. No one was there, and he moved quickly toward another smaller storage room at the far end. He opened the door with a key, turned on the light, pointed out the proper filing cabinet, and closed the door after I entered.

I had barely gotten the first file open when I heard a woman's voice asking Karl what he was doing there. I didn't hear a response, but I imagined Karl holding up his mop remorsefully to show he was merely doing his job. The lady must not have been buying it, and a second later, the door to the storage room was yanked open. Was accessing adoption hospital staff records a felony under HIPAA laws?

"What are you doing here?" the short, sturdy lady in a skirt and jacket demanded.

I'd never seen anyone with their hands on their hips, impatiently tapping their foot before. First time for everything. I had no idea what to say and couldn't think of an even remotely plausible excuse. I just stood there, speechless. Maybe I was Karl's younger brother, and he was training me to be a janitor who spoke very few words?

She stared at the papers in my hand for a few more seconds, and I figured I would soon be filing information request forms and threatening lawsuits when she whipped around to confront Karl.

"I know what you're doing," she snarled with a sneer. "You're selling access to our files, aren't you?"

Karl was taking this surprisingly well. He reached into his pocket, calmly took out my original set of twenties, fanned them out to show there were ten, then slowly peeled off five and offered them to her. I had to stifle a laugh as her expression changed from anger to resentment to interest. She slowly reached out, took the twenties, folded them once, put them in her jacket pocket, then turned to me. "Hurry up in there. The others will be back from lunch soon."

I looked at Karl, who merely shrugged and resumed mopping. Karl was quickly becoming my design muse. He had the innate ability to produce the desired effect with maximum efficiency and minimum effort. I wondered if he'd ever designed any sculptures.

Fortunately, Father Tom had selected a home for unwed mothers that kept meticulous employment records. I quickly determined three ladies were on midwife rotation on the day of my birth. Given more time, I might have narrowed it down further, but the incessant toe-tapping outside the door was making me crazy. I took pictures of the relevant pages, texted them to Dean, reinserted the file in its original location so the next miscreant could locate it, and exited the storage room.

Once the door was closed and relocked, our new partner in crime was visibly relieved. I was about to say thank you, but I didn't want to get hit up for an exit fee, so I nodded at her and followed Karl back to the main entrance.

I smiled as we shook hands. "Thanks, Karl."

He nodded, patted the pocket that held the remaining four hundred dollars, and resumed mopping. He really should put some water in that bucket one of these days.

Chapter Twenty-Three

Saturday, May 6

At exactly 5:00 A.M. Saturday, I received the first text from Dean. I didn't know it at the time because I was still sleeping, like the rest of civilized society. It didn't help that my phone was on silent from yesterday's excursions, so all I would have heard was a slight buzzing. The second text came in exactly ten minutes later. The precise timing meant Dean probably created an app called "Annoy" that continuously sent messages at preselected intervals until the recipient responded. My brother could be quite persistent when he couldn't wait to share something he found online. So it went on for the next thirty minutes until I finally woke to the buzzing at 5:40.

I turned on the nightstand light and opened the messages app to see what he was sending. The messages were all the same—**Big News—check email.** Good enough for me. I switched over to my Gmail account. Dean had emailed me at 3:15 A.M. At least he was kind enough to wait until five before Annoying me. I opened the email with the subject line "Big News."

Dean had been up late researching the people in the texts I'd sent him from Wilkes, and he summarized his findings in the email. One of his previous bosses must have insisted on receiving information in well-organized reports because that was his default format. I would have expected to receive an invoice if this email had come from anyone else.

He had searched the names of the three hospital staff members working the day I was born. After weeding through a considerable number of false positives for each person, he used their locations, demographics, and work histories to search public social media platforms and triangulate on them. He might also have accessed a few private databases, whose existence he could neither confirm nor deny. Okay, sometimes he went a bit overboard on the reporting, but I was finally getting to the good stuff.

According to his research, which he believed to be accurate to ninety-eight percent probability, two of them lived in the northern metro area, and the third lived in St. Cloud, which was about sixty minutes northwest of the Twin Cities. He provided addresses and phone numbers for all three, noting two were retired and the third semi-retired.

Just then, I received another text, which contained the same message. It was now 5:50, and I was absolutely getting annoyed. I replied to get it to stop, saying, **News received—check email.** Then I replied to his email saying I was planning to visit them in person, once it was a decent hour of the morning, starting with the local ladies and then driving to St. Cloud if necessary. I figured it would be harder to close the door on a visitor than it would be to hang up on a caller. After sending the message, I wondered if he would realize I was ribbing him for Annoying me so early.

Since it was the weekend, I didn't want to arrive at the first house until 9:30 at the earliest, which meant I had some time to kill. I fired up my laptop and did some searching of my own. I opened the midwives' Facebook pages using the links Dean had provided. He truly was a talented researcher. Okay, maybe I'd let him slide on the annoying text messages. After wasting the rest of the time on meaningless clickbait articles, I drove to north Minneapolis and parked in front of the home of one Beverly Lewis.

The home was halfway down the first block off North Dowling Avenue. It was a pleasant neighborhood, which must have been developed in the 1920s. The houses were older, and most were well maintained, with large hardwood trees towering overhead and a short walk to a park. It seemed like a cozy place to retire.

I knocked on Beverly's front door, hoping she'd be willing to talk. In a few minutes, the door opened a crack. "Can I help you?" said a voice. There was a chain that stopped the door from opening any farther. I thought I could see the frame of a walker through the opening.

I tried turning on the charm. "Hello. I'm looking for Beverly Lewis."

"You've found her, honey. What can I do for you?"

"I'm sorry to bother you, Ms. Lewis. My name is Grayson Dyle. I was wondering if I could ask you a few questions about your time as a midwife at the Wilkes Hospital."

"I don't have any records here if that's what you want. You need to contact Wilkes Home directly. Maybe they can help you. Goodbye."

Beverly was trying to close the door, but the front wheel of her walker was blocking the way. Before she could clear it, I quickly interjected, "Ms. Lewis, I've already been in touch with Wilkes House, but they couldn't help me. I'm looking for information on a specific young lady that died right after giving birth. Would you know anything about that?"

She stopped struggling with the walker for a moment. "I worked with so many girls over the years. You can't expect me to remember all of them." The way she said it gave me the distinct impression she remembered this one but didn't want to admit it.

"I believe that young lady was my mother."

"Are you an attorney?" She squinted at me.

"No, ma'am. Just a lost son looking for closure on his mother's death."

Beverly was silent for a few moments, and I could see her considering me through the door opening. "I guess I have a few minutes to spare." As she stepped back, the walker wheel no longer blocked the door, which she closed to remove the chain. The door opened again to reveal a medium-framed African American woman with hoop earrings and glasses nestled into her nearly white hair and a dark-blue dress dotted with small white crescent moons. I was about to enter when she stopped me. "I don't let strangers in my home. We can sit on the front steps if you want to talk."

"That's fine, ma'am. Perfectly fine."

"Call me Bev. What did you say your name is?"

She moved her walker to one side, and I noticed it was a seriously souped-up version of the standard old aluminum walker. There were no tennis balls on the front feet of this one. It had large six-inch wheels in front and smaller wheels in the back with a padded fold-down seat and ergonomic handles with hand brakes—a well-designed piece of equipment. If you put taillights and a license plate on it, it might even be street-legal.

"My name is Grayson Dyle. Nice to meet you, Bev." I would have shaken hands, but she had moved the walker aside and was stepping onto the porch stoop while holding on to the side rail for precious life. She didn't seem to want any assistance, so I didn't offer any, although it pained me to watch her struggle.

In a minute, she was seated on the top step, to both of our immense relief. "What can I help you with, Grayson?"

I explained I'd been born at Wilkes and had been trying to locate my birth mother when I discovered she died after giving birth to me. Since Wilkes girls rarely died from childbirth complications, I thought maybe she would remember this one.

Bev looked away wistfully. "That was an awful time. All those girls having all those babies. It was rough being with child if you weren't married. The home started working on those girls as soon as they arrived…messing with their heads. 'How're you going to bring up that baby all by yourself? You should give up that baby to a nice married couple. They'll know how to raise them right.' Most of those poor girls were so confused. They just followed right along."

"I'm sorry to bother you about this." I hoped to get back to my reason for being there before I lost her to more bad memories. "But I can't help feeling there was something suspicious about my mother's death. Her name was Maggie Fitzgerald, and she would have given birth in October of 1980. Does that help you?"

"This was a private adoption, wasn't it?"

I had a glimmer of hope. "Yes, it was."

"I remember that day." She sighed heavily, and it looked like the weight of her memory was deflating her. "It happened during my shift. There was another girl whose water broke earlier that morning. I got her, and Colleen got Maggie. Everything went fine with my girl like usual. I heard

Colleen's girl delivering in the next room, and she seemed fine, too. It wasn't five minutes later when there was a big commotion, and everyone came running. Colleen ran in with her girl's baby..." She looked at me with a sudden realization. "Why, that would have been you."

"Yes." It was all I could muster.

"Anyway, I saw the whole thing from the baby room next door. Colleen ran in and gave me her baby to watch because her girl was bleedin' real bad. That was no problem for me—I could watch her baby and my girl too. Next thing I knew, it was too late. Then they brought a priest in to do the last rites. It was a horrible, sad day that day." She sighed heavily again. I didn't say anything, hoping she'd continue.

"Sure, every once in a while, there was a breach baby, and we had to call a doctor from the big downtown hospital, but we never lost a mother—not on my shift. Funny thing was, I saw a nun with Colleen's girl, and they never showed up for the deliveries. They waited until afterward to make sure the girls didn't try to keep their babies. This nun was with that girl, and then I never saw her after that. Course, I had my girl to tend to, so I might have missed her. I don't know what else I can tell you. You might want to talk to Colleen, though. She would know more than me."

"Good idea." Since I already had Colleen's info, I didn't bother asking for it.

It sounded like there was nothing else to discuss, but I couldn't leave her like that. "Did you stay at Wilkes after they turned it into a youth home?"

"I delivered the babies and taught the girls, too. How to feed their babies, when to feed them, like that. When they were closing down the hospital, they asked me to stay on as a counselor. Said I'd probably be good at it. I guess I did okay 'cause I spent another ten years there. Then I retired and tried to put those memories behind me."

"Weren't there any happy times? I heard some of the girls kept their babies. Did you ever hear from them?"

That finally brought a smile. Bev told me stories about girls whose babies she had delivered and who she taught to be mothers that brought their young children in to see the place they'd been born. Some of them had gotten married and brought their husbands along. Usually, she saw them at Christmastime, and they brought a plate of cookies or donated presents for the new mothers to open. Some of her neighbors occasionally walked by as we talked, and she smiled and waved.

"I guess that place wasn't all bad, really," she said at last.

That sounded like my cue to leave. "Bev, thank you so much for spending time with me today. It was great hearing about Wilkes. I feel like I made a connection with my birth mother for the first time and know a bit more about what she must have gone through."

"I'm glad you stopped by, Grayson. I hope I helped you somehow."

"You certainly did." She didn't seem like the type to take offense at being assisted, so I asked, "Can I help you up the stairs?"

"No. I think I'll sit here awhile and watch the world go by. It's one of my favorite things to do."

Since I was already on the road, I decided to try my luck with another midwife. Bev mentioned Colleen, but she lived in St. Cloud, which was ninety minutes away, so I decided to try Evelyn Goodland next. She lived on Seventh Street NW in New Brighton, which was only fifteen minutes away, and was also retired. I soon arrived at her home on the corner of the block and parked a few doors down. The light tan stucco on the narrow, two-story home had severe cracks, and overgrown bushes completely blocked the crumbling sidewalk to the front door. Through the windows of the fully enclosed, sagging front porch, I saw piles of boxes and bags that looked like they hadn't been moved in years, which made me itch all over. I walked around to the back door, which, strangely, was ajar.

"Evelyn?" There was no reply, so I knocked on the wooden doorframe, whose paint had mostly peeled off.

"Evelyn Goodland?" Still no answer. I trusted Dean had given me the correct address, and since the door was already open, I walked in, despite my dread of discovering dozens of cats or, even worse, mice. "Evelyn? Are you here?"

Laying on the floor next to the kitchen table was a small-framed, gray-haired woman in a faded housedress who had been shot once in the head. I rushed to her but could find no pulse. The spattered blood was slowly dripping down the appliances, and the blood pool on the floor was fairly small for a head wound, which told me she had only recently been shot. Houses in this neighborhood were close together, so the gunshot would have been heard, and the police were probably on their way. Just as I stood to leave, a squad car screeched to a halt next to the house, lights on but running silent. I watched through the kitchen window as one cop headed toward the back door and the other toward the front. I ran into the living room and hid behind the couch, wondering how to get out.

One of the cops banged loudly, trying to force the door to the front porch, while the other entered the kitchen and was probably doing a pulse check. The front door cop radioed the kitchen cop the outside door was stuck and he couldn't get in. The kitchen cop replied that he found a gunshot victim and the front door cop should come around and search the house. The kitchen cop called in for backup and the medical examiner while the front door cop came around and started the search.

I scanned the living room windows but saw they had been painted shut, and I had no time to find one that would still open. The couch was next to the door that led to the front porch. While the cop was clearing the first room off the kitchen, I silently reached up and opened the door, only to be bombarded by a disgusting stench that I imagined could easily have been coming from the dead woman's long-deceased husband if he were still in there. As the cop moved to clear the next room across the hall, I quickly crawled onto the porch, trying to cover my nose with my shirt and stifling the urge to retch. I closed the porch door as the cop entered the living room. As he cautiously searched the room, I slowly tugged a few bags over me as cover.

Just then, an intrusion of cockroaches spilled out of one of the bags onto my side. I hated cockroaches more than all other creatures, dead or alive, and it took all of my willpower to stop myself from jumping up, shaking them off while screaming bloody murder, then begging to be arrested. The cop looked out the porch window and must have decided anyone desperate enough to hide there had earned their freedom as he moved away and went upstairs to continue the search. I figured there was no way to get through the front door without bashing it open and making a lot of noise, so I crawled back into the living room, the last few roaches making a mad dash for the dark space under the couch.

After clearing the second floor a few minutes later, the cop went downstairs to search the basement. I stuck my head up from behind the couch and scanned the grimy windows. Semicircular scratch marks were on the windowsill beneath one of them where Evelyn must have let fresh air into the house, probably as a way to celebrate national holidays. I snuck over and opened the window, checked to make sure I wouldn't be seen, and dropped to the ground, doing my best to close the window behind me. Fortunately, the small hopper windows in the basement walls were so dirty that the cop couldn't see through them. I straightened up and slowly walked back to my car as the cops' reinforcements were arriving.

Holy crap, another murder. I drove away. *And probably with the same gun.* I supposed this death could have been a major coincidence, but it was much more likely James's murderer was trying to eliminate more sources of information about the past. While I wanted to drive straight home, burn my clothes, and scrub off the cockroach poop in a two-hour shower, I had to contact the third midwife before it was too late.

Chapter Twenty-Four

Saturday Afternoon, May 6

Ninety minutes later, I parked in front of Colleen Hayes's 1960s-era, single-family home made of reddish brick with yellowing aluminum siding on the garage. There was a small propane grill near the front door, alongside a long wooden picnic table and a portable cooler. An old, rusty push lawn mower sat idle on the right side of the cracked asphalt driveway, and a basketball hoop without a net occupied the left side.

I walked up to the front door and rang the bell.

In a minute or so, a friendly-looking man in his sixties or seventies opened the front door. "Hello—what can I do for you?"

"Hello, sir. My name is Grayson Dyle. I'm looking for Colleen Hayes. Do I have the right house?"

"That depends. What do you want with her?"

"I have some questions about her time at Wilkes Hospital. A former coworker of hers thought Colleen could help me out." I figured the coworker reference would help convince him I was legitimate.

"Wait here." He closed the door most of the way, and I heard a muffled discussion. Soon the door was reopened by a lady who resembled the man in age and demeanor. He hovered nearby in case she needed rescuing.

"I'm Colleen. What did you say you wanted?"

"Hello, my name is Grayson Dyle. I'm looking for some information on a young lady that gave birth at Wilkes Hospital many years ago. I spoke with Beverly Lewis, who was very helpful. She suggested I contact you as well."

"I left there a long time ago. How did you get my address? Did she give it to you?"

"No, she didn't, ma'am. I looked you up online. I hope you don't mind."

She was noncommittal. "What is the name of the lady that gave birth?"

"Maggie Fitzgerald."

She looked as if a jolt of electricity had gone through her. She put her hand to her heart, breathing heavily. The man, who I assumed was her husband, closed in behind her to make sure she was okay.

"Are you with the police?"

"No, ma'am. I'm a private citizen."

"I don't think I can talk about this."

The man put his hand on the door and was getting ready to slam it shut.

I figured I had one more shot. "Maggie Fitzgerald was my mother. She died right after I was born."

The initial shock was wearing off, and now she knew I wasn't there in any official capacity, she seemed to calm down a bit. "I know she did. It's okay, Henry."

He gave me a don't-try-anything-funny look and stood down.

Colleen opened the screen door to let me in. "Would you like some iced tea? I just made a pitcher."

"Yes, please." I wanted to be friendly. The home was well kept, with a blue-and-green plaid couch and a worn leather reclining chair that both faced a widescreen TV.

"Please have a seat." She gestured toward the couch. "I won't be a moment."

I sat on the couch and studied numerous pictures of what must have been the same three kids at various ages on the wall and end tables. It looked like a happy family home upon which I was encroaching.

Henry wisely retreated to a back room, so when Colleen returned in a few minutes with the iced tea, it was just for us. She sat on the other side of the couch, staring at the drops forming on her glass.

"I always thought someone would call me one day about that situation.

For the first few days, I waited by the phone and wasn't sure whether I would answer it or not, but no one ever called...not the hospital, not the coroner, not the police, no one. That was the only girl I ever lost. I never really put it out of my mind. Then the years went by. I don't think of her as often as I used to." She looked at me directly. "I'm still not sure what happened. I used to have dreams...more like nightmares about that day...but they've gone away, too. I'll never forget Maggie, though. She had so much energy and so much love. She was a free spirit, that's for sure, and I think that's what got her into trouble..." She looked down again.

"What can you tell me about that day?" I asked gently, trying to soothe her feelings and let her know it was okay. I wasn't going to blame her for anything.

Tears were forming in her eyes.

"It's okay," I said. "I know this must be painful. But I need to know what happened so I can make peace with this, too." That might not have been the whole truth, but it was certainly true enough.

Colleen wiped the tears with the back of her hand and drew herself up as if accessing some internal source of resolve. "I remember it like it was yesterday because it was so...horrific. Everything was going well. It was a routine delivery. Maggie was in good spirits for someone who was so young and who was having a baby. She had been telling me she'd already had a child who she'd given up for adoption. Kieran, she called him. She told me this baby would go to the same family so they could grow up together and help each other. That was pretty unusual—a lot of the girls were upset, some of them hysterical when they realized they would soon be giving up their baby. But not Maggie. She just smiled and said it was all part of God's plan. She was hoping for a girl but thought it would be a boy because of how hard he kicked. She adored the baby's father and said that he was going to watch out for both of her children." She paused to take a sip of iced tea.

"She was from Rochester. I remember that. She had a friend who was a nun with her, and they both worked at the same Catholic Church."

"Sister Anna," I said softly.

Her eyes went wide with recognition. "That's right. It was Sister Anna.

208

She was so devoted to her friend and very helpful to me. Maggie told me she had been at Kieran's birth, too, and she smuggled out a letter Maggie had written to Kieran's adoptive parents. She said she was going to write one to you...too." The tears began again. "You never got a letter, did you?" She already knew the answer.

There wasn't anything to say to that, so I just shook my head no.

She composed herself again. "After you were born, I noticed the amniotic fluid wasn't draining from your lungs. I thought maybe we would have to put you in an incubator, so I asked Sister Anna if she would keep an eye on Maggie for me. She said she would see to it and that it was okay if I took you to the baby station to get you looked at by another nurse. It was right down the hall, and Sister Anna seemed very competent, so I followed her suggestion. The next thing I knew, Sister Anna was calling for help. I asked Bev to watch you and ran back to Maggie's room...there was blood on the floor...so much blood...I left for five minutes at the most...I don't know how it could have happened. Sister Anna said Maggie started hemorrhaging. She didn't realize how serious it was and waited too long to call for help. By then, it was too late, and Maggie was gone. I'm so sorry, Grayson."

"It's okay," I repeated over the lump in my throat. "I'm sure you did everything you could. There was no way you could have known what was going to happen."

"Thank you for understanding. That means a lot to me." Her voice was raspy with emotion. "The odd thing was that by the time I got back to the room, another of Maggie's friends was in there with them. I think his name was Frank."

It was my turn to have a jolt go through me. Frank was there when I was born? How the bloody hell could that have happened? I knew that bastard was involved in this somehow. Then I realized I was missing what Colleen had just been saying.

"...seemed to come out of nowhere. By the time I got there, they were already cleaning up the room. I told them we had a cleaning crew for that, but he insisted. The whole thing was so strange..."

My blood was starting to boil, and I looked down. I had clenched my hands clenched into fists. Henry must have sensed something was wrong because he came out of the backroom just out of Colleen's sight to glare at me.

What was Frank doing at the delivery? If this were going to be another routine delivery, like Dean's, there would be no reason for him to be involved. The only reason that made sense is he was there to make sure Maggie didn't make it, but why? Something was seriously wrong here, and I couldn't figure out what it was. I swore I would nail that self-righteous jackass as soon as I could prove he was a double murderer. But it was time to calm down, so Henry didn't kick me out.

"...I stayed at the hospital for another year after that, but my heart wasn't in it. It got so the sight of the place made me sick. Henry could tell I needed a change and said we should move somewhere else. He had some relatives in St. Cloud, so we moved here, and I got a job as a nurse at St. Cloud Hospital. He recently retired, so I went part-time."

"What can you tell me about Sister Anna?"

"We talked for a bit between Maggie's contractions. She seemed nice. She was kind of old-fashioned, even for a nun. I noticed she was wearing a scapular of St Benedict...I hadn't seen one of those in years." Colleen got quiet, and it seemed like it was time to leave.

"Colleen, I know it was difficult for you to relive these memories again. But I want you to know you've been tremendously helpful. It sounds like Maggie was a wonderful person, and I feel proud to be her son. I know my brother will feel that way, too."

"Your adoptive parents didn't name him Kieran, did they?"

"No. They named him Dean. They never knew Maggie had picked out a name for him. She told them not to give him the letter until he turned twenty-one, but we didn't find it until recently." I didn't see any point in getting into the whole story about my adoptive father's death. I finished my iced tea and stood to leave. "I appreciate your sharing all this information."

"I'm glad you stopped by, Grayson. I always wondered what happened to Maggie's baby boy. Now I know he's doing just fine."

210

Now that I knew Colleen had Henry around, she seemed like a less likely target. But I had still warned her to be careful. I texted Dean from my car, saying I met with two of the three midwives, and we needed to talk. He texted back he was free for dinner the following evening, and we agreed to meet at my place at six.

As I drove off, a troubling thought occurred to me. Colleen had barely known my birth mother, yet she had taken an immediate liking to her. Maggie seemed to have a gift for making people happy. I loved my adoptive parents dearly and had no reason to complain about how we'd been brought up. Yet, I couldn't help wondering how different we would be if Maggie and James had raised us. Would I still be the person I think of as 'me?' There was no way to tell.

Chapter Twenty-Five

Saturday Night, May 6

T he reservation for my date with Kate was at a restaurant in an up-and-coming area of Minneapolis called the North Loop. It was a popular place, and the closest parking spot I could find was a couple of blocks away, which wasn't ideal, considering the killer could open fire at any minute—the things we did for love. I met Kate at the reception desk about ten minutes early and checked in with the maître d'. As we waited for our table, I noticed Kate looked charming in a white silk blouse, black slacks, and low heels. I had gone crazy and wore a light blue button-down dress shirt with black slacks and a sports jacket with a discrete blue and black plaid pattern. The prospect of spending the evening with her was exhilarating.

I thought I'd break the ice with what should be a safe topic. "Do you come from a big family?"

"I have an older sister and a younger brother. My sister is our resident scientist. She has a Ph.D. in biology from the University of Minnesota. They offered her a research position, and she's been there ever since. My brother is an outdoorsman and was always interested in law enforcement, so he's a conservation officer with the Department of Natural Resources."

"And you're the high finance person. What a talented family!"

"Why, thank you. You and Dean are doing pretty well for yourselves, too."

On it went, the usual banter of two people getting to know each other during their first official date. In a few minutes, our table was ready, and we went in. The building was a smartly reworked, turn-of-the-century farmhouse. The tables and fixtures were white, the bench seating was black, and the chairs had both black and white in a diamond pattern, which made the reddish hue of the original brick walls pop. It was one of the trendiest spots in town, and I was glad I'd made the extra effort to snag a reservation.

Since we had no celebrity status, the maître d' took us to a table in the middle of the large dining room. The chef was a James Beard award winner, as was apparent once we perused the menu. I could have sworn the governor was seated at one of the primo tables near the door. The two beefy men in dark suits at the next table seemed to confirm my suspicion. With that kind of muscle around, James's killer was going to have to take the night off.

Bison Tartare—wasn't that raw buffalo? The next item was Seared Foie Gras. I was pretty sure this was duck liver and was usually served cold. It looked like being trendy meant preparing a recipe in exactly the opposite manner of the traditional approach. In the end, I went with the pork chop, and Kate went with the lamb, both of which seemed safe for a first date.

Dinner was delicious. Halfway through, Kate said with a smile, "Okay, Grayson, let's have it."

"Sorry, Kate?" I had let my mind drift back to the discussion with Colleen. I couldn't help wondering why Frank had been at my birth and what he had to gain from Maggie's death. It just didn't add up.

"It seems like something is bothering you. Do you want to talk about it?"

"Something's been bugging the hell out of me, but it's about James and Frank, and it doesn't seem like a good topic for a dinner date."

"Does it have to do with Frank being on the wrong end of the stick for once?"

"Most likely."

"Then let's have at it. After the way he's been treating me, I'd love to see that guy get his comeuppance."

Dean would have thought it still too risky to bring Kate into the investigation, that she was still on the suspect list, but I didn't care. I didn't think she was the murderer and wanted to confide in her. Besides, Dean and I would figure out whodunit, even if it was Kate, so I didn't see much downside.

"As long as you don't mind...." I told her the whole thing. From Dad dying, finding the letter, and discovering we were adopted, up to the investigation Dean and I had been conducting to find out what happened to James and Maggie. I also told her about my theory that the monsignor killed James to prevent him from telling us the truth.

Her initial fascination quickly turned to disgust. "Oh my gosh, that's horrible."

"That's what I thought." It suddenly sounded so much worse, and we both sat there in shock for a minute.

"You two aren't going to let this go, are you?"

"Not after hearing how suspicious Maggie's death was, no."

"Sister Anna and Father Frank were both in the room right after you were born."

"Yep. By the way, have you ever met Sister Anna?"

"I've never even heard anyone mention that name. Maybe there was a falling out, or maybe she moved to a different parish."

"Colleen said she was an old-fashioned nun, even though she was about the same age as Tom and James. She said she wore a scapular of St. Benedict. You don't see those much anymore."

"What's a scapular?"

"It's made of two fairly small swatches of cloth that are held together by two long strips of cloth. You put one strip over your head so one swatch rests on your chest and the other on your back. The swatches have the names or images of certain saints. It's a reminder of the wearer's devotion to them." Then it hit me like a bag of cement.

"I think I just figured something out." I got out my phone and typed furiously to do a quick web search.

"What? What is it?" Kate's wide eyes and big smile said she was getting caught up in my enthusiasm. Damn, she was good-looking. What was she doing out with me, and why hadn't she been snatched up a long time ago?

I found what I was looking for on my phone. "Oh my gosh, I just figured it out. St. Scholastica and St. Benedict were brother and sister!"

Kate looked at me like I was crazy. "Do you need to go home and blog about that? Because I'm pretty sure that's common knowledge. I like your blog posts, by the way."

"Thanks." Wow, it was good to know she read them. "But that's not the new part. The new part is that Sister Anna and Principal Jane Walsh are the same person!"

"What? How did you figure that out?"

"The Scapular. Colleen said Sister Anna wore a scapular of St. Benedict, and when I met with Jane, she was wearing a scapular of St. Scholastica. It must have been the same scapular, but she must have had it on backward when I saw her. I just Googled it. A scapular with St. Scholastica on one side will almost always have St. Benedict on the other side. They must be the same person. Holy crap, wait until Dean hears about this."

"Wait a minute. That doesn't necessarily prove anything. I'm sure lots of people still wear scapulars...well, some people anyway."

As the server was clearing our plates and refilling our wine glasses, I realized I needed to fill her in more. "No, you're right. That doesn't prove anything. But listen to this. When I had dinner with Cathy, I showed her the letter Maggie had written to Dean. It's quite touching, by the way. I'll show it to you the next chance I get. Anyway, Cathy was quite upset by it. She said it was because it reminded her that James was a cad, but she already knew that about him. But maybe she realized Sister Anna and Jane are the same person, and that's why she stormed out."

"Let's assume Anna and Jane are the same person. Why would that upset her, and how does that help your investigation?"

"I'm not sure." My initial enthusiasm for this breakthrough was waning. "Let's think about this. If Jane and Frank were both there when Maggie died, they're obviously in this together. If they were involved in Maggie's death, they were probably involved in James's death, too. Maybe Frank really did kill James to keep him from telling us the truth, but why? As much as I like the idea of Frank being involved in both murders, killing James merely to stop him from disclosing he had two illegitimate sons seems like a real stretch."

215

We both sat back. The server must have been wisely holding back from bothering us during our lively discussion because he quickly came over to ask about dessert. Kate suggested the Crème Fraiche Torte, and I was skeptical until reading it featured chestnut pudding with blood orange ice cream. That, I would enjoy. We agreed to split one serving.

We were mostly silent until the dessert came as we tried to figure out how this new puzzle piece fit. The date was in danger of ending on a down note when another thought popped into my head. A small smile crept onto my face.

Kate smiled back. "I'm learning to like that wicked grin you get when you have an idea."

"Thanks. Frank is a master of deception, and he's been at it a lot longer than we have. The only way we're going to catch him is by setting a trap of some kind."

"Hmm, I'd be happy to help with that. He's been a thorn in my side ever since that whole accounting thing. What do you have in mind?"

"Not sure yet. Let's meet with Dean and come up with a plan."

"Count me in." She took a big spoonful of the dessert. Just then, a big glob of whipped cream slid off her spoon onto her slacks.

"Nice move." I quickly realized I would have mockingly said that to Dean and looked up in a panic, thinking she'd be mad.

"Thanks," she replied with her trademark smile. "It matches the spot on your shirt."

I looked down to see a glob of juice from the pork chop that was already beginning to set. We both burst out laughing. It seemed like the start of a beautiful friendship. I was excited about the prospect of Kate helping us solve the murders and got the sense she was feeling the same way. I was going to fall hard for this woman if I wasn't careful. We quickly finished the dessert and looked into each other's eyes. I abruptly called for the check so we could get out of there and perhaps have some alone time.

I offered to walk her to her car, hoping the presence of the governor's limo would keep any killers at bay. She accepted, but when she told me where she had parked, I offered her a ride instead. We walked briskly to my car, arm-in-arm, and I held the door for her to get in. The side street was somewhat secluded and even dodgier now as it was getting late. We stared into each other's eyes, and I moved toward her, planning to kiss her. I could have sworn her smile was giving me a green light, but as I moved closer, she turned her head away, and I awkwardly kissed the side of her face. Not my smoothest move ever. I thought maybe she turned to look at something on the street and looked out the side window but didn't see anything unusual.

It seemed like the moment had passed, and I leaned back to start the car when she suddenly turned around, pulled me close, and kissed me. I didn't ask why she hesitated the first time. I didn't care. Her lips were soft and warm. The night had cooled off a bit, and in a few minutes, the windows were getting steamy. If I didn't take her back to her car soon, things could get out of hand.

"How would you like to meet at my place?"

Kate frowned and looked skeptical, and I realized my question could easily have been misinterpreted. "I mean tomorrow. Dean and I are meeting for dinner at my place at six to figure out how to nail the killer."

"That sounds great." We kissed again, and she told me where she'd parked.

I pulled up behind her car to make sure she would be okay when she got out. "See you at my place. I'll text you the address. I text you the code for one of the guest spots in the underground parking, too."

"Sounds great. Thanks, Grayson. I had a wonderful time."

"Me too." I snuck in one last kiss, and she headed off.

Chapter Twenty-Six

Sunday, May 7

I spent Sunday afternoon tidying up to make a good impression on Kate. I ordered takeout for the three of us to keep things informal, then used the remote to set the robot vac loose on the floor. I considered scouring the kitchen but decided against it. Better to keep her expectations in line with reality.

At six on the dot, Kate rang the doorbell, and I buzzed her up.

"Wow, great place."

"Thanks." What was the appropriate greeting here, a kiss or a hug?

Fortunately, Kate put her arms out for a hug. Then she smiled at me expectantly, and we kissed. I didn't know what she was thinking, but I was falling for her hard.

"I couldn't help noticing your offices are in the same building. That's mighty convenient."

"There's a gym here, too. It doesn't get that much use, so I have the run of the place quite a bit. I'm a pretty lucky guy." I hoped she realized I wasn't talking about the building. "Did you get into the underground parking, okay? Sometimes the guest spots are full, and it won't let you in."

"Yep, all set."

"Great. Would you like some coffee?"

"No thanks." Kate walked over to the large windows along Lake Street with the partially unobstructed view of the lake. The walkers, joggers, and sailors entertained us for a few minutes, and I was seriously thinking about kissing her again when the doorbell rang. I hit the buzzer, and Dean came up with the food, having run into the delivery guy in the lobby. I introduced them, and we sat at the island counter to eat.

After chatting over dinner, I got down to business with a review of my meetings with the two midwives. To avoid any unpleasantness, I said that Evelyn Goodland did not answer when I visited her home, which was the absolute truth. Kate updated Dean on our realization that Sister Anna and Principal Jane must be the same person. I was glad to hear her taking ownership of the theory. Dean agreed and said that that would explain why he couldn't find anything online about Sister Anna after the year I was born. I gave him an update on my discussion with Cathy and the theory it must have been the reference to Sister Anna that had upset her.

"Where do we go from here?" Kate asked at last.

"We need to think of a good place to set a trap, right? How about Bingo Night at the church? Someone shot at DeeDee and me the last time I was there, so it would probably be a good place to try again."

Dean seemed skeptical. "Maybe they'll want to stay away from there for a while."

"It's been almost three weeks since the last shooting, and the cops have chalked it up to gang warfare and already moved on. I don't think the killer will have any issues now."

Dean gave in with a wave of his hand.

"Hasn't he been wearing a mask every time he's shown up in the past? If he sticks with that plan, how do we get him to take it off without physical threats or by holding him at gunpoint?" Kate asked.

"Wait a minute," I said. "Dean, can your facial recognition app scan someone's face underneath a mask?"

My brother was in his element. "As the system sits today, no, it cannot. However, if I replace the regular camera with a thermal infrared camera, it will capture the heat emitted by the subject and form something called a thermogram. Then, it will be a simple matter of reprogramming...."

He must have noticed the bored looks Kate and I were exchanging and realized this was way too much information. "The short answer is no, but I can add that feature in a few hours."

"Great." I was thankful he could get the app to work on someone in a mask and that he had stopped explaining. "Once we prove he's the man in the mask, he'll have to admit he was somehow involved in the murder."

Dean said, "Do either of you have any pictures of Frank? I'll need to scan one, so the software can match it with the image taken by the IR camera."

"I don't," said Kate. "But maybe we can find one from a newspaper story online."

"I have a picture of the whole group I found in one of the books James used to own. It's not a close-up, and it's a few years old. Do you think it will work?"

"Shouldn't be a problem," Dean said. "The scanning software can get the resolution we need from a picture like that."

"It works like Facebook, where it locates the faces when you scan in the picture, then you tell it who is who, right?"

"Yep."

"That's great, but how do we get him to show up at Bingo Night? We could be killing a lot of time setting traps for no one," Kate said.

It seemed obvious to me. "Let's just use the letter as bait. We can say we'll give him the letter if he meets with us."

Dean appeared skeptical. "No, I don't think so. I mean, it might get him there, but once he reads the letter and realizes there's nothing in it worth killing for, he's going to come after us to keep us quiet."

I threw up my hands. "Then we're screwed no matter what we do." I looked at Kate, hoping for support, but she didn't say anything, so she must have agreed with Dean.

I got up to stare at the partially unobstructed lake and think while Dean refreshed our glasses.

"Maybe there are a few facts about the murder that aren't public yet that we can use for leverage," Dean said after a few minutes.

I shot him a stern look. Where was he going with this? Why would we have information like that unless one of us had been at the crime scene? Was he going to tell Kate I found the body next? I sat back down in case I needed to kick him under the kitchen counter for making another dumb comment.

"What about the bloody prints from the shoe? We could try to pin those on him somehow," Kate said.

"Umm, what bloody shoe prints?" asked Dean.

"You know, the prints next to the body."

Wait a minute. Andy Murphy told me James's office had been cordoned off for the police and then immediately cleaned and restored. Dean and I glanced at each other nervously. He knew about the prints from my description of the clean-up effort after leaving the scene, but we both realized there was no way Kate could have known about the prints without having been there on the night of the murder. Could she have been the person I heard when I was staring at the body, who was leaving the building after plugging James twice?

"This is the first I've heard of them," he said with mock innocence.

Kate's face was turning red. She must have realized she might have been admitting she had been there. I figured I'd better help her out.

"Wait a minute. Copeland asked me if one of my shoes had blood on the sole. I'll bet he asked you, too, right?"

Kate was noticeably relieved. "Of course he did."

While I had just scored some major league points with Kate, the problem was Copeland wouldn't have asked her about the prints because, based on their size, they were from a man's shoe. Damn, I hoped like hell she wasn't the murderess. Could Frank have forced her to kill James in exchange for clearing her of embezzling funds from the church? But if he did, why was she helping us trap him now? Did she think Frank would let himself get caught without giving her up as an accomplice?

"I don't know if that will work. The killer may not have even realized he left them."

One thing I knew for certain, I didn't mind covering for her now, but there was no way I was going to cover for her if she had been involved in James's death. I decided to ask her about it later.

"It looks like the letter is the only bait we have," Dean said.

Kate and I quickly agreed.

We talked through the details of the trap over and over, how we would lure the killer there, which room would be the best for setting up the equipment, where we would be positioned, and so on until we had what seemed like a solid plan. The first step was for me to text the killer by replying to his latest message.

Let's call a truce. We figured most people wouldn't carry their regular phone and a burner phone around with them, so we were prepared to wait for a day or two, if necessary, before trying again. But it only took fifteen minutes to receive a response.

Go on.

I'll give you the letter if you leave us alone.

Why would I do that?

You want us to stop investigating, right?

I can make you stop by myself.

Time to take a different approach.

I spoke with Colleen and Bev—we know what happened to Maggie.

Who are they?

Midwives at Wilkes on the day I was born.

There was a long pause. This was likely bombshell news, and the threat should be clear.

When/where?

I paused to make it seem like I was thinking about it like we didn't already have it planned out.

My office, tomorrow morning.

No, it needs to be a public place.

Considering I had unwittingly walked into his trap at the Rectory, this was exactly how we thought he would respond. Still, I breathed easier, knowing he had turned it down. Now for the actual location. I waited another minute for effect and texted, **Fine—the church during Bingo Night.**

In less than a minute, I received a reply. **Fine.**

8:00 main hallway.

Fine.

I resisted the urge to text something snarky like "come alone" or "see you later, jerk." It was best to leave well enough alone.

We talked for a while longer, but now that the plan was in motion, Kate said she had to head out, and Dean took it as his cue to leave. I went to the bedroom to retrieve the picture from James's book and gave it to Dean. It looked like a beautiful night, so I went down the lift to see them out. I gave Kate a quick kiss goodbye, and she took the lift to the underground parking. It was only about eight, and I was considering taking a walk around the lake. I said goodbye to James, sat on a bench in front of the building, trying to decide what to do next, and saw my brother turn south down James Avenue, which was one block down. It was just like Dean to park on a side street to avoid paying a meter.

I wasn't sure why I noticed the black Crown Vic making turning onto Lake Street a few minutes later. Maybe nearly being run over by one had something to do with it. It slowly drove down Lake, then turned right on Irving Avenue, the next block down from James Avenue. That was odd. You didn't see many Crown Vics in this neighborhood. I decided to skip the walk and started up the stairs to my apartment when it suddenly seemed like too great of a coincidence to have that car going in Dean's general direction. He should have been long gone before the Vic got near him, but I thought I'd better check it out, just in case. I ran down the stairs, bolted from the lobby, and dodged pedestrians and cars until I reached James Avenue. There was a body lying on the road about halfway down the block. I ran down the middle of the street, hoping it wasn't my brother. I pulled out my cell to call 911.

"Dean...Dean!" I shouted as I knelt next to him. He didn't respond. He had a large gash on his forehead and a bullet hole in his left shoulder. The bloodstain on his shirt was steadily growing. I whipped off my polo shirt and applied direct pressure to the wound. Then I heard a pop and the crack of metal right next to my head. Dammit, the shooter was still trying to kill us. He must have parked the Crown Vic on Irving Avenue and snuck between the houses to access Dean, who would have been unawares.

I couldn't run for cover and let my brother bleed to death. So, I lay on the

223

ground next to him, holding the shirt in place while trying to remain calm enough to explain the emergency to the 911 operator. I hoped the shooter wouldn't finish us off execution-style in the middle of the street.

"Come on, Dean, stay with me," I begged, knowing he couldn't hear me. The pool of blood oozing out from under him was getting bigger, and I was starting to panic. How could I dodge bullets and put direct pressure on both sides of my brother while he was sprawled out in the street, all at the same time?

Sirens emerged from the background din, and a squad car soon arrived. Two policemen got out with their hands on their weapons. They scanned the surrounding area. Where the hell was the damn ambulance?

"My brother's been shot."

"An ambulance is on the way. It should be here any minute."

More squad cars arrived, and police began securing the street with crime scene tape. Soon we were surrounded by cops and gawkers. The EMTs arrived moments later and immediately took over. They checked Dean's back, then put him on a gurney and hustled him into the ambulance. I jumped in, and we headed off, lights flashing and sirens blaring. The ER staff at Hennepin County Medical Center were experts at dealing with gunshot victims, so that's where we headed.

As we whizzed through the streets, I texted Kate to let her know Dean had been shot. She was horrified and offered to meet me at the ER, but I told her to wait until we knew more. It could be a very long night. When we finally arrived, the ER staff bolted into action, taking Dean into the surgery unit. I was escorted to a waiting area, which was frustrating as hell as I wanted to be doing something, anything, to help.

As I sat there trying not to think about the worst-case scenarios, I hoped my meager actions had been enough to get Dean through this. Oddly, it reminded me of a time when Dean had saved my bacon. Growing up Catholic, our parents had signed us up to be altar boys, and we usually served at mass together. On one particular Sunday, Dean had the flu, so another boy was called to take his place. At the end of the service, the other boy quickly left so he wouldn't be late for a baseball game, leaving me to put away the vestments from the service. Father Timothy startled me by sneaking up from behind and putting his hands on my shoulders.

"I'm glad you stayed behind to help out, Grayson. You're a good boy. I've been watching you, and I have something special I want to show you."

Something didn't seem right, and I was getting scared. I thought about running away, but the priest had me by the shoulders and wouldn't let go.

"You don't have to be afraid, Grayson. I'm not going to hurt you." Father Timothy lowered himself and turned me around to look me squarely in the eyes. "I'd like you to come back to the Rectory with me right now, okay? I have something there for you to see."

The priest took me by the hand, and I did as I was told. We were soon walking through the narrow corridors of the Rectory to the priest's room, which was small and confining. Father Timothy closed the door and began massaging my shoulders. He brought me closer and began moving in when the door burst open. Dean was standing there, breathing hard, in a cold sweat.

"Father, please stop. Let him go."

Father Timothy looked at Dean. "Sure. Grayson, you run home. Dean, why don't you stay here with me until you catch your breath?"

Dean walked into the small room, grabbed me, and pushed me toward the door. "Go home. Run home. I'll be right there."

As the door was closing, I saw Dean turning and bravely looking the priest in the eyes. I had no idea why he was going to stay with Father Timothy, but it didn't seem right. I sobbed all the way home and tried to tell my parents Dean was in some kind of trouble, but I didn't know what it was. My parents checked his bedroom and realized he was gone. They decided to head over to the church when Dean walked in, his clothes disheveled, his face betraying intense pain and disgust. As Mom embraced him to make him feel better, she noticed he was burning with fever again.

"My gosh, Ben, he's burning up! Help me get him back to bed."

Dad scooped up his son and headed upstairs to his room.

Mom followed closely at his heels. "We've got you now, Dean. You're going to be okay."

I stayed in the living room, trying to make sense of the situation. Later that day, I told my parents what had happened and asked them to explain why Father Timothy wanted Dean to stay with him. They told me it was nothing. He just wanted to take care of Dean because he looked so ill. A few weeks later, I heard Father Timothy had transferred to a new parish in another state.

As I got older, I realized the true nature of the sacrifice my brother had made for me. By some unspoken agreement, we never discussed that day again. I only hoped I had somehow helped even the score.

After a few hours, which seemed like days, an ER doctor came out with an update. One of the bullets had nicked an artery, which was why he had been bleeding so much. They had been able to patch him up and move him to a regular room. The doctor told me he should fully recover, but anything strenuous, such as setting a trap for a killer, was out of the question for the next few weeks. Kate and I were going to have to handle this on our own.

I texted her with the good news and asked if she still wanted to go through with the plan to catch a murderer. Of course, she did, she said—anything to bring them to justice.

To add insult to Dean's injury, a few minutes later, I received a text from the killer's number. **Now I know you will be alone for our meeting.**

I didn't dignify that with a response. He must have figured Dean and I were at my apartment planning the meeting together, then drove over and waited out front for Dean to leave. What a son-of-a-bitch. I wanted to push my hands through the screen and rip out his throat.

I pulled up at the main entrance of Hennepin County Medical Center on Tuesday morning to pick up my brother.

Dean walked out and let himself into the car. "Thanks for picking me up."

"No worries." He had a large bandage covering six stitches in his forehead from where his head hit his car after he'd been shot. Considering he had recently been shot in the chest, the hospital staff undoubtedly wanted to bring him to the car in a wheelchair, but he would have none of that.

"All that lying around gave me a great idea for improving the facial recognition device."

Nothing about Dean surprised me anymore. "Really, what would that be?"

"I think I'd rather show you when it's done. It should only take a day or two. My company is insisting I take some time off to *recuperate*," he said with air quotes. "I'll have it ready in plenty of time for Bingo Night."

One thing was still bugging me about the night he was shot. "The Crown Vic passed my place about five or ten minutes after you left. Why were you still there? You should have been long gone."

A sheepish look crossed Dean's face, and he mumbled something I didn't catch. Then it hit me.

"You were still trying to unlock your car with the fingerprint scanner!"

Since his fancy, malfunctioning car security system had turned him into an open target, I needled him the entire way home. That was what brothers were for, right? As I pulled up to his house, he suddenly got serious.

"Thanks for saving my life, Bro."

"It was nothing. Consider it payback."

"Payback? For what?"

"For the time you saved me from Father Timothy. You made quite a sacrifice." I used my most sincere voice.

Dean burst into laughter and then put a hand on his chest. "Ow. Stop it. You're killing me here."

Now I was pissed. It was just like Dean to turn a poignant moment into something stupid.

"How can you laugh at something so horrific?"

"Don't you think it was hilarious?"

"What, getting molested by a priest?"

"Holy crap! I never told you, did I?"

My blood was boiling. "Never told me what?"

"Gray, don't you remember how sick I was? I had a horrible fever and ran all the way to the church. As soon as you closed the door behind you, I threw up all over him and his room."

Chapter Twenty-Seven

Wednesday, May 10

I met Dean at his house on Wednesday afternoon so he could show me his new and improved facial recognition rig. It was awesome. Then I met Kate at the church at five, so we could move it into place without the early-bird Bingo practitioners seeing us. We figured the monsignor would show up about six-thirty after the players had become engrossed in the game, so we'd agreed to be in position by six twenty. Dean had simplified the use of the scanner, but I had to admit I was a bit nervous without him there.

There were two smaller meeting rooms just down the hall from the Bingo room. We set up the rig in the larger one, which usually sat about twenty people. It should give us enough privacy to unmask the killer without too much risk to the general public.

We were ready by five fifteen, so Kate and I put on our bright yellow Bingo Night volunteer shirts and went over to the main hall to help with the setup. I wouldn't be able to hang out with Kate or even talk to her while we were volunteering, but it was better than the two of us sitting around in the side room waiting to serve justice.

The Bingo Night crowd started filing in, and I was soon busy peddling Bingo cards while Kate was making change and coercing new volunteers. DeeDee and Harry were at their usual table near the back, and I managed to avoid her gaze. I feared she would soon start waving to get my attention, but once the first game started, she got down to business. I checked the time on my phone—6:15, which gave me five minutes to get into position. Someone waved for more cards, and I was heading toward them when a subtle change swept over the crowd. Boisterous laughter became subdued, and people were whispering in reverent tones and glancing at the main entrance. Even the caller noticed, and he held the next ball for a few moments.

I turned around to see the bishop and monsignor had arrived and were working the crowd, probably to say thanks for supporting the church and whatnot. Kate and I looked at each other in a panic. If, for some crazy reason, the monsignor went to our meeting arm-in-arm with the bishop, we'd have to change our plans dramatically and on the fly or maybe just cancel them altogether. I started drifting toward Kate but strayed too close to DeeDee's table.

"Psst, Grayson." She spoke in the hushed tones Catholics always seemed to use in church or when clergy members were present. "Good to see you again."

"Good to see you too, DeeDee," I whispered back. When in Rome, right?

"Isn't it exciting the bishop is here tonight? He only shows up now and again. It's a real thrill to see him."

"It sure is." I agreed to keep the conversation moving along. "I'm running out of cards. I need to get some more from Kate."

DeeDee pulled on my arm so I'd lean over, and she could whisper into my ear even more conspiratorially. "I see the way you've been looking at her, Gray. I think you two are up to something."

That hit me like a taser, and I almost dropped the Bingo cards. She was perceptive, but how much had she figured out? Then the knowing grin on her face made me realize she was talking about our relationship.

"You're the only one here clever enough to spot us, DeeDee." I winked at her. "But please don't tell anyone. We want to keep it to ourselves until we know where this is going."

DeeDee seemed flattered to be in on the love conspiracy. "Of course, Gray. You can count on me."

I put the remaining cards on the table under Harry's urn. "Thanks, DeeDee.

229

Here, you and Harry play these cards as a gift from me for helping us out. I'll pay Kate for them."

She smiled, and my face warmed a little.

That was my cue to extricate myself and go directly to the main entrance to get a new batch of cards. I tried to give the new guests a wide berth, but the monsignor turned around, and our eyes locked. His face grew dark. He was onto us. He must have brought the bishop along so he could turn the tables on us later. I smiled, nodded once, and kept moving.

I drew near to Kate, trying to look nonchalant.

"What do we do now?" she asked.

"If he brings the bishop along, we'll have to abort. But if he shows up alone, we should be okay." My phone read 6:35 as I put it away. Considering he was in the same room, we probably had schedule flexibility, but I wanted to get this done. "Let's go to the meeting room and see what he does."

Kate nodded.

Before leaving, I turned back to check Frank's whereabouts one more time, but he was nowhere to be seen.

"Kate, he's gone. Frank's gone. We've got to get over there."

She looked around, nodded at me, and asked one of the other yellow shirts to cover the operation. We headed toward the main entrance as quickly as we could without seeming suspicious. I turned to scan the hall for the Monsignor one last time and noticed DeeDee giving me a thumbs-up with a twinkle in her eye. I smiled back and left.

I ran down the hall to the meeting room with Kate right behind me. The monsignor didn't pass us in the hallway, so I figured the room would be empty and rushed in. But a masked person in loose-fitting black sweats was standing near the left wall, pointing a gun at us. Okay, this wasn't going to plan. How could we call for help without being shot?

I no longer cared about unmasking anyone. My concern now was for Kate's safety, but the gun didn't seem to scare her. "You don't need the mask anymore. We know who you are," she yelled. She must really loathe Frank because she was sticking to the plan.

"I don't think so," was the response.

There was a slight bump near their mouth. The person must have been using a voice modulator as the words came out garbled and in a low register. It sounded like a reporter interviewing an anonymous witness on TV. The sweats made it difficult to tell the size of the person underneath. But he was Frank's height, so it must have been him. I wondered how he had changed clothes so quickly. But that didn't matter. With Dean's new and improved rig, all I had to do was push a button on the remote, which I could do through the material of my pants. I slowly moved my hand but didn't feel anything in my pocket but some coins. A quick downward glance confirmed the small remote was on the table a few feet away. In all of the excitement, I must have left it there.

"Did you think you could get away with it?" I asked to stall for time as I slowly moved toward the table.

"Get away with what? I didn't do anything."

"Then why are you wearing a mask?" Kate asked.

"I don't want to be accused of murder. Just give me the letter, and you'll never hear from me again."

"Fine. It's in the bag over there." I indicated the bag I'd used to bring in the rig and had left by the wall.

"Stay where you are," the voice croaked as the killer moved toward the bag. As soon as they looked down, I reached over and hit the button on the remote. The top panel on the rig slid open, and a small drone deployed. It raised a few feet and then started scanning the room. The killer pointed their gun at it, but it was too late.

"Hello, Jane." Stephen Hawkins's voice rang out from the drone. "Welcome to my world."

Chapter Twenty-Eight

Wednesday Evening, May 10

J ane stripped off the mask and threw it at Kate, who instinctively ducked. Jane took advantage of the distraction and bolted into the hallway, but I ran after her. She didn't get far before I grabbed her. She elbowed me hard in the stomach and broke free, then backed away and pointed her gun at me in what was quickly becoming a hostage situation.

"Give me the gun, Jane."

"No way, Grayson. Try to get it away from me. I dare you."

Just then, the bishop and monsignor arrived in the hallway, probably on their way back to the Rectory. The monsignor must have gone to the restroom when he left the main hall. DeeDee was right behind them, holding Harry and looking inquisitive as usual.

"What's all this about?" The pleasant look on the bishop's face turned to anger and fear when he saw the gun. "Jane, what are you doing?"

She didn't respond as she desperately looked for a way to escape. I was blocking one end of the hall, and Tom, Frank, and DeeDee were blocking the other. Jane knew she was trapped and seemed to be thinking about shooting her way out.

"Get out of my way," she screamed.

That wasn't going to happen. I dove for her arm, which spun her away from Kate and me, but she must have panicked because she pulled the trigger. The sound was deafening in the narrow hallway. It took a moment for me to realize she had hit the bishop, who started staggering. The monsignor, ever the one to immediately assess and fix any situation, grabbed him by the waist and slowly sank to the floor with him so he wouldn't get hurt by the fall. He also took out his phone to call 911.

I clutched Jane by the arm and grabbed the gun. She let it go as she broke away to rush to Tom's side, looking horrified. As she put direct pressure on the wound in his abdomen, she screamed, "We have to save him. Get me some towels." Then she turned to face him directly. "Don't worry, Tom. I'll take care of you. I always have."

Kate ran to get some towels from the kitchen. I ran down to the bingo hall entrance while tucking the gun into my waistband behind my back and grabbed the nearest volunteer. I told him there had been a shooting and asked him to close the doors and keep everyone in the room until the police arrived. I returned to the room. Kate came rushing back and handed Jane some clean towels to help stop the blood flow.

Tom was wounded but still coherent. "Jane, what is going on? Why did you have a gun?"

In the meantime, my mind was reeling. I had been so focused on Frank being the killer I'd never considered Jane. Now that I knew it was her, the reasons for James's murder became apparent, especially after her last pronouncement. Every last loose thread came together. Why hadn't I thought of this before? "She's in love with you, Tom. She's been in love with you since Rochester."

Tom looked confused, and Frank was scowling at me, but neither of them said a word. DeeDee was cowering next to them, probably having a flashback to when she'd nearly been shot if Harry's urn hadn't taken the bullet.

"She's so obsessed she killed James for you."

"That's crazy. Jane, is that true?"

Jane didn't respond, so I continued.

"Jane's been in love with you for years, Tom. I read the letter in your filing cabinet she wrote to you when she was still a nun."

A shocked expression covered Jane's face, yet she seemed oddly pleased. "You kept my letter?"

"Yes, but it's not what you think," Tom stammered. "I thought you loved me for my faith in God and the church...for what we were doing for the community, not in love with me as a person. But never mind that. You killed my brother? Why would you do that?"

Before Jane had a chance to respond, I looked Tom straight in the eye. "I know why. It all goes back to one simple truth. James isn't our father." I paused to drum up the courage. "You are."

Anger took over Tom's face as he struggled to get up, but neither Frank nor Jane would let him.

"There's no point in denying it, Tom. I'm going to have proof in a few days. Remember when someone broke into the Rectory? That was me. I borrowed a sample of your hair from the floor and submitted it to a lab for DNA testing. The results will confirm you're my biological father and Dean's, too."

Tom winced as he tried to talk. Jane was successfully holding back the blood flow, but it must have been painful.

"You must be delirious," he finally stammered.

"No. I don't think so. It's the only thing that makes sense. You were having an affair with Maggie at Holy Redeemer in Rochester when she got pregnant. You paid for her stay at Wilkes and arranged for the Dyles to adopt the baby. You asked Jane, who was known as Sister Anna back then, to support her, and she was happy to help. You convinced James to tell those in your inner circle that he was the father. You would have been kicked out of the priesthood if the truth had come out. No one knew you were Dean's father but Maggie, James, and you. Frank figured it out later, but you bought him off with a monsignor-ship.

"You had covered it all up, but you couldn't stay away from Maggie. She became pregnant again, so you ran the same routine. When Maggie died, you must have figured your secret was safe. If we came looking for you, James would claim to be our father, and there would be no one left to deny it. But you couldn't have foreseen the availability of DNA testing."

I looked at Jane. "After James agreed to meet Dean and me for dinner, he called you, asking for advice. I'll bet he was going to tell us Tom was our birth father and figured we'd keep it quiet. Even if we didn't, it wouldn't matter that much because it all happened so long ago. But you didn't want to risk Tom's secret getting out, and you made him promise to tell us he was our birth father. Then you waited outside the restaurant and went back to his office with him to make sure he had."

Jane looked down and sighed. "After your dinner, he changed his mind. He said you deserved to know the truth. I couldn't let that happen. Tom would have been disgraced, and it would have ruined everything." Something wasn't quite right here, but what was it?

Tom seemed to be struggling to grasp the depth of her devotion. "That's why you killed James?"

"You would have lost your position as bishop, and they would have forced you out of the priesthood."

"Then I would have gotten what I deserved. Nothing is worth taking a life."

Jane continued. "But they found Maggie's letter—after all these years. I should have destroyed it when I had a chance. James said Grayson wouldn't show it to him, so I didn't know if you had been named. I had to have it to see what they knew."

I jumped in again. "That's why she shot Dean and shot at me, too, to stop our investigation and get her hands on that letter. The incredibly tragic part of this whole thing is that Maggie didn't reveal any other names in that letter."

Jane's face fell as the realization that she had almost killed Dean and me for nothing hit her hard.

The sirens were getting louder, and I was glad to have finally caught James's killer, but something was still bothering me. Then I realized we still had another murder to solve, and another flash of insight struck.

I turned on Jane again. "Wait a minute. When Dean was born, you thought James was the father, like everyone else, right? You didn't know Tom had been sleeping around."

Jane looked down as the tears began to flow. "I had no idea. They both lied to me about James being the father. So, I decided to help them out and watch over Maggie at Wilkes. I even delivered that damn letter." She trailed off, sobbing.

"Then you found out Maggie was pregnant with me, and you went up to help her again. She must have confided in you that Tom was the birth father. She told you how much in love they were, and you couldn't stand it. You decided Maggie needed to go away for good so no more love children would be born."

Jane sobbed even harder. Now that her final secret was out, she seemed to want to confess everything. "When they came to take Dean away, and I cut the ID band from his tiny little wrist, it felt like I was cutting his umbilical cord...as if I were freeing him from being bound to this girl and to the birth father, who, I thought, was James. I was setting him free and was setting them free, too. I thought everyone would have a fresh start. But then she got pregnant again and asked for my help. Right before she delivered, she told me the truth—that Tom was the birth father. I was shocked and appalled. I must have lost my mind for a moment and yanked at her afterbirth because the next thing I knew, it was on the floor, and Maggie was hemorrhaging badly. There was blood everywhere. Then Frank was telling me we needed to get out of there right away."

Frank wasn't about to let that go without an argument. "Wait a damn minute here—"

I jumped in. "Shut up, Frank. You weren't trying to kill anyone. You were trying to prevent Sister Anna from doing anything stupid, but you were too late. You couldn't stop Maggie from bleeding to death, so the fixer kicked in and cleaned up the evidence so Anna wouldn't be blamed."

Frank's evil glare was probably a warning there would be payback for telling him to shut up, but his silence confirmed it was true.

"After that, I realized I couldn't live with being a nun anymore. I left the convent and went back to my original name." She looked at Tom lovingly. "I thought you'd leave the priesthood to be with me, but you didn't, so I followed you instead."

"But you were worried about yourself, too," I continued. "You figured James would tell us everything and maybe even accuse you of causing

Maggie's death, so he had to go. You also cracked me on the skull and pushed me into that hole. You bribed the receptionist at Wilkes to watch for Dean and me so she could warn you if we ever showed up looking for information. And you killed Evelyn Goodland, who was one of the midwives at Dean's birth, so we couldn't question her. My god, the depth of your depravity is truly disgusting."

Jane scowled at me. "Yes…No…I don't know anymore." She looked at Tom. "What have I done? I'm so sorry for everything. Now your secret will get out for certain."

I realized she was right. Nobody wanted Tom's secret to get out, least of all me. As much as I disrespected the man for getting a young girl pregnant—twice—I didn't want to see him disgraced, and stripping him of his position wouldn't bring anyone back. Truth be told, I was watching out for my own best interests, too. The thought of Dean and me being known as the adopted guys whose birth father was a Catholic bishop and whose mere existence had resulted in multiple murders was mind-numbing. There was no way to escape that kind of notoriety once it tainted you.

I also realized that, despite her meager confession, there was no way to prove Jane had killed Maggie. The only potential witness was Frank, and he wasn't going to implicate her. If anything, he would claim Maggie's death had been an accident and Jane was innocent. But, I was betting that she used the gun currently tucked into my waistband to kill both James and Evelyn Goodland, which would implicate her in that murder as well. So, even though we were talking about my birth mother's life, convicting Jane of two murders would have to be good enough.

I leaned down and whispered so that only Jane could hear me. "I'll make you a deal. You confess to killing James because you didn't want him to admit he was our father so it wouldn't embarrass the church and to killing Evelyn to hide the truth. We'll tell the police James was our real father, and Tom's secret will be safe."

Her face lit a tiny bit as if a heavy burden had been lifted, and she nodded vigorously.

At that moment, the police and paramedics swarmed in. Among them was

Detective Copeland, who quickly took control of the scene. I immediately handed the gun to one of the uniformed officers and explained what had happened. Within a few minutes, the police ascertained there was no imminent threat, so they cleared the way for the paramedics to do their job. While they were distracted, locking down the scene, I told Kate about the deal I'd cut with Jane, and she quickly agreed to follow along. I knew Dean would, too, however reluctant he might be to be involved in something untoward. We obviously didn't have to worry about Frank or Jane saying anything, so Tom's secret should be safe.

DeeDee was a bit of a wild card, though. I knew she'd readily agree to keep silent and was undoubtedly delighted to be in the know, but could she keep her story straight if anyone asked about this in the future? I guessed we'd just have to trust her.

As I brainstormed options for tying up this potential loose end, I realized I had become a fixer. Not at Frank's level, of course. It would take years to get there, but a fixer, nonetheless. The terrifying part was it had come so easily that it almost seemed natural. I wondered if this was how Frank got his start, covering up a crisis for a worthy cause and then spiraling downward toward a path of no return. It suddenly struck me as a design flaw in the human condition. Most people had the best of intentions but were unwilling or unable to stop themselves from doing the wrong thing. I guess that was why they called it free will.

Detective Copeland spotted me in the crowd and interrupted my gloominess by starting right in. "A shooting at the church, and look who's here. Grayson Dyle. Why am I not surprised?"

Chapter Twenty-Nine

Sunday, May 14

C opeland and a host of other detectives grilled us for hours that night, dragging us through every detail over and over again. I worried the entire time one of us would say something suspicious or slip and refer to Tom as our biological father, but we all managed to hold it together. Once Jane knew we claimed James was the biological father and Tom's reputation would be intact, she admitted she killed both James Brennen and Evelyn Goodland. The case was going to be closed, and Jane was going away for a long, long time.

Tom had been lucky. Even though he had been shot at close range, the 22-caliber bullet had missed his vital organs. But a bishop getting shot while visiting his flock at the church during Bingo Night made national news. They tracked his condition hourly for the first day or two until it became clear he was out of danger. Then most of the national news outlets moved on to the next political crisis, while the ones that covered religious news changed their reporting to a human-interest angle. The press wrote any number of puff pieces about Tom's dedication to the community, his courageousness in the face of danger, and the damn-near miraculous way he had escaped death. There were pictures of Tom posing with various dignitaries, famous well-wishers, and other hangers-on.

Frank must have loved the attention because he could be spotted skulking in the background of most of the pictures, usually with a devious smirk. He looked as if he was trying to figure out how to work this newfound interest in Tom and his parish to their mutual advantage but was coming up short. At least, that was how he looked to me.

The spin on the church's report regarding Sister Anna/Principal Jane was nothing short of genius, and it had Frank's fingerprints all over it. The story went that a local school principal accidentally shot the bishop in a case of mistaken identity. She had been exhausted from fundraising for the school, and after a particularly taxing Bingo Night, she was walking through the darkened corridor outside the main hall when two men approached. Fearful they were there to steal the Bingo money, she drew the pistol she carried for protection and accidentally discharged the weapon, striking the bishop in the abdomen. She was incredibly sorry, and Bishop Tom magnanimously forgave her completely, which made him even more of a hero in the eyes of many. The need for a principal to carry a gun for protection within her own grade school was chalked up to the country's sorry state of affairs.

Frank must have convinced the St. Paul Police to delay the announcement that they had solved James Brennen's murder because it hadn't hit the news cycle yet. I figured a certain reclusive nun named Sister Anna would get the blame. Maybe they would say she'd become delusional after forty years of cloistering, blamed the bishop for her current situation, and shot his brother to death thinking she was shooting him. I could see a lot of people thinking it wouldn't take forty years for them to open up on someone in those circumstances.

When the story finally did break, the local press would heap praises on the police for solving the murder of a prominent local attorney, and the dignitaries would take a victory lap. It probably wouldn't even hit the national news. They would bury the ballistics report that showed the bullets that killed James matched the one that injured the bishop, and life would go on. With Sister Anna going to jail or a psych hospital, Frank would have to explain the disappearance of Principal Jane, but I had no doubt he'd pull that off, too. It would probably involve her taking early retirement at her remote cabin in Montana due to her embarrassment at shooting a member of the clergy.

Kate and I had been through a lot together in the relatively brief time we knew each other, and we managed to squeeze in another date on the Friday after the shooting. She told me she was looking for another volunteer to replace her in doing the parish books as she didn't know if she could work with the bishop after everything that had happened. She was surprised when I told her I was thinking about visiting Tom.

"You've got to be kidding me. After all of his coverups and lies, why would you do that?"

"I don't know why, Kate. I can't explain it. I'd like to know about my birth family. Now that I've found my real birth father, I want to know…need to know what kind of person he is."

"Maybe you should wait six months or a year, so neither of you will say something you'll regret later."

"That's a definite possibility, but I'd like to spend the next six to twelve months trying to decide if I want him in my life over the long term. I can't do that now because I don't feel like I know the real Tom."

"Are you going to invite Dean?"

"Of course, but I doubt he'll go. He's still pretty bent out of shape about the whole thing. If anyone needs a year to cool down, it's Dean. Hey, why don't we get together after I meet with him? You can talk me down from the edge."

"Grayson Dyle, are you hitting on me?"

I loved the wicked grin she used to say things like that.

"Maybe. Who wants to know?"

I'd called Dean the next day, and, to my great surprise and sudden suspicion, he agreed to go. After that, I'd called the hospital to see when Tom would be receiving visitors and was told to contact a certain monsignor, who was screening the bishop's meetings. Frank begrudgingly consented to ask Tom if he'd meet with us. Tom must have agreed with great enthusiasm because Frank called me right back to set a date for Sunday afternoon. He reminded me that if any of the hospital staff or, God forbid, members of the press asked about our relationship with the bishop, we should say we were his nephews who were concerned for the welfare of our uncle as if we needed to be reminded of that.

Dean and I had met at one of the trendy restaurants along Mears Park to plan our approach to the meeting. He was simultaneously proud his device helped solve the murders, disappointed he missed all the action, and miffed that I had suspected Tom was our father without telling him. I explained I didn't want to accuse Tom of anything until I was sure. As usual, he got over it quickly, and we moved on.

Airing grievances with Tom would be an entirely different matter. Now that he privately acknowledged his parenthood, our relationship was going to change, and it was going to get a lot more complicated before it got easier. Dean wasn't sure he wanted to have a relationship with Tom, biological father or not, because of his secret affair with Maggie and the deceit he had displayed over the past forty-plus years to cover it up. While I agreed Tom certainly was no saint, it only seemed fair to allow him to explain himself. I also pointed out we had already lost an adoptive father whom we dearly loved, and it would be a shame not to establish a relationship with our birth father while we still had the chance. In the end, we both wanted to see what he had to say for himself.

On Sunday afternoon, four days after the incident, Dean and I checked in with the security guard controlling access to Tom's floor at the hospital. Frank had been gracious enough to add our names to the list of approved guests, but just for this one meeting. We would have to discuss who controlled access to our biological father, but that could wait for another time.

"Grayson, Dean, how good to see you again."

We walked over and shook the bishop's hand. The bed had been arranged with the back tilted up so Tom could receive visitors from a more dignified sitting position. He might be in a hospital bed, but he wasn't going to show signs of weakness.

"Good to see you again...Bishop," I said as Dean and I sat in the chairs arranged along the bed.

"Please. Call me Tom."

"Good to see you, Tom," said Dean.

"Thanks for making time to see us," I said. "According to the press, you should be released in a couple of days, which is good to hear."

"I have a feeling the doctors are keeping me here longer than necessary to be certain nothing goes wrong. You wouldn't want to have the national news saying they botched a simple gunshot wound."

Was it me, or was he enjoying the attention a bit too much? "Is the hospital food as bad as they say?"

"Worse. Of course, we don't have gourmet meals at the Rectory, so it's not much of a change. What would you like to talk about?"

I went first. "It's hard to know where to start. I have to admit I was crushed to find out James had been killed right after he told us he was our biological father, especially coming so soon after we buried Ben." I paused, considering what to say next.

Tom waited patiently.

"While James's death was certainly tragic, I'm grateful to know he wasn't our biological father after all, and you're still here with us. But, as thankful as I am for that, I have a tough time accepting your actions, especially coming from a priest and not only a priest but a bishop."

Tom looked down and pursed his lips.

Dean could contain himself no longer. "Tom...you left us. You abandoned us. You got a young girl pregnant, twice, and then you abandoned us, your own flesh and blood. How could you do that? What would you have done with Maggie if she hadn't died? Abandon her, too? Maybe get her out of the way by sending her off to a convent so you could go on with your wonderful life, being loved by all? Then, after all of that, you told Cathy her recently deceased husband, James, was our father, so no one would think it was you. How can you call yourself a man of the cloth, a bishop, no less, when you've done all these things? And who knows what else you've done. How is it that a bishop needs a fixer? What other nasty things have you done that Frank has made go away? You disgust me." After that tirade, I thought he might bolt from the room, but he sat back down, seething.

Tom must have known this was coming. He also must have known there was no way to defend his actions, and he didn't even try. "I'm not going to deny my role in all of this, but I lost a brother because of you two. If you and Grayson hadn't gone around stirring up the mud, James would still be alive, Jane wouldn't be in jail, and I would never have been shot."

Dean was furious. "You're trying to pin James's death on us? How about Maggie? Is that our fault too? Maybe you shouldn't have been having sex with an innocent young girl. Did you ever think of that?"

Tom looked down and was quiet for a minute. When he finally did speak, his voice was halting and full of remorse. If it was an act, it was one of the best I'd seen. "Of course, I thought of that. I've thought of that every day since she died. I loved her, you know...really loved her...and she loved me. It just wouldn't work. It couldn't work." Tom's face scrunched up in pain. "I was dedicated to the priesthood...there were things I wanted to do... that I needed to do. I wanted to help people. I have helped people...lots of people. How could I do that if I'd been defrocked? Maggie didn't want that either. She supported me and my calling one hundred percent."

"Maybe being kicked out of the priesthood would have been the best thing for you and Maggie." I spoke in a low tone, trying to de-escalate, but Dean wasn't having it.

He was livid. "You're saying the ends justified the means?"

Tom looked up, his face turning red. "Who are you to judge me? I've done a lot of good for a lot of people. I taught the priests in my parishes how to look out for the people, how to help them out with their daily struggles when they can." He turned to me. "Didn't you ever wonder why Mike Wilson called your company out of the blue and asked you to bid on his new project? Frank set that up. I'd been keeping an eye on both of you through social media and news stories, and when I read that a Chinese company had purchased one of your big clients, I thought maybe your business would be in trouble. I asked Frank if he could help out somehow. He called Mike, who was already working for the church, and asked him if he had any work he could farm out to you. Mike said he did, but he would only use you if you could get the job done. Frank agreed. It was all he could ask. Mike loved your design work, by the way. You earned that business on your own merits."

That explained a lot. "It's your network of priests in action." I was stunned he had the foresight to see my company was going to have financial issues, had convinced Frank to help us out, and he'd already heard we'd won the business with Mike—we'd only closed the deal two days ago, which was after he'd been shot.

"That's right, Grayson. We try to help wherever we can. There are dozens of stories just like yours. Hundreds. You thought Frank was a big bad fixer whose only purpose was to save the church from various scandals. Well, he might be a fixer, but he spends the vast majority of his time trying to help people fix their own lives. They can make such a mess of things sometimes."

At that moment, I knew he was referring to himself, and I also realized something else. "Falling in love, having children, Maggie's death...you realized your life was out of control. You used that experience to turn your life around, didn't you?" This put a whole new spin on Tom and the entire situation.

"Dean—Grayson—as human beings, we're flawed. We were created that way by God so we would have free will. Love is only real when you choose it for yourself. Look into your heart. You know that to be the truth. If the church had forced Ben and Linda to take you in, they might have done it, but they wouldn't have loved you. It was when they chose to adopt you that you became precious to them. How ironic is it that God, who could create anything He wanted to with perfection, purposely created us with a design flaw and, in doing so, He found the perfect design."

The perfect design was the design with a flaw in it. It would take me a bit of thinking to wrap my mind around that one. There was one thing I knew for certain. Being shot had in no way diminished Tom's ability to preach.

Dean still didn't seem to be buying it, but he seemed to have lost his will to fight. "You're just using this as an excuse for your crappy behavior," he said, almost under his breath.

It would be difficult to get past our angry feelings for this man any time soon.

"I'm sorry," Tom said. "I'm sorry for everything bad that happened. I hope you can find it in your hearts to forgive me."

"We're working on it...Tom," I said halfheartedly. "We should probably go."

As we headed out, one thing was clear. It was going to be a complicated relationship. Now that we finally found our real biological father, I couldn't see abandoning him. But it would take some time to forgive him, no matter how good his intentions might have been.

That evening, Kate came to my place to get caught up and help make dinner. She looked gorgeous in a simple royal-blue cotton T-shirt and faded jeans. I thought it would be nice to chat for a bit first, so I opened a bottle of red, poured two glasses, and passed along Dean's update about the drones while we stared at the calm, dark-blue water of the partially unobstructed lake. "X loved the idea. He started acting like a kid with a new toy. He told Dean to stop what he was doing, and they spent an entire afternoon coming up with phrases that were short enough for the drones to spell but still make sense as clues. His fiance loved it, too."

"So, she accepted his proposal. That's great!"

"Yep, now they're off planning some elaborate wedding. Thanks for your help with that, Kate. You're amazing." Then I told her about the meeting with Tom.

"You're the amazing one, Grayson Dyle," she said.

As glad as I was to hear her say it, I wanted to know more. "Why is that?"

"I don't think I'd be able to do what you're doing."

"Which is what?"

"Trying to forge some kind of relationship with your father. He's been such a deceitful man. I can't imagine you wanting to be around him."

"That's one way to look at it."

"What's another way?"

"He made a lot of mistakes in his life, no doubt, but he's learned from them, which made him realize he wanted to serve people, to give something back. In a way, I think he learned a lesson a lot of other church leaders never did. That being a priest isn't just about saying mass and doling out sacraments. That it's first and foremost about helping people, and he's trained the younger priests around him to serve that way, too. If there was ever a way to save the church from itself, this could be it."

Kate considered this for a minute and must have agreed. "Maybe I don't have to give up my volunteer work for the church after all."

"That's the spirit. Besides, if it weren't for his indiscretions, you'd be talking to yourself right now."

It was good to see her smile. Unfortunately, there was one more thing I needed to clear up.

"Kate, I have to ask you something. Remember when we were at my place planning the trap for Frank, and you mentioned the bloody sole prints? Copeland never asked you about them, did he?"

Kate looked down. "No, but you knew that when you gave me the excuse, didn't you? Thanks for doing that, by the way."

"No worries." I paused, then hit her with what could only be called an accusation. "You were there the night James was killed, weren't you? Why didn't you say anything?"

"The whole thing was so surreal. I guess I panicked. I didn't want you to think I was involved."

"What happened?"

Kate's voice was getting thick, and she was tearing up a bit. I hated pressing her on this, but I had no choice. I was pretty sure I knew what had happened, but I wanted to hear it from her. If we were going to make it over the long term, she needed to know I had this intense curiosity that I sometimes couldn't avoid. She would have to decide if that was a deal-breaker for her.

"I was working late when James came back after your dinner, and I could tell he was upset. Being alone in the office with him was nerve-racking, especially with his odd mood, so I went down the hall to the restroom before he got any ideas. A few minutes later, I heard the shots. I didn't know what to do. I know I should have run out to see if anyone had been shot so I could call 911, but they say it's best not to confront an active shooter, so I stayed in the bathroom."

She seemed to be reliving the events of that night as she retold them, the self-recrimination evident in her voice. She took a sip of wine and haltingly continued. "Not knowing what was happening in the office was making me crazy. After about ten minutes, I couldn't stand it, so I ran back to the office and realized James had been shot. By then, I knew he was dead, and I couldn't help thinking I might have saved him if I hadn't been such a coward. I was so scared. I knew I should have called the police, but I'd never seen a dead body before. I just…froze. Then Frank's voice started echoing around my head. It kept saying he would get me out of this mess…as if I was guilty and needed his help. I hate to admit it was oddly reassuring. I got my phone out to call him, but I was tired of being under his thumb. I was trying to figure out what to do when I heard someone at the front door. I ran to my office and turned out the lights. After you walked by, I snuck out."

"How much did you take?"

She crossed her arms and looked up, frowning. "Gray, what do you mean?"

"It's okay, Kate. I know. You can tell me. How much money did you take?"

I'd never seen anyone burst into tears before, never even understood the expression until that moment. I handed her a nearby box of tissues, and she took a couple to wipe her eyes.

"Ten thousand dollars…from the Bingo fund at the church. How did you know?"

"It's the only reason you wouldn't have told me you were there. We could have given each other alibis, and we would have called the police right away. You were there returning the money, weren't you?"

She looked down again, her face turning beet red. "Yes. It was the last payment. My brother was in a boating accident on his job with the DNR and hurt his back. He got hooked on OxyContin. After his injury healed, he couldn't get a prescription, probably because he worked for the State. He kept asking me for money to buy drugs off the street, but I wouldn't give him any. I found an inpatient treatment center for him, and he got serious about getting his life back. He's been clean for over six months now. But it was expensive, and I got in over my head. I didn't want to ask the firm for help because of James, and I didn't want to ask the church because of Frank, so I 'borrowed' the money, fully intending to pay it back, which I did—in full." Kate's eyes were puffy, and her nose was running. Not her best look, but I still found her irresistible.

"James caught me making personal deposits into the church fund that we manage and was trying to blackmail me into having sex with him. I wasn't about to let that happen, and I think he ratted me out with Frank. You can see how it would have looked to have the police find me hovering over James's body."

"Is that why you've been hanging out with me, so you could help find James's killer and clear yourself?"

Kate turned to me with a shocked look. "No, Gray. No! I really like you. I can see a future with you. Well, I used to see it. I don't suppose you'll be interested in me now."

Oh, Kate, if you only knew. "I have a confession of my own to make."

She drew away from me to look into my eyes. "Yes?"

"I almost took some money from the Bingo cash box myself a few weeks ago. It was so tempting to use it to help save my company." I paused to swallow down my emotions.

"What happened?"

"I was reaching for a big stack of twenties when DeeDee walked in and startled me. I closed the box without her noticing." At least, I didn't think she noticed. I still didn't know if I really would have taken the money, and being that close to doing it scared the hell out of me. I leaned over and gave Kate a big, long hug, then pulled away for a moment so I could look into her eyes, which were as royal blue as her top.

"Thanks for telling me, Kate."

"Thanks for not giving up on me, Grayson."

She nuzzled in close, and we stayed like that for what seemed like an hour. I doubted I would get the mascara stains out of my shirt, but I didn't care. I had fallen for her, flaws and all.

A Note from the Author

As with many first books, parts of this story were inspired by real-life events.

Acknowledgements

To my Agent, Dawn Dowdle, and Publisher, Shawn Simmons, thank you for believing in me.

Thanks to the following friends and family who assisted in the writing process through their support and subject matter expertise. Any errors are my sole responsibility.

Sheila Anderson, Kari Baumbach, Bill Bloedow, Doug Dorow, Tracy Dyer, Alexa Golemo, Diane Heideman McDanel, Kathi Koehn, Jim Lewis, Melissa Logan, Georgine Madden, Terry McDanel, Andy Morgan, Lisa Morgan, Nancy O'Brien, Jon Parshall, Anthony Scarpelli, Barb Strandell, Margaret Sullivan, Kori Wistrcill, Kristen Witte, Suni Zmich

About the Author

When he's not working on his next murder mystery, Joe is a Partner with a Management and IT Consulting firm. He is originally from Chicago and holds a Chemical Engineering degree from the Illinois Institute of Technology. He moved to Rochester, Minnesota, to work for IBM and fell in love with the Land of 10,000 Lakes. Joe has a lovely wife of over 30 years, two adult children, and a crazy dog named Marco.

SOCIAL MEDIA HANDLES:
   https://www.facebook.com/JoeGolemo/ (business page)
   @JoeGo7
   https://www.linkedin.com/in/joegolemo/

AUTHOR WEBSITE:
   www.joegolemo.com

Printed in the USA
CPSIA information can be obtained
at www.ICGtesting.com
LVHW090317260923
759261LV00002B/287

9 781685 124137